The chute gate rattled. Shallie swung back around in time to witness a freeze-action picture of perfect bareback riding form: The "dude's" free hand was held high, and the horse seemed to be suspended in midair, all four hooves off the ground, his body bowed in a shuddering arc. This man was not the first-time novice he'd fooled Shallie into believing he was. Anger surged through her as she realized she'd been made a fool of.

As the horse landed hard, the sunglassed cowboy absorbed the shock effortlessly, his right arm seemingly welded to the leather rigging. His timing was so perfect that he and the horse appeared _____ choreographed their moves. For eight seco_____ n cowboy epitomized the best in rode_____ t was much more fluid grace than bru_____ e became so caught up that she forgot _____

The crowd was abso_____ he horn blared out, signaling the end of _____ s. The rider, timing his movements pe_____ se loft him in the air so he landed on hi_____ ned crowd broke into bleacher-pounding applau_____ e cowboy stopped directly in front of Shallie. With exaggerated chivalry, he swept his hat from his head, unloosing a thick headful of dark, sweat-dampened hair, and bowed toward her.

ALSO BY TORY CATES

HANDFUL OF SKY

TORY CATES

POCKET BOOKS

New York   London   Toronto   Sydney   New Delhi

Pocket Books
A Division of Simon & Schuster, Inc.
1230 Avenue of the Americas
New York, NY 10020

This book is a work of fiction. Any references to historical events, real people, or real places are used fictitiously. Other names, characters, places, and events are products of the author's imagination, and any resemblance to actual events or places or persons, living or dead, is entirely coincidental.

First Pocket Books paperback edition November 2013

POCKET and colophon are registered trademarks of Simon & Schuster, Inc.

For information about special discounts for bulk purchases, please contact Simon & Schuster Special Sales at 1-866-506-1949 or business@simonandschuster.com.

The Simon & Schuster Speakers Bureau can bring authors to your live event. For more information or to book an event, contact the Simon & Schuster Speakers Bureau at 1-866-248-3049 or visit our website at www.simonspeakers.com.

Interior design by Lewelin Polanco
Cover illustration by Craig White

Manufactured in the United States of America

10 9 8 7 6 5 4 3 2 1

ISBN 978-1-4767-3244-2
ISBN 978-1-4767-3260-2 (ebook)

To my "editors,"
Mary Kay and Debbie

Chapter 1

lano Estacado. The Staked Plains. Shallie Larkin mentally assessed the name the early Spanish explorers had given to the region whizzing past her high window. She'd heard this part of New Mexico which she called home referred to as "desolate," mostly by tourists from the East accustomed to tree-shrouded landscapes. Shallie couldn't imagine living anyplace where trees and buildings and mobs of people blocked out the sky.

Shallie rubbed a mittened hand over the frosty patch of glass where her warm breath had condensed. From her lofty perch in the big truck her vision swept out across the wind-raked mesa, dusted in spots with patches of late spring snow, stopping only at a strip of cobalt-blue mountains rising in the hazy distance. Her spirit soared, unleashed by the majesty of the land.

She couldn't understand how anyone could perceive such a vista as being desolate. For her it was a land of possibilities where limits were set only by the boundaries of a person's imagination. Maybe it was this unfettered view, she theorized, that had caused her to set her sights so high.

A wisp of cirrus floating all alone in the vast sky caught Shallie's eye. Nervous tension abruptly knotted her stomach as she felt herself riding all alone as well and, very possibly, too high.

Let my spirit be big enough, she wished fervently, almost as if offering a silent prayer to the grandeur of the land she loved.

The strident shriek of gears grinding together brought her awareness back suddenly to the diesel-smelling confines of the huge truck's cab. She glanced at the driver, her hired hand, Wade Hoskins. Although she was his employer, Shallie had difficulties making herself speak to the man, much less give him orders. She'd overheard enough of his conversations to know that he was a man to whom women were either "skanks" or "heifers." Just sitting next to him made her feel unclean.

"Thought that'd get your attention." Wade Hoskins parted his lips in a wolfish imitation of a smile, revealing the black space where an incisor had once been. His lower lip bulged with a wad of chewing tobacco.

Shallie's tight smile was the only reaction she let herself show. She fought the revulsion that rose in response to the leering, sidelong glance he shot her way. She wanted to scoot her slender, jeans-clad body even closer to the window she already hugged. But she couldn't allow Hoskins to see that he intimidated her. Today she was taking her first, unassisted step into a world where she would have to hold her own against men like Hoskins. It was crucial that she win, if not their respect, at least their cooperation, or all her dreams would be lost.

Hoskins openly stared at Shallie's determined profile. He was pleased to note the rigid set of her spine. His scrutiny made her so stiff that each bump in the road set her palomino-gold curls bouncing.

"I ain't never had a boss woman before," he drawled, overplaying his Texas accent. "Leastwise none that could prove to *me* that they was a real woman." He watched for her reaction and was delighted to see a sudden burst of color suffuse her apricot-toned cheek.

Shallie continued staring grimly ahead. She could just imagine how a man like Wade Hoskins, his gut spilling so far over his belt that the buckle was lost, would define a "real woman" and what he would demand in the way of proof. Her pansy-brown eyes grew cold as iced coffee as she contemplated the stomach-turning image. It infuriated her that Hoskins felt free to make comments like those. He certainly would never have dared to in front of her uncle. For one chilling moment she was afraid she wasn't ready to take her uncle's place. Being a rodeo contractor, responsible for supplying the animals and ensuring a smooth-running show, was a difficult enough job for a burly former rodeo cowboy like her Uncle Walter. What had ever made her hope that a five-foot-four, 120-pound woman could handle it?

Suddenly she wished she'd cultivated more orthodox ambitions. Why couldn't she have been content doing something with the business degree her mother had insisted she earn? Something other than keeping the Double L's books and negotiating the contracts that came in. Shallie didn't have to ponder that question long. The answer came as a memory of those long years spent inside four walls and the suffocating, claustrophobic feeling that had accompanied her years of study. She'd always done well in school, but not through any native love of studying. She considered it a trade-off she'd had to make. Seven hours of imprisonment in a classroom in exchange for a few hours of freedom outside at the end of the day.

Beyond that was the irrefutable fact that she loved rodeo and wanted to carve out a life for herself in it. She'd wanted that for fourteen years, ever since she was ten and her father, over her mother's strenuous objections, had started taking her to rodeos to watch him and his brother, Walter, win all the prizes in the team roping competition.

At first she loved rodeo just for the escape it offered from a world ruled by a mother who spanked "bad little girls" who committed unpardonable offenses like scuffing their patent-leather party shoes or missing a word on their spelling tests. On the rodeo circuit there were no party shoes and no spankings. Freed from their white-picket-fence prison, she saw her father, taciturn and unsmiling at home, blossom into a happy man with a joke and a kind word for everyone. But, even after the accident that claimed her father's life, Shallie remained smitten by the highly infectious malady that those afflicted can only describe as "rodeo fever."

It was in her blood. Two years ago, on the day she'd finished her last college class, she'd gone to work fulltime at the Double L Rodeo Contracting Company, which her uncle anwd father had started ten years earlier. Five short years before her father was killed.

Her mother, who had come from a wealthy Denver banking family, had packed Shallie off to an exclusive women's college in that city shortly after the accident. Her mother had hoped to end forever her daughter's unseemly fascination with the sport she held responsible for ruining her life, although she herself had experienced that same fascination when rodeo had taken the breathtakingly handsome form of John Larkin—Shallie's father—the man who was to become her husband. She had married him assuming that rodeo was merely a whim for the soft-spoken man whose kisses made her forget her exalted position in society, and that he would, of course, eventually be absorbed into her family's banking establishment. She thought that her husband would be given a job with high pay and few responsibilities just as her sisters' husbands had.

But John Larkin had harbored other plans for his wife and the child she was carrying when they were married. He'd never wanted nor accepted a cent of her family's money. Over her loud protests, John Larkin, just as he'd promised he would before they married, moved his new wife to a small ranching community outside of Albuquerque where he and his brother ran a few head of cattle and practiced doing what they did best—roping steers as a team. When they weren't practicing they were doing what cowboys do when they answer rodeo's siren song—they were "going down the road" chasing after jackpots and prize money. They won consistently and put aside every penny they could save in hopes of one day starting their own rodeo company.

Their dreams had materialized in the Double L, each "L" standing for one of the two Larkin brothers. Shallie remembered her mother, who had long since moved her and her daughter into a "respectable" house in Albuquerque, pouting and refusing like a spoiled child to ever set foot on Double L property. Shallie had visited the ranch, though, and soon her father's dream had become her own. The burden of proving that she was worthy of it weighed heavily on her. It had been thrust upon her quite unexpectedly.

That morning her uncle had been up and dressed when Shallie had come down to start off on the long drive to the rodeo in the Panhandle of Texas that they'd contracted to produce. He was issuing orders to their two hired hands, Wade Hoskins and Pecos Cahill, about which livestock was to be hauled hundreds of miles to the rodeo. But, even with his cane, he could barely hobble about. The hobble was the legacy left by the car wreck that had ended her father's life and her uncle's roping career. The long cold New Mexico winter had taken its toll that year on his shattered knees. He'd grimaced with pain as he tried to bend them enough to haul himself up into the eighteen-wheeler's cab.

"Shallie, girl"—her uncle had shaken his head in weary resignation as he'd backed away from the truck— "it doesn't look like this worn-out old body is going to carry me to the rodeo."

Shallie too had backed away. The pain and worry that clouded his eyes, however, halted her timid retreat. The Double L had never failed to honor a contract. She knew that a blemish on that record would hurt her uncle far more than the ache in his injured knees.

"Don't worry. I can handle everything." Shallie's words had tumbled out before she could allow herself to think about the enormity of the task she'd just committed herself to, before she had time to see a smirk spread across Wade Hoskins's face.

Walter stared at her as if somehow trying to reconcile the image of a potbellied, cigar-smoking rodeo contractor with the slim, fine-boned girl standing before him. It wasn't her words, though, that finally allowed him to put the two together. No, they quavered and had a hollow ring to them. It was the look in his niece's eyes. For Walter Larkin it was as if he were staring into his brother's eyes thirty years ago when John had announced, "Walter, you're almost thirty-three and I'm crowding thirty. We both know that the day will come, and it will come soon, when we'll have to hang up our ropes. Now, neither one of us is ever going to be completely happy unless rodeo is part of our lives. So, what we're going to do is start a rodeo company."

Walter had laughed. Between the two of them they didn't have the price of a hot dog for dinner. But they hitched rides to Denver, borrowed horses, and roped themselves into the first-place money. The only thing that stood in his way—from the moment John had made his announcement until they owned the Double L—had been love. A strange kind of love. Walter had never been able to understand how John could have taken the wife he did or why they ever stayed together. It was one of the few puzzles in Walter Larkin's straightforward life and one of the reasons he'd remained a bachelor.

But even John's wife hadn't been able to keep him from fulfilling his promise. Walter had seen the same determination in his brother's eyes he now saw hidden deep in Shallie's, so deep that she probably didn't even know its strength. But she would, Walter had thought that morning, if she's bound on this course she's chosen for herself. She'll have to draw deeply on every inner resource she possesses.

So, he'd made his voice sound jovial and carefree and he'd said: "Hell, you don't need me anymore. You've been doing most of the work now for the past two years. You can run a rodeo as well as I can any day."

Then it was Shallie's turn for a display of false bravado. She swung into the cab of the truck and gave her uncle a jaunty wave as Hoskins headed the truck loaded with bucking horses, bulls, and steers east toward the Texas Panhandle.

The truck lurched as Hoskins applied a lead foot to the brake. Shallie was thrown forward, her head banging against the windshield. From the trailer behind them came startled neighs as the horses were thrown against each other.

"Could you use a gentler touch on the brakes?" Shallie fought to keep the annoyance out of her voice. The one thing guaranteed to bring her to anger more quickly than any other was the slightest hint of mistreatment of an animal. "I'm responsible for the safety of that stock."

"Why are *you* responsible? They ain't your horses."

Hoskins's surly statement managed to both challenge Shallie's authority and completely change the subject from his erratic driving.

"Actually they are half mine." Shallie's statement came out tight and stilted. She knew that she had to establish herself, and that with employees like Hoskins it was a tricky process, but nervous tension goaded her into a hasty response. "My father left his half of the Double L to me in his will. But that's not what's important. Part of your job is to make sure that all of Double L's stock is treated well. If you can't or won't do that, maybe this isn't the job for you."

"Does that mean you're firing me?" Hoskins asked with a smirk.

Shallie knew she'd made a mistake. She wasn't prepared to back up her threat. Without her uncle, they would be desperately shorthanded. She needed all the help she could get, even if it had to come from a reptile like Wade Hoskins.

"Ma'am?" Hoskins prodded her when she didn't answer. "Or maybe you'd be happier if I called you sir?"

He was testing her, exploring her limits. Knowing that she couldn't produce today's rodeo without his help, Hoskins felt free to use any means he could to assuage the affront to his pride which a female superior represented.

"Shallie's always been fine in the past. Why don't we just stick with that?"

"All right, *Shallie*." Hoskins pronounced her name with a drawn-out slur which hinted at an intimacy that made her shudder.

The remainder of the long drive passed in a grim silence punctuated by an occasional lurch when Hoskins tromped on the brake or accelerator pedal to express his continuing protest against the "boss woman."

Chapter 2

By the time they reached their destination, a tumbleweed-blown town, a tight band of tension was squeezing Shallie's forehead. They drove through the High Plains town to the small arena on its outskirts. The sun had taken the bite out of the late spring air. Shallie shrugged off her jacket and mittens.

A few rows of wooden bleachers surrounded a freshly plowed area. They pulled the truck to a halt at the end of the arena, where the bucking chutes for the horses and bulls had been constructed. A homemade sign reading "Not Responsible for Accidents" was posted above the rickety wooden chutes. Another truck bearing the Double L logo pulled in behind them. Shallie jumped out and went to the back to check on the horses. They neighed gently at the approach of the familiar figure who was always so generous with chunks of apple and carrot and scoops of sweet, molasses-laced grain.

Shallie was relieved to find all the horses fit and frisky-looking, as if they were itching to be turned loose in the soft dirt of the arena where they could buck and snort to their hearts' content. At least she never had to worry about her rapport with the horses. That had been a source of joy for her ever since her father sat her on her first pony. If only humans could be as amenable, she thought, searching for Hoskins and Pecos Cahill. Hoskins had already reached her other hired hand, the driver of the truck containing a load of calves and steers for the roping events. Shallie was certain that Hoskins was wasting no time in relating to his shorter, plumper counterpart all the indignities he had suffered at the hands of the boss woman. Cahill looked her way. When she caught him staring, he turned back guiltily.

Feeling alone and isolated, Shallie headed for the area behind the chutes where the rodeo cowboys rigged up for their events. She was intercepted by a tall, thin man carrying a clipboard. His face was stretched long with worry.

"Shallie, thank God you're here. Where's your uncle? I need to consult with him about which horses have been drawn for the bareback."

"He's not here, Mr. Eckles," Shallie told the rodeo committeeman who had hired the Double L to put on his town's annual rodeo. "I'll be producing this show."

"You?" Eckles looked at her in disbelief.

"Yes, *me*," Shallie sighed. "Is there something wrong with that?"

"Not a thing." Mr. Eckles smiled and Shallie realized how defensive she'd become during her years in rodeo, having learned through experience that it was a world where women are generally regarded first as potential conquests. If they wanted to be thought of as anything else, they had to fight for that recognition. It was a struggle Shallie sometimes wearied of.

"Here's a list of the horses that were drawn and their riders," the committeeman said, handing her a sheet of paper. "Think you can have them up by starting time? We've already got some spectators filling up those stands."

Shallie glanced up. The stands were indeed beginning to fill up. A teenage couple sauntered in, both wearing identical floral-print Western shirts and tall straw hats. They were followed by a slim woman holding a baby in one arm and leading a three-year-old with the other. Both children wore tiny pairs of leather boots. Her husband sashayed in after her, twirling a toothpick between two back molars.

A covey of potbellied old men in white shirts and suspenders had congregated close to the trucks and were talking and pointing toward the deceptively docile-looking horses. Shallie had overheard enough old-timers' talk to know that they were commenting on what a sorry-looking lot of horseflesh they used in rodeos nowadays.

Then they'd trade tales about the "really rank" horses that had bucked and snorted across the prairies and later the arenas of their youth. And how if these drugstore cowboys thought they were so hot they should have tried to "fork down into the saddle on the back of one *them* boogers."

Shallie nodded a hasty good-bye to the rodeo committeeman and ran as fast as her boots would allow across the spongy earth of the arena. She scrambled up the metal gates leading to the catwalk that ran behind the chute and overlooked a dusty sea of denim and leather churned up by a dozen bareback riders preparing for their event.

In the center of the chaos of cowboys rifling through the canvas duffel bags containing their gear, helping one another to pin contestant numbers onto the backs of shirts, and testing their rigging, was one cowboy limbering up. He was seated on the dusty ground, his legs angled out from him. As he bent his long torso forward, the muscles of his shoulders swelled and strained against the tight cloth of his yoke-back shirt in a way that caused her breath to catch. He stretched still more, grabbing a polished boot with both his hands and pulling himself down even farther to limber the powerful muscles in his thighs. Shallie couldn't see the cowboy's face but noticed a knot of scar tissue at the base of the middle finger on his right hand.

Shallie watched the almost ritualized movements

with satisfaction. This was the one single moment she liked best. There was something about the quiet intensity of the contestants as they prepared for their few seconds in the arena that made her feel she knew what the director of a ballet, the producer of a play, went through in those final backstage moments before the curtain went up. Being a rodeo contractor wasn't so terribly different. Without her and the stock she provided, this drama between man and beast couldn't be played out.

As she turned from the scene a knot of tension tightened her nerves. Hoskins and Cahill were stretched out in a patch of shade beneath the bleachers, finishing off both a cigarette and their dissection of her.

"Wade, Pecos," she called, capturing their unwilling attention. "Get those broncs unloaded. We're here to put on a rodeo." Her tone held no room for argument. The pair lethargically dragged themselves up and moved toward the horse trailer.

Shallie had to work twice as hard as her hired hands to compensate for their deliberately sluggish pace. Her anger seemed to fuel the determination that had driven her for the past two years: She *would* be taken seriously in the world of rodeo. She wasn't going to be defeated by a couple of Neanderthals like Hoskins and Cahill just because they had trouble taking orders from a woman. Working from the list Mr. Eckles had given her, Shallie separated out the broncs that were slated for the first go-round.

"Hoskins," she called out as she drove the fractious horses from the truck down to the bucking chutes, "get the gate on six." With an exaggerated slowness, the beer-bellied hand crawled up on the catwalk and manned the sliding metal gate that partitioned off the last enclosure. Shallie drove a snorting dun-colored bronc down the metal-sided aisle. Pecos stood above the chutes on the catwalk yelling until the dun reached the end, then Wade lowered the gate to trap him. The air filled with the sound of steel gates clanging, horses snorting, rough cries, and dust as they repeated the same procedure until each of the six chute divisions held a bareback horse raring to be turned loose.

By the time Shallie had gotten the bareback broncs sorted out and ready for the first event, the stands were filled. Nervousness hung in the air as thick as ozone behind the chutes. She looked into the contestants' faces and saw nothing there except iron concentration as they set their minds to the task at hand. The public-address system crackled to life and the rodeo announcer began his spiel.

"Welcome, folks, to our thirty-eighth annual Rodeo and Cowboy Reunion. As you know, the rodeo is held each year at this time to give all our local hands a chance to show their stuff and pick up a little of that prize money. This year, for the fifth year in a row, stock is being furnished by the Double L Rodeo Contracting Company out of Mountain View, New Mexico. Walt Larkin and his crew have always done a real fine job for us and we're pleased to have 'em back with us. Take a bow, Walt, wherever you are."

Shallie glanced up at the wooden box built over the bucking chutes, which held the announcer and a few officials. Mr. Eckles was whispering in the announcer's ear. The announcer, a florid man in a maroon double-knit Western suit and string tie, covered his microphone and pointed down to where Shallie stood. She saw disbelief crease the man's chubby face.

"Heh-heh, folks, excuse me," the announcer chuckled over the PA. "Appears I've made a mistake. Walt's niece, Shallie Larkin, will be producing this year's rodeo. Let's wish the little lady the best of luck."

Because you think I'll need it, Shallie fumed as she turned on a smile she didn't feel in response to a thin smattering of polite applause. On a couple of the older, male faces in the crowd, she read open resentment. *They're mad*, Shallie realized. Mad that a "little lady" was trying to invade their cozy, masculine world. Well, she thought determinedly, it would take more than a few sour stares to chase her away.

"Now, let's welcome the Cavalcade Riding Academy," the announcer continued over the scratchy PA. A troupe of flamboyantly costumed equestrians thundered into the arena, executing a series of intricate maneuvers on horseback. The announcer broke in.

19

"It gives me great pleasure to introduce this year's rodeo queen from Coalla County, Miss Bridgie Sue Gates." A heavily made-up young woman wearing a kelly-green pants suit with a white hat and white boots galloped full tilt into the arena, carrying an American flag unfurled behind her.

"Ladies and gentlemen, our National Anthem."

Those words signaled a halt for Shallie, and suddenly the banging of steel gates and the shouts of her helpers stopped. As a vintage recording of the "Star Spangled Banner" blared over the loudspeaker, hats were whipped from foreheads that the sun rarely touched, and heads were lowered.

Shallie too lowered her head, but it was to sneak a surreptitious glance at the list of horses and riders to double-check that each one had been loaded in the right chute. She went down the list: Zeus, Mercury, Vulcan, and the others. She knew each of them like an old friend and had named them accordingly. Zeus, a dun-colored gelding, was the strongest horse in the string; Mercury, the fleetest; Vulcan, the most explosive. She'd taken the names from mythology, feeling they fit the animals' innate nobility better than the standard, hackneyed rodeo names—Rocket, Midnight, Widowmaker. Once people accepted the novelty of the names, she was often asked why she hadn't used the most obvious name of all—Pegasus, the mythical winged horse. But

Shallie was saving that name, keeping it in reserve for a truly special horse. There could only be one horse fit to be christened Pegasus and she hadn't seen that animal yet.

Before the final chords of the National Anthem had scratched into silence, Shallie was hurrying the bareback riders along.

"Come on, gentlemen," Shallie called down to the cowboys, repeating the words she'd heard her uncle use so many times, "let's ride some horses."

The cowboys swung up onto the catwalk carrying their leather riggings. With some help from her, they set the riggings on the back slope of the horses' withers. Shallie watched one cowboy, a fresh-faced boy no more than sixteen, wearing bright red chaps. After he and a buddy had gotten his rigging cinched down tight on the horse he'd drawn, he grabbed hold of the railing and squatted, bouncing up and down to loosen the muscles in his legs, which were drawing tight with fear.

"The first event this afternoon will be bareback riding," the announcer began his stock commentary. "Most cowboys will tell you that riding these bareback broncs is the most physically demanding event in rodeo. All that holds the cowboy to that keg of dynamite under him is a leather rigging twenty-two inches long. He can use only one hand to hang on to that strip of leather. The rider must spur the horse in the point of the shoulders the first

21

jump from the chute and continue spurring throughout the eight-second ride . . ."

Shallie tuned out the announcer's voice. She'd heard the same spiel hundreds of times at hundreds of rodeos. She looked over the men who would be trying to win money riding her horses. She knew that the nervous young cowboy in the red chaps would get nothing more than a short flying lesson for his entry fee. Next to him was an old veteran on the amateur rodeo circuit. Laughter, hard weather, flying hooves, and gouging horns had all left their mark on his wrinkle-pleated face. She remembered hearing that he'd tried making it on the professional circuit and had ended up with a dislocated shoulder and a concussion. The concussion had passed but the shoulder had never been strong enough again for him to try and take on the big boys. She guessed he'd make a solid, if unspectacular ride.

Her appraisal slipped to the next contestant. He was a short, stocky fellow who looked as if a horse might have put a hoof in his face at one time. He was buried beneath a mountain of angry concentration, like a man looking forward to taking his revenge. Shallie checked the horse he was to ride: Odin. That was a relief; he was one of her stoutest animals. He'd give the angry cowboy a run for his money.

The next contestant puzzled Shallie. He was wearing aviator sunglasses and the bottom half of his face was hidden behind a bandanna. Either one would have set him apart from all the other contestants and most cowboys anywhere. But on top of that, he was wearing a tailored shirt of cream-colored challis tucked into a pair of jeans sporting a crease that only a laundry could put on denim. Her gaze traveled up to his face, unreadable behind the reflector lenses.

Shallie wondered why this mystery man was trying so hard to keep his identity a secret. Probably some city dude who wanted to play cowboy for a day. Whatever. As long as he paid his entry fee, he had the right to make as big a fool of himself as he liked.

Judging by the relaxed set of his broad shoulders, however, the dude didn't even know enough to be scared. Shallie glanced down to the chute below him and shuddered inwardly. Of all the luck, the poor sucker had drawn her most powerful horse, Zeus. She cringed, thinking of his coming humiliation. He's going to need all the help he can get, Shallie thought and began edging toward him.

But as she approached him, something began to bother her. The dude in the aviator sunglasses projected a quiet, sure intelligence unlike the usual braying jackass who thought that with one eight-second ride he could prove he was a man.

"Would you like me to hold on to your glasses while you ride?" Shallie asked.

The cowboy turned toward her. All she could see was

her own reflection in his lenses. "No, ma'am. Believe I'll just wear them." His answer, even muffled by the bandanna, had a calm, masculine strength.

Shallie knew only too well that rodeo had a way of magnifying the male ego and she'd learned to tread carefully around that volatile area. "Of course, I wouldn't presume to tell you what to do," she went on, trying to hide her dismay at the man's foolishness. "But when you get thrown the glasses could be dangerous. And it wouldn't be too safe for the other cowboys if you were to leave the arena littered with broken glass."

"Who says I'm going to get thrown?" His question had more understated assurance than the kind of blowhard cockiness she usually encountered in onetime rodeoers. Still, she was tempted to abandon him to his fate. But there was the very real chance that he could be seriously hurt, so she tried again.

"Have you limbered up?" At least, Shallie thought, if his muscles are loose he'll stand less of a chance of having them jerked out of his shoulder. When he didn't respond, Shallie demonstrated to him how he should swing his arms in wide arcs like the cowboys.

"You mean like this?" He imitated Shallie's propeller motions.

"Right." In the dusty area below the catwalk she caught a glimpse of her two hired hands watching her with amused smirks on their faces. "Come on." She stopped the arm-flapping demonstration. "I'll help you get rigged up."

The dude stood back, obviously not knowing the first thing about setting a rigging.

"Here, hold it like this," Shallie directed him when she had the rigging in place.

As he bent near her, Shallie experienced an odd claustrophobic feeling as if his smell, his nearness, his gaze, all had a physical weight that was pressing down on her, driving the air from her lungs. It was a strange sensation. To hide her discomfiture, Shallie brusquely grabbed the latigo and cinched the rigging down tight on Zeus's back. As she recoiled from the hurried motion, however, she was thrown into even closer contact with the stranger. Large, strong hands closed around her shoulders, steadying her.

"Whoa. There now, are you all right?"

"Fine, fine. Perfectly fine," Shallie babbled, completely flustered. She stumbled quickly away, her thoughts scattered about like flushed quail. She forced herself to fix her thoughts on the announcer's words.

"In chute number one we have Willie Poteen. Willie's a local boy and he's riding a horse called Mercury. As we go down the list today you will notice that a lot of the Double L bucking stock have the names of pagan gods and such like. Walter told me last year that his little niece, Shallie, picks them out."

Shallie arched her brow in annoyance. Would she

ever be thought of as anything other than a "little lady" or a "little niece"?

"Looks like Willie is getting set."

In the first chute Shallie watched the young cowboy in red chaps ease down onto his mount's back. He jammed his hat down so hard on his head that his ears stuck out like the handles on a jug. With a jerky nod he signaled for the gate to be thrown open. Mercury bolted out with all the speed of his namesake and the chaps became a red blur hurtling through space. The embarrassed hometown cowboy landed right where the chaps didn't cover.

"Ready on two?" Shallie asked the next contestant.

"I was born ready, ma'am," the leathery old veteran shot back.

"Then let her rip." Shallie laughed, turning her attention to the next contestant. Shallie didn't watch the ride, she was too busy hurrying along the stumpy, muscle-bound cowboy who'd drawn Odin. Uncle Walter always prided himself on running a fast, well-paced show.

"You let too much time pass," he always said, "and the people in the stands are going to start noticing how hot it is or how hard the seat is and next thing you know they're asking themselves why in blazes they ever left their plasma TVs and their internets to come out to some old rodeo. Then you've lost a paying customer, and we've got too few of them as it is."

"The judges have given J. T. Watkins a whopping big eighty-one for that last ride, folks." The announcement brought a round of applause for the battered old veteran.

The dude, who was the fourth rider, after the angry cowboy had his turn on Odin, was standing back helplessly. The third contestant was almost ready to call for the gate. There wasn't much time. If she didn't baby him along he'd hold up the action.

"Okay, mister." She eased alongside of him. "Step aboard." She indicated Zeus's back. The dude straddled the planks above the horse and settled gingerly down. In the next chute the third contestant nodded for the gate.

"Grab ahold of the rigging," Shallie coached the dude. He gripped the rawhide handle with both hands as if he were picking up a heavy suitcase. Shallie sighed and shook her head. She hoped this town had a good emergency room.

Out in the arena the last rider picked himself up from where Odin had thrown him and beat the dust out of his hat, looking angrier than ever.

"Let's hear a big round of applause for Elroy Stivers on Odin," the announcer coaxed the crowd, "because your applause is all he'll be taking home tonight."

"Here, hang on to it like this." Shallie demonstrated to the dude how he should slide just his right hand in underneath the grip with his palm pointed upward. Her pupil shook his head in understanding and switched his handhold.

"Scoot up on your hand," Shallie directed, holding her fist in front of her hips to demonstrate the position he needed to assume. Down by the gate Wade and Hoskins were elbowing one another and snickering at her impromptu bareback riding lesson. She was again about to give up the effort when she realized he wasn't wearing a glove.

"Your riding glove. Where is it?" When the dude shrugged she turned and borrowed one from the nearest cowboy.

"Here, stick this on your riding hand."

He held up his right hand. Shallie tugged on the leather glove. As she did, she noticed a mound of pink scar tissue. This was the cowboy she had been so entranced with as she'd watched him limbering up. She stepped back, a sick feeling gathering in her stomach. It spread as she watched the "dude" settle his firm buttocks down on Zeus's back and scoot forward until he was nearly sitting on his gloved hand. Zeus kicked a hoof against the chute in protest. Then, in a low, commanding voice she heard:

"Turn him out, boys."

The gate rattled as it sprung open. Shallie swung back around. She witnessed exactly what she was afraid she might see—a freeze-action picture of perfect bareback riding form: The "dude's" free hand was held high, and both his dull spurs were planted high in the horse's shoulders. Zeus seemed to be suspended in midair, all four hooves off the ground and his body bowed into a shuddering arc. It was the image of a prize-winning champion, not the first-time novice he'd fooled Shallie into believing he was.

Zeus landed hard on his forelegs with a shock which almost always unseated whatever pesky human was attempting to stay on his back. The sunglassed cowboy absorbed the shock effortlessly, his right arm seemingly welded to the leather rigging. His timing was so perfect that he and Zeus appeared to have choreographed their moves. For eight seconds this unknown cowboy epitomized the best in rodeo, the mastery that was much more fluid grace than brute strength. Shallie became so caught up in it that she forgot the anger which had surged through her when she realized she'd been made a fool of.

The crowd was absolutely silent as Zeus bucked into two more high, wild jumps that didn't even jiggle the cowboy's sunglasses. The horn blared out, signaling the end of the eight seconds, and the rider, timing his moves perfectly, let Zeus loft him up into the air so that he landed on his feet. The stunned crowd broke into bleacher-pounding applause. As the cowboy retreated to the back of the chutes, he stopped directly in front of Shallie. With exaggerated chivalry, he swept his silver-gray hat from his head, unloosing a thick headful of dark, sweat-dampened hair, and bowed toward her.

Embarrassment and anger heated Shallie's cheeks. Cahill and Hoskins weren't merely snickering anymore, they were laughing openly, delighted by the humiliating trick that had been played on the boss woman by the obviously experienced rider.

"Pecos," she barked. "Get up here and finish running the bareback. Wade, get the calves ready for the roping."

Shallie's boot heels pounded a furious tattoo on the planks of the catwalk, then down the metal steps at the end of the chutes. She looked over her shoulder and saw the bronc rider coming after her. The soft earth slowed her escape, but she plowed forward determined that he was not going to enjoy any more cruel sport at her expense. The ecstatic cheering rang in Shallie's mind like one long jeer.

His hands broke through the nimbus of rage whirling about her and gripped her shoulders. The full length of his taut, muscular body pressed against her back, the rider held her the same way he'd ridden the bronc; with a pressure that was both firm and masterfully light. Again Shallie felt the inexplicable, smothering claustrophobia. She could smell the freshly laundered scent of his shirt combined with a mild tang from the sweat he'd worked up riding Zeus. As his body slid next to hers she could feel its warmth envelop her, penetrating the thin material of her blouse. His thumbs pressed against the taut muscles at the back of her neck. His hands spanned her shoulders, his fingers plunging over her collarbone. Their size made Shallie feel as if her shoulders—well-developed from years of riding and ranch work—were tiny, delicate as a bird's wing beneath his palms. She knew her heart was beating rapidly as a trapped bird's too and wondered if he could feel it. She was infuriated by everything, by the joke he'd played on her, by her own gullibility, but most maddeningly of all by his effect on her.

"Look, I'm sorry if I've upset you. I wasn't intending to make a fool of you."

"Well, then I congratulate you." Shallie heard her words come out tight and angrier than she really felt at that moment. "Because you succeeded in doing exactly that without even trying." Whether to add emphasis to her words or to make herself believe them, Shallie folded her arms in a furious barricade across her chest.

The instant she did, though, she realized she'd made a mistake because the action pushed her breasts upward until their plump tops lay beneath his fingertips. She felt the four points of his fingers on the swell of each breast as eight separate sensations. The effect was breathtaking. She spun from his grasp.

"Do you get your kicks from ruining people's reputations?" she demanded. "You obviously know something about rodeo so you know that it's a sport where reputation is everything. That little trick you didn't intend to play might just have cost me mine."

"Hold on a minute." Shallie had difficulty concentrating on his words; the mouth forming them had claimed her attention. "You work for Walt Larkin, right?"

"I'm his niece and we work together. I'm half owner of the Double L."

"So you're John Larkin's daughter."

The mention of her father's name cooled Shallie's anger instantly. She nodded her head.

"He was a great roper," the bronc rider said, his voice low and respectful. "One of the greatest rodeo ever had."

"Thank you." Shallie's mouth quivered and she jerked it back into a grim, tight line. "For the last two years, I've been working hard to be taken seriously. I'm sure that at this very moment the two men who work for me are busy telling everyone who'll listen about the 'greenhorn in sunglasses' who made a fool of the silly female who thinks she can be a rodeo contractor. That story is going to spread as fast as men in pickups can carry it. Given the efficiency of the rodeo grapevine, it'll be all over the circuit by next week, and whatever credibility I *have* managed to build up will be destroyed."

"Aren't you taking this all a bit too seriously? I doubt that your credibility has been destroyed. It wouldn't even have been dented if you had been the first one to laugh at yourself."

Shallie's anger flared anew, burning now as hot and bright as ever. "Why, of all the presumptuous things to say . . ." She sputtered. "'Laugh at yourself.' That's easy for you to say—a man. You can afford to look like a fool. But I—"

"Ladies and gentlemen," the announcer's voice cut into Shallie's tirade. "I can't believe the score the judges have come up with on that last ride. A ninety-six! I can't remember when I've seen one higher."

The crowd came alive again.

"May we have that last rider back out in the arena again."

"Your fans await you." A chilly tone frosted Shallie's words. The cowboy looked from her to the arena full of stomping, whistling fans. "Better get back in there before they tear the stands apart."

He stood undecided for a moment. Then that slow, supremely arrogant smile cut his strong face. "You haven't seen the last of me, Miss Larkin. I promise you that." He jammed his hat down onto his head and stormed back to the arena.

Shallie fled to the safety of the cab of the semi-truck with the intertwining L's painted on the side. She wasn't ready yet to face Wade and Hoskins and whomever they had told their amusing story to. She needed time to rein in her stampeding emotions. That brazen son of a buck, who did he think he was? Making a fool of her, then telling her she should lead the laughter at herself?

Far behind her she heard the applause die away. It was soon replaced by the crunching of pebbles against boot leather. He was coming back to look for her!

Shallie slid far down in the cab so that her head was hidden. The crunching grew louder. Then it stopped near the truck. Shallie prayed that he wouldn't have the audacity to peer inside the cab and find her crouched down like some frightened animal in its burrow. The crunching started again. As the sound faded Shallie peeked up over the dash.

He stopped at a mahogany-brown pickup and tossed his duffel bag in the back, then quickly stripped off the fancy shirt he'd worn to ride in.

Shallie gasped. His torso was taped from his waist to just below his armpits. He had ridden Zeus, the best bronc in her string, with a chest full of broken ribs! He pulled on a nondescript T-shirt and climbed behind the wheel of the truck.

As he slammed the door, Shallie's anger gave way to an intense curiosity. Who was this backwater champion who wasn't even staying to pick up the prize money he'd won? A tall plume of dust rose in the still, cool air to mark the truck's departure. It fell back to earth as the truck disappeared in the distance. Curiosity and anger both dissolved, giving way to a sentiment she rarely experienced—regret—regret that she would never see the eyes behind those dark glasses.

Chapter 3

In spite of having stayed up late the night before, checking over all the stock to make sure that none had suffered any cuts or scrapes during the day's performance and giving each one an extra ration of grain in reward for their good work, Shallie still awoke before dawn the morning after the rodeo. In the dozy state between sleep and consciousness, she rubbed the scoops beneath her collarbones where his hands had been. She half expected to find an imprint on her neck as clear as the one his touch had seared into her mind.

Outside her window a flock of killdeer trilled their good mornings to one another. Off in the distance, a horse nickered. Shallie tugged on a cuddly-soft flannel robe and went to the window cut into the thick adobe wall of the ranch house. The milky light of early morning glinted off the crusty patches of snow dumped by the late spring storm that had blown through a week before. The

Sandia Mountains looming to the northeast shimmered a chilly blue. Albuquerque lay on the other side. It was almost as if the serrated peaks were a demarcation line separating one life from another—the stifling suburban life of cell phones and shopping malls her mother had wanted for her, from the life of freedom she had found here. Even with her mother gone—remarried and living in Denver—the Sandias still seemed to divide her past from the future she hoped to build.

Shallie wondered vaguely how her mother was doing. It was so hard to tell anything from her phone calls. Her mother always made her voice sound cheery and bright, the beautiful bird in the gilded cage who never failed to sing for her supper. People used to remark on how much they resembled each other. At least they had when Shallie was younger and her mother had insisted that they dress in identical clothing, even when it meant paying a seamstress to stitch up the expensive outfits. They did have the same wheat-streaked hair, the same delicate build, and the same porcelain-doll features. Or they used to until Shallie had let the sun and hard work resculpture her.

She had consciously begun to reject the similarities after her father had exposed her to another, happier world. That was when Shallie stopped wearing her hair in a neat, meticulously flat-ironed style just like her mother's. She let the silky strands find their own curls and waves. And where her mother abhorred even the slightest hint of muscularity, years of working with animals, putting up fences, and cleaning out stalls had put wiry strength into Shallie's slender limbs. When she looked into a mirror, Shallie didn't see the pert chip of a nose or the rosebud lips that were copies of her mother's. She saw the warm chocolate-brown eyes and thick dark lashes and brows that had been her father's.

She wondered what her father would have thought of that impudent cowboy yesterday. It was certain that her mother wouldn't have liked him—she rated rodeo cowboys just slightly above child molesters, and Shallie usually agreed with that evaluation. She'd overheard enough behind-the-chutes banter to know that the average cowboy's outlook on women was prehistoric and that most were faithless as tomcats. Of course, there were exceptions, her father and uncle proved that. Might the cowboy in sunglasses be another?

Before the question was fully formed, Shallie was berating herself for her foolishness. Surely, a man so devastatingly male had honed his attractiveness on the hearts of dozens of women who had hoped he might be the exception—the rodeo cowboy who could be happy with one woman.

Still, she couldn't stem the tide of memories that washed over her. Each one came as a distinct image: a cream-colored Western shirt camouflaging a panther-quick body; a silver-gray hat jammed down on sweat-dampened ringlets; sun-darkened muscles contrasting sharply with the stark white of adhesive tape.

From the kitchen, the sound of water spilling into the old metal coffeepot jerked Shallie out of the dangerous vortex of emotions swirling within her. Uncle Walter was up already. His knees must be bothering him, Shallie deduced. She pulled the cozy robe more tightly around her slim waist and went to join him.

"Good morning." Uncle Walter's hearty greeting betrayed no hint of the pain he suffered constantly from his old injuries. "Sorry I wasn't up to help you unload last night, but I didn't think I'd be much use to you anyway. Not the way this damned cold weather has sunk into my bones."

"Here, let me do that." Shallie gently relieved him of the pot of water he was struggling with while balancing on his cane and lighting the burner at the same time. Walter Larkin hobbled to a seat behind the old wooden table. Shallie ached to see him so crippled. She wished there were some way to send her uncle to a warmer climate. But the Double L was a hard mistress; she provided only enough to survive on and not a cent more.

The day's first light slanted in through the kitchen window, falling golden across her uncle's face. It illuminated a quality that Shallie had always loved in her uncle.

It was the kind of unblinking innocence captured in old photographs of turn-of-the-century cowboys. Like them, Uncle Walter had never known the stress and unavoidable compromises that city life imposes. He was sixty-three years old and he'd never married. There had been rumors, snatches of whispered conversations Shallie had overheard when she was barely old enough to understand the words, about a sweetheart who had left him for another man. But she'd never had the heart to speak to him about it.

"So what kind of rodeo did you put on for old Johnnie Eckles?" The creases carved out by sun and laughter around his dark eyes deepened in amusement.

Shallie cringed. Should she tell her uncle about Wade and Pecos? About how she had been made a fool of by that infuriating cowboy? Should she tell him that there was probably little sense in her continuing to masquerade as a rodeo contractor? That the double L's would always stand for the Larkin brothers? She looked into his face. It filled with happy anticipation.

"Couldn't have gone better," she answered. There was no point in dumping her problems on Uncle Walter. She'd either have to solve them herself or admit that there was no room in rodeo for a woman contractor. Eager to change the subject, she went on, "Had a fellow goose-egg on Mercury."

"That dink," Walter snorted. "I could ride that horse

41

myself if somebody'd help me climb aboard. Any complaints on the roping stock?"

"Not a one. Mr. Eckles said that, as usual, Double L supplied the best roping calves and dogging steers of any outfit around."

Uncle Walter smiled with pride. He spent an exorbitant amount of time and energy seeking out and developing Double L's roping stock. Shallie believed they needed to put more emphasis on what the majority of fans came for—the bucking broncs and bulls. She was convinced that they would never be recognized as truly first-rate, never have a chance to advance beyond the ranks of the amateurs into professional rodeo, unless they also had the finest in bucking stock. But Uncle Walter's loyalties lay with his former colleagues, the ropers.

Shallie decided that now was not the time to reopen their good-natured debate on the subject. "I ran into a cowboy who said you and Daddy were two of the greats."

Uncle Walter was as transparent as a clear stream and his pleasure at the compliment was obvious. "Must have been an old-timer," he laughed.

"He wasn't that old. Early thirties, I'd imagine." Shallie tried to sound casual, unconcerned about the mysterious praise-bearer. "You and Daddy did win every buckle they gave out in team roping until ten years back. That's not so long ago."

"Didn't happen to catch the fellow's name, did you?"

"No. No, I didn't." *But I can describe him for you.* Shallie's rebellious mind added the haunting details: *an arrogant son of a buck with powerful, yet gentle hands, a crown of dark curls, and—*

"He a team roper?" Her uncle interrupted the pestering mental image.

"No. Bareback rider."

"Who'd he draw?"

"Zeus."

"Did he get his gourd thumped?"

"No. He rode him. Scored a ninety-six."

"A ninety-six!" Stupefaction froze his features. "You wouldn't kid a crippled-up old man, would you, Shallie?"

"Not my favorite crippled-up old man," Shallie laughed. Anxious to change the subject before she inadvertently revealed just how unsettling she'd found her brief encounter with the nameless bareback rider, she asked, "What about those steers we got at auction last week? Which pasture do you want me to put them in?"

"Don't worry about that." Walter waved aside the question. "I've got much bigger fish for you to fry. You'll never guess who called me late last night." He stared expectantly at Shallie. She couldn't think of a single person who would elicit such delight.

"I don't know." She shrugged. "Tell me."

"Guess," he insisted. When Shallie clucked in mild

annoyance, he prompted her: "Who's the biggest contractor in the business?"

"Jake McIver?" Shallie leaned forward incredulously, seeking confirmation.

"You guessed it." Walter beamed. "Mr. Rodeo himself. They're going to be running a rodeo school down there at his ranch and he's short a few dozen dogging steers. Said he'd heard we have the best Mexican steers around for wrestling. Asked us to ship down as many as we could spare. Old Jake is stuck, Shallie. I expect we'll get a good price out of him."

Shallie was puzzled. She was surprised that a big-time contractor like Jake McIver would have called up for stock, especially when he was close to seven hundred miles away. But she didn't want to dampen her uncle's enthusiasm.

"That's great," she declared enthusiastically. "Now we'll be able to pay off our feed bills."

"I've left word with Wade to get the steers loaded up. I'm sending you and him down to deliver them as soon as you can get ready."

Shallie felt her stomach lurch sickeningly. "Me and Wade?" she echoed miserably, hoping she hadn't heard correctly. "The McIver ranch is down near Austin, Texas. That means I'd be fourteen hours cooped up in the cab of a truck with Wade Hoskins."

"Something wrong with that?" Shallie looked into her

uncle's face. He was so far removed from the Wade Hoskinses of the world and their sleazy attitudes that they didn't even occur to him. Shallie couldn't bring herself to admit to him that the prospect of spending fourteen hours in close quarters with Wade Hoskins made her physically ill.

"Couldn't you send Pecos?" she asked, hoping for the lesser of two evils.

A look of slightly irritated puzzlement crossed her uncle's face. "With you gone I'll need Pecos to keep the ranch running. You know that Wade isn't worth a damn if someone doesn't keep after him every second. At least Hoskins won't be tempted to sleep on the job if he's behind the wheel of a semi."

"But why do I need to go?" Shallie asked, trying to camouflage her misery.

"Look, Shallie"—her uncle leaned forward over the scarred wooden table—"I've thought long and hard about this. With me fading more and more out of the picture—" Shallie opened her mouth to protest, but her uncle silenced her and went on—"it's important for you to get to know the movers and shakers in rodeo. A contact like Jake McIver could be invaluable."

Shallie knew he was absolutely right.

"You're not worried about old Jake's reputation, are you?" he asked with a grin. Jake McIver was a man who had come to favor ever younger girls as he grew older until, at seventy-seven, he was usually to be seen in the company of a cute young thing who could be, not his daughter, but his granddaughter.

Shallie laughed. "I'd like to see an old goat like that just *try* to chase me around the barn."

Her uncle joined her laughter. "Doubt that the old coot could remember what he'd been chasing you for, even if he was to catch you."

Suddenly Shallie felt foolish for having let a worm like Wade Hoskins get her in such a dither. She'd been taking him much too seriously. Perhaps that arrogant cowboy *had* had a point when he told her yesterday that she ought to laugh at herself. And so it was decided: She was going to the Circle M, Jake McIver's ranch. Shallie got dressed, pulled on her fleece-lined rawhide jacket, and stepped out into the cool, clear early morning air.

The Double L. She'd loved it even before she ever set eyes on it. She loved her father's dreams for it, which he had shared with his horse-crazy daughter while his wife made noises of disapproval in the background. She looked over the collection of tumbledown stalls and the practice arena where half the wooden slats had been kicked out by crazy broncs and wild bulls. So much work needed to be done and there was never the time or the money to do it. She thought of her father and how he had dreamed that the Double L would one day be a contracting outfit to match any in the country, even Jake McIver's.

"Someday," he'd promised her, "there'll be Double L stock at the National Finals Rodeo."

Just as every rodeo cowboy dreamed of earning enough points to compete in the National Finals, rodeo's World Series, every contractor dreamed that his bronc or his bull or his steers would be chosen to challenge the finest the sport had to offer. Shallie shook her head at the memory and kicked a rust-red clump of caliche out of her path. The Double L hadn't even managed to break out of the amateur circuit yet, much less work its way to the top of the pros. They had so far to go and didn't seem to be getting any closer.

As Shallie approached the loading pens, she saw Wade surrounded by his sidekicks, Pecos and two other hands. His back was toward her but he was clearly doing a wildly exaggerated imitation of the "riding lesson" she had unsuspectingly given yesterday. His audience collapsed in laughter as he drove his stumpy body through a series of jerky flailings. Shallie felt embarrassment and anger churn her stomach. Her uncle's words about "fading out of the picture" rang in her ears and Shallie made herself march forward in spite of those emotions. If her father's dream was ever to be realized, she would have to act, and act decisively, conquering her natural inclination to retreat and forcing herself to act like the contractor she claimed to be. A memory from yesterday's rodeo gave her a notion of how to do just that.

"Hey, Wade," she called out, acting as if she were sharing their amusement, "you're almost as good a riding teacher as I am, except that I only give lessons to champions." She stared straight at the runty man, dazzling him with her brightest smile. Something in Hoskins's face quirked uneasily as the other hands, including Pecos, began laughing *with* Shallie and not at her.

"Have you got those steers loaded yet that we're hauling down to the Circle M?" Shallie's question came perilously close to a direct order, something she'd never dared before in front of an audience of Hoskins's cronies. But she'd decided, if she truly was going to be a contractor, now was as good a time as any to start. Hoskins sensed the balance of power between them shifting.

"No, I ain't." His answer was a surly challenge that stopped the laughter cold.

"Pecos, give him a hand." She completely ignored his challenge. "We need to be on the road within the hour." Pecos looked from Shallie to Wade, then moved off toward the pens. The other hands drifted off to their chores.

As she stepped away, Shallie marveled at just how right the bronc rider had been, at how easy it had been to defuse Hoskins's undermining of her authority simply by being the one to lead the laughter at herself. Too bad she would never see him again. She would have liked to meet him once more to thank him for that bit of advice. Just that, nothing more. Just to say thanks.

Chapter 4

She was there at last—the National Finals in Las Vegas. The stands were packed and he, the nameless bronc rider, was up. A jolt of pleasure shot through Shallie as she realized he was riding Double L's Zeus. The odd thing, though, was that while all the other cowboys were in their fanciest spangled outfits, he was dressed in nothing more than jeans and adhesive tape from his waist to beneath his armpits. No one seemed to notice.

At the height of the arc of a wild buck, the rider was thrown free. He floated in slow motion, coming to a gentle landing at Shallie's feet.

"Miss Larkin," he said, sweeping the hat from his dark head, "I just wanted to tell you that you have the rankest, meanest string of broncs I've ever had the privilege of attempting to ride."

Shallie opened her mouth to speak but his sunglasses

were like a barricade repelling her thoughts. She watched the distorted reflection of her head in the lenses as it bobbed from side to side trying to see around the glasses. Then he understood! He had to take the glasses off before she could speak. He raised his hand and Shallie felt an unearthly exultation. She would see his eyes!

"Hey." An elbow bit into her ribs. "Hey!"

Shallie's head jerked up and a keen disappointment bit into her. Even awake she carried the thought from her dream that she was about to learn something of great importance. But instead of staring into the face of the bronc rider who so disturbed her thoughts, the light from the dashboard of the truck shone dully on the grizzled features of Wade Hoskins as he tapped futilely on the GPS screen.

"Piece of crap ain't workin'. Check the map." He didn't bother to soften his harsh order with a "please." "Find the turnoff for McIver's ranch."

Shallie shook off the webs of sleep and shuffled through the stack of maps to find the one Uncle Walter had marked. It wasn't there. She glanced around the cab and saw the map propped up on the dash directly in front of Hoskins.

"It's right in front of you."

"Oh yeah. So it is." Hoskins pulled the map off the dash and shoved it at Shallie. "Where's the turnoff?"

Uncle Walter had clearly indicated the road leading

to the Circle M, but Shallie knew that navigation was not the issue. As always, the real issue was her authority. "Take the next right. It should put us onto the spur road to the McIver ranch."

The big truck lumbered off the highway and onto a narrow, potholed country road. Shallie's head ached dully. She'd taken the second shift, driving for an hour and a half after they'd left the Double L. Wade had promptly fallen asleep beside her, his mouth gaping open in his slack face. She'd let him sleep another two hours beyond the time when he should have taken over. Then, when she'd tried to waken him, he'd moaned in his sleep and mumbled incoherently.

Shallie suspected that he was playing possum, but she didn't care to pursue it. Even if it meant driving straight through herself, a sleeping Wade, even if he was faking it, was vastly preferable to a wakeful, leering Wade. So, she'd let him slumber on until he roused himself an hour outside of Austin and took the wheel.

"Take the next gate." Shallie made her command as unpleasant as she could, hoping to show Hoskins that two could play at surliness. They passed under a high arching gate of black wrought iron. A large M was welded inside a circle at the top. The McIver brand. To Shallie it stood for the biggest and the best in her business. The private road through the McIver property was considerably smoother than the one maintained by the county that they'd just turned off. The cab was filled with the soft scents of cedar and fresh-cut grass. Shallie took a deep breath. Her nose, attuned to the various nuances of grass, told her it was coastal Bermuda, a species that made excellent hay. They drove on for several miles before spotting a light at the top of a rise.

The light shone on a full-scale rodeo arena complete with bucking chutes and concrete stands. It appeared that a full-scale rodeo was taking place as well. Hoskins parked the truck and they got out. On the far side of the arena, milling about in the darkness, Shallie saw a solid acre of corralled horses.

"Looks like they're having a buckout." Hoskins's voice in the darkness startled Shallie nearly as much as the sight of so many horses penned in one spot.

"Looks that way."

In the arena, the horses were being run through the chutes and ridden as fast as they could be rigged up. A short cowboy with a face as broad, open, and friendly as Howdy Doody's made notes on each horse's performance.

Shallie circled around the bright pool of light flooding the arena, left Hoskins to watch the buckout, and went to the corral full of horses. The animals' heads churned about catching flashes of moonlight like waves on a midnight sea. She hung on the gate and scrutinized them. For the most part they were a scruffy lot of dinks, sluggish animals that lacked animation. Perhaps that was why the dappled white roan, tinged a ghostly blue, captured her attention so quickly.

A proud, indomitable spirit flashed from the roan's eyes. He held his head aloft, nostrils quivering, as if being jammed against such a common herd offended his sensitivities.

Over the years, Shallie had learned that a contractor had to be part cowboy, part lawyer, part veterinarian, and part politician to survive, but that he would never succeed if he was not, above all, a good horse trader. And that, Shallie knew, was her long suit. As good as her uncle was at juggling all the other roles, he bowed to her expertise when they stepped into the auction barn. Judging horseflesh came more as an intuitive gift to Shallie than as a skill she'd had to consciously cultivate. She seemed to have an instinctive knack for knowing which horses, with the right treatment and feed, could be turned from lackluster dinks into high-bucking champions. From the first time she ever accompanied her uncle on a buying trip, she'd been able to pick out those animals with hidden fire.

That first trip out, though, she hadn't been able to convince her uncle to trust her instincts and bid on a scruffy-looking chestnut gelding. The horse had gone to a producer in Montana. After the chestnut gained sudden notoriety as the rankest horse on the amateur circuit, Uncle Walter had begun paying serious attention to her perceptions. On her advice, they had acquired Zeus and Odin, the two best broncs in their string.

Shallie never questioned her intuition about horses, which was why, from her first glimpse of the blue roan, she was unshakably certain that this was the horse that could carry the Double L brand to the National Finals. She calmed herself, remembering that she hadn't even seen the animal buck yet. Still, she thought of the load of steers she'd hauled up and her mind immediately fell to horse trading. If this horse were only half as rank as he looked, he'd be worth a feedlot full of steers. Somehow, she had to see this horse buck and she had to do it before Jake McIver did.

"Miss Larkin?"

Flustered with guilt that someone from the Circle M had caught her in the middle of her scheming, she whirled toward the voice in the darkness. "Yes?" All she could make out was a tall shadow topped by a cowboy hat.

"Welcome to the Circle M. My grandfather and I have been waiting for you."

Shallie extended her hand. It was an automatic response she had adopted when meeting anyone connected with rodeo. Anyone male. She had found that a firm, no-nonsense handshake was a good method for convincing would-be Romeos that she had no intentions of ever mixing business and pleasure. She was surprised by the feel of his hand. An uneasy prickling that she couldn't stop to analyze caused her to shiver. The hand that grasped her own was rough, obviously well-acquainted with hard work, and large enough to make her own seem frail and smooth in comparison. Shallie recorded all these impressions in less than the blink of an eye. As her thumb slipped over the back of his hand, she was jolted by one more discovery: a lump of scar tissue at the base of the middle finger. She ripped her hand from his, thoroughly disconcerted to be standing in front of the man she had been dreaming of such a short time before.

"So, you remember your old riding student?"

How could she have failed to recognize that voice? Shallie wondered, then realized that the uneasiness she'd experienced upon first hearing it had been a warning signal. One she shouldn't have ignored.

"I told you we'd meet again." It was clear from his tone that he was not someone accustomed to having his wishes denied. "I'm sorry you had to spend fourteen hours in a semi, but that was the only way I could arrange it."

"*You* arranged it?"

"Sure. Don't you think we have dogging steers down here in Texas? I had to convince my grandfather that Double L's were really something special to get him to call your uncle."

Shallie was flabbergasted. First, to have this phantom

figure materialize as if out of her dreams, then to learn not only that he was Jake McIver's grandson, but that he had actually maneuvered their reunion.

"Just what made you so sure I'd come?" she challenged him with considerably more starch in her voice than she felt at that wobbly moment.

"Well, I was pretty sure you *wouldn't* come if I called myself. That's why I got Jake to get in touch with your uncle, and what contractor worth his, or her," he added with elaborate emphasis, "salt would pass up the chance to meet Mr. Rodeo himself?"

"I guess that makes me pretty predictable, but at least I'm worth my salt," Shallie retorted, remembering his lesson about being the first to laugh at yourself.

His laughter at her self-mocking comment rolled deep and gentle in the darkness. "Seems you don't take yourself quite as seriously when you're away from a rodeo arena."

Shallie took his amusement as a compliment, responding to his warm friendliness. "I suppose I'm learning to do what you advised me to, laugh at myself."

His face above hers was shadowed, his expression unreadable. Her own was clearly visible, upturned to the moonlight. She turned away from him, feeling too exposed, too vulnerable. She looked back at the horses, eager to turn the conversation away from herself. She needed a moment to collect her emotions.

"Are you planning to have an auction?"

"Early next week. Soon as we pick out any horses worth keeping. Most of them are pretty sorry." He took a place beside Shallie. His nearness triggered those same baffling sensations she'd first experienced when helping him to rig up at the rodeo. She had to concentrate to come up with a halfway intelligent remark.

"Where did they all come from?" she asked, already knowing the answer as well as any contractor.

"Everywhere. Every rancher and farmer between here and Butte, Montana, who buys his kid a horse, then finds out that Junior can't ride the pony, thinks he's got another Midnight on his hands."

Shallie laughed at the comparison between the mangy creatures in front of her and the legendary bronc Midnight.

"It *is* pretty funny," he went on. "They all think they'll sell their 'killer' horse to the Circle M and make a fortune. Turns out most of these 'outlaw' animals couldn't buck off a wet saddle blanket."

Shallie knew there was one horse in the pack that could do that and much more. She climbed up on a wooden railing to find his bluish mane. As hard as she tried to ignore the disturbing presence of the man beside her, she was acutely aware of his gaze following the curves of her body as closely as the jeans and tailored shirt she wore.

"How long . . ." Her voice came out squeaky and high. She cleared her throat and started again. "How long will it take for you to buck out all these horses?" She turned toward him and the answer to her question was lost forever.

She was standing above him so that now it was his face that was lit by the moon's radiance. It was precisely the face she would have seen in her dream if she hadn't been awakened. There was an uncompromising ruggedness to his high cheekbones, and his eyes held a wildness that matched the panther quickness of his body. Looking into those eyes for the first time told Shallie everything she would ever need to know about the secret to this man's success at bronc riding—he was united with the wild mounts he rode.

"You said Jake McIver is your grandfather?"

"I did indeed."

"That means . . . you're Hunt McIver."

"Last time I checked my driver's license that's what it said."

"What in God's name is a four-time world broncriding champion doing competing at an amateur rodeo?"

The cocky lilt abruptly faded from Hunt's voice. "Those four buckles happened a long time ago."

Shallie riffled through her mental files searching for any bit of gossip she'd heard about Hunt McIver. For the first time she regretted her lack of interest in the sport's personality parade. All she could remember was that after winning four consecutive world titles at the National Finals, Hunt McIver had had a couple of bad years compounded by some severe injuries. She also vaguely remembered that he'd earned quite a reputation as a rakehell in a sport that had more than its share.

"But you're still riding on the pro circuit, aren't you?"

"Some folks would argue with you about whether what I've been doing lately is actually riding or not, but, yes, I'm still holding my PRCA card," Hunt answered, referring to the membership card issued by the Professional Rodeo Cowboys of America that entitled the cowboys holding it to compete in any of the more than 650 PRCA-sanctioned rodeos held annually.

"You wouldn't have that card for long, would you, if the Association knew you were riding in amateur rodeos?" Shallie already knew the answer, but she was hoping he might provide the response to an even larger question.

"Of course not," Hunt answered edgily. "They'd jerk it so fast my head would spin. That's why I didn't ride under my own name or pick up the prize money. Why? Are you planning to report me?"

"No." Shallie watched the roan's head, colored the thin blue of skim milk, rise above the others. No, she wouldn't give away Hunt McIver's secret, but she was careful to file it mentally in a convenient spot. It could prove quite useful in the future. "Why did you do it then if you weren't even planning on collecting the prize money?"

She felt his shoulder, lightly touching the outer side of her thigh, shift uncomfortably. She knew she was treading on touchy ground. She glanced down at him. His burning, intense eyes were fastened on some invisible object in the dark distance.

"I was never intending to make off with some hometown hero's prize money. I just wanted to ride. I was lucky I drew your top bronc. I needed a good ride. Needed it bad. Just me and an honest horse. Not Hunt McIver, one-time bronc-busting champion with a couple thousand fans waiting to see if he still had it or not. For one afternoon I wanted to be any cowboy putting down his money and taking his chances. I wanted to rodeo, pure and simple. To get down into that chute without feeling like I had a business manager and contracts for commercials and offers from Hollywood and a big, fat, bloated reputation all riding on my back. Just me and a good horse, that's all I wanted. Can you understand that, Shallie?"

"I think anyone who really loves rodeo can understand." Shallie's tone spoke more than her words about the bond of understanding between them. It was a bond forged by a mutual love of the raw heart of rodeo which had much more to do with the sport's beginnings on a forsaken prairie somewhere when men and mounts faced one another in contests played out for survival, not for the cheers of crowds seated in concrete arenas.

"Good," Hunt boomed out with a heartiness that sounded forced to Shallie's ears. "Now that we've got that all squared away, I'm taking you to meet my grandfather. He heard you were pretty and—" Hunt stopped. He scooped Shallie off the fence and into his arms. "I want to show him that the rumors were true." He held Shallie against his chest, his arm crooked around the swell of her buttocks. The combination of being swept off the railing and feeling the hard press of his body against hers left Shallie temporarily short of breath.

He grinned triumphantly up at her, his full lips split by the gleam of solid, white teeth. It was a smile that Shallie reckoned a goodly number of women had succumbed to over the years. She put her hands on the broad muscles of his shoulders to steady and to lever herself away from him. He lowered her slowly until his taunting lips were level with Shallie's breasts. If he were to turn his head to either side their tips, pressing against the thin cotton of her blouse, would be at his mouth.

A scuffle and the snort of unsuccessfully suppressed laughter burst from the darkness behind them. Shallie distinguished Wade's dumpy form in the shadows. Once again he'd caught her in a less than authoritative position. She tried to reclaim what shreds of dignity she might have left by demanding icily, "Mr. McIver, if you would be so good as to put me down, I would appreciate it greatly."

With an agonizing slowness he lowered her, managing to graze every inch of her body with his own during the descent. When she was finally on the ground, Hunt turned his attention to the intruder lurking behind them. In two surprisingly swift steps he had closed the distance between himself and Wade and was confronting him face to face.

"Who the hell are you?" he roared at the eavesdropper. "And what are you doing prowling around like a thief?"

"He works for me," Shallie interjected.

"Are you in the habit of peeping on your boss, mister?"

"Nuh-nuh-no," Hoskins stammered meekly. "I was just looking to find out what I should do with the steers we brung."

"What do you think you should do? Serve them all punch in demitasse cups?" Hunt's sarcasm bit like a whip. "Get the stock unloaded, man. My livestock superintendent will tell you where the stock tank is and show you where you're bunking tonight. And, as long as you're on Circle M property, don't go sneaking around like some damned sewer rat. Is that understood?"

"Yuh-yuh-yessir." Hoskins sounded like a frightened bully called up in front of the principal. As he turned to leave, however, he slashed Shallie with a glare burning with smoldering resentment.

"Can't say I'm too impressed with your hired help," Hunt announced.

"We can't afford to pay much," Shallie admitted. "We take what we can get."

"Well, you don't have to take weasels like him. Come on, let's get up to the house. Jake McIver isn't used to waiting for anyone."

Chapter 5

I t's about damn time you two showed up. You shouldn't keep an old man waiting like this." Jake Mc-Iver's age-rusted voice bellowed out at the sound of the heavy, carved front door opening. Shallie was astonished by the size of the stone house as well as the magnificence of its furnishings. A chandelier lighted one entryway lined with antique photographs of McIvers long since gone to their eternal reward. It opened onto a sunken living room, where the elder McIver held court before a fireplace that extended from the floor to the vaulted ceiling. The floor was of smoothly polished stone taken from the nearby riverbed. Western paintings by masters like Frederic Remington graced the walls, which were paneled in a light oak. Sculptures sitting about the mammoth room on their own individually lit pedestals caught bucking horses at the peak of their leaps and ropers chasing calves, their lassos frozen above the fleeing beasts.

The only sour note in the baronial room was sounded from the thronelike chair Jake McIver occupied. It was composed entirely of long, curving cattle horns, fitting for McIver's majestically dominating air, which Shallie had come to associate with contractors who were either trying to live up to the stereotype of the rodeo producer or who had had a hand in producing it. McIver belonged to the latter group. From the crown of the Stetson hat that Shallie was sure he only removed at bedtime and reluctantly even then, to the diamond Circle M stickpin glistening on his hand-tailored Western shirt, to the tips of his ostrich-skin boots, Jake McIver was every inch the stereotypical contractor.

As if completing the image, a young woman of dark and sultry beauty was curled at his feet like a royal attendant. Her slender, manicured hand rested on the old man's knee. A long, silken curtain of ebony hair framed her elegantly high-cheeked face. Meticulously applied makeup added an extra note of hauteur to her aloof features. Shallie became uncomfortably aware of her wind-tossed locks and grimy jeans. As she looked more closely, she realized that the woman's sophistication belied her youth—she couldn't be out of her early twenties. She recalled her uncle telling her that McIver had seen the sunny side of seventy long ago. So, she concluded, the old goat had earned his reputation.

"Granddad, I'd like to introduce you to—"

"Who the hell are you introducing?" Jake McIver cut his grandson off. "You think I don't know who this little filly is? This is John Larkin's little girl. And just as pretty as I heard she was." The old man's agate-sharp eyes glittered as they surveyed Shallie's lean curves. To Shallie it felt as if he were drinking in her youth, feeding vampirishly upon it with his eyes. The demeaning appraisal irked her. Not only hadn't old McIver accepted her as a business associate, he was treating her like a bit of feminine fluff to be admired, then acquired. Any hope of being recognized as an equal would vanish if she didn't act quickly.

"And you," Shallie said, her voice low and calm, her gaze pointedly taking in the woman at his side, "appear to be everything that I heard *you* were."

For a stunned moment old McIver didn't speak. A brooding grayness lowered his thick eyebrows. The heavy mood, though, lifted as suddenly as it had fallen and he burst out in a booming laugh. "You can bet your boots on that, gal. You can just bet that Jake McIver is everything, and more, that folks say he is. Come on over here and sit down. I don't bite, do I, Trish?"

"Not where it shows, Sugar," the dark-tressed beauty purred, giving him a feline smile.

Shallie descended the low steps into the living room and seated herself at a chair somewhat removed from the others. Hunt followed, sprawling out on a richly upholstered, ivory-colored sofa. But Shallie detected something of the crouched predator in his determinedly casual pose, putting a wary distance between himself and his grandfather. No one spoke until Jake McIver cut the silence.

"What the hell kind of a name is Shallie?"

Shallie hated the question and the reply she always had to issue to it. "It's short for Shalimar."

"Shalimar? You mean like the perfume?" McIver continued to probe, insensitive to her embarrassment.

Shallie nodded.

McIver looked puzzled for a moment, then roared out his by now familiar laughter. "That's probably how you got started, wasn't it? Your mama's perfume. Is that it? Did old John name you after your mama's perfume?"

Shallie was grateful for the dim lighting, otherwise McIver would have had another object of ridicule—her flaming red cheeks.

"You don't have to answer that, Shallie." Hunt's voice, low and tight, cut through the bray of laughter. "The old man's only kidding."

Shallie was grateful for Hunt's intervention, but to remain silent would be to allow Jake McIver the upper hand, something she didn't intend to let happen.

"Yes, I suppose my mother's perfume did have something to do with my start in life," she answered in a light, bantering tone. "I guess I'm lucky she didn't wear Opium."

Old McIver eyed her as if sizing her up for a second time. A surprised chuckle accompanied the glance. "You're right, it could have been a lot worse. Most folks, if they had been named after the romantic potions that put the twinkle in their daddy's eye, would have ended up being christened Wild Turkey."

Shallie forced herself to laugh, aware both of its falseness and of Hunt's eyes upon her. His lips were sealed in a grim, tight line. That was when Shallie noticed that he and his grandfather shared the same sort of full, sensuous mouth. When not laughing, the corners hung down with a slight petulance. They were mouths which had demanded, and known, more than their fair share of pleasure.

"What kind of mangy steers did you bring down for this rodeo school Hunt's putting on?"

Shallie let her reply fall into the rhythm of McIver's repartee. "Just the flea-bittenest, motliest bunch I could come up with." Sometimes she felt almost bilingual in her ability to switch into the speech patterns favored by rodeo folk.

"We'll have a look at your sorry beeves tomorrow. Come on, Trish, time for me to put this old body to bed." McIver negated his words by springing spryly to his feet. He was well over six feet tall, every inch as trim as he had been half a century before. Trish trailed behind him as he swept out of the room. Shallie detected the electric glance that passed between Trish and Hunt. It sparked a flicker of jealousy that she was quick to extinguish. The last thing in the world she needed was to become embroiled in the twisted affairs of the Circle M. At least she had an explanation now for the hostility that flared between Hunt and his grandfather. Hunt too knew the prick of the green-eyed monster.

The gargantuan room seemed to shrink once Jake and Trish had left. Hunt stood suddenly very close. Shallie's thoughts spun in a futile attempt to come up with something resembling polite conversation.

"It would appear you've learned that a sharp wit can be a handy weapon." Hunt's words were as quiet as his grandfather's had been raucous. They also made Shallie suspect that Hunt too might be a bilinguist who reserved one way of speaking for rodeo people and another for the rest of the world. Shallie felt oddly flattered that he didn't feel he had to use his rodeo camouflage with her.

"Actually I have you to thank for teaching me that lesson. Besides, what other way is there to deal with your grandfather?"

"The only way I know of dealing with him is very carefully." A frostiness crept into Hunt's words, which hung in the air long after they had been spoken. Shallie cast about for another topic of conversation. Unfortunately, she blurted out the only one she could come up with before she'd had a moment to consider it.

"Trish. She seems so much—"

"Younger than my grandfather," Hunt finished for her. "Chronologically she's twenty-four, but as far as experience goes she's at least as old as he is."

Shallie wondered about this cryptic comment, but it was clear from his impenetrable expression that he did not care to explain it. Shallie could only assume that he had firsthand knowledge about the depth of Trish's experience. She made one more stab at conversation.

"From your accent," Shallie hazarded, "I'd guess that you haven't spent your whole life in Texas."

"And you'd be right. My grandmother packed me off to an Eastern boarding school as soon as I hit my teens. At the time I thought it was the cruelest kind of punishment. But once I got over the shock of using my legs for activities other than gripping the sides of a horse, I was grateful to her for opening up a larger world beyond rodeo to me. Sounds like you're acquainted with that world too."

"I guess I have my mother to thank for that. Like your grandmother, she insisted that I study something unrelated to horses while I was at the university." The mention of horses turned Shallie's thoughts back to a matter that pressed urgently for quick action: the blue roan. She looked at the man lounging on the sofa and felt her supply of nerve shrink away. In the dim light his hard-carved face fell away in angled planes and deep, hard shadows. His eyes, she'd discovered in the light, were a blue as changeable as a wild sea. One minute they sparkled in his tanned and weathered face, the tranquil azure of a tropical cove. The next, they shifted to a stormy shade closer to black. At the moment they were a dark Prussian blue.

Under any other circumstances Shallie would have retreated from a man like Hunt, from the dangerous aura of sensuality which he exuded. That is precisely what she had been doing for the past two years. It was simpler that way, she told herself. There was no room in her life for emotional complications. But she couldn't avoid the danger that Hunt McIver represented, not if she was going to have any chance at the magnificent outlaw roan in Jake McIver's corral.

"Hunt, I have a favor to ask of you." Her voice quavered in the dusky room.

He turned his gaze on her without answering.

"I'd like to see one of the auction horses ridden."

"No favor there, just stay around a day or two and you'll see them all ridden at the auction."

"Not all," Shallie contradicted him. "You'll have the best ones culled out by then."

"Of course. Jake didn't get to be where he is today by selling off his best stock."

"I know. That's why I'd like to see one particular horse ridden tonight, before anyone else has a chance to see him."

"I take it that I'm your candidate to stage this little moonlight buckout."

"Would you, Hunt?" Shallie couldn't stop the eager note of pleading that colored her request. "There's one horse I just have to see. It would mean so much to the Double L. You and your grandfather already have so many champion broncs. All I want is just a chance at this one. He might not turn out to be anything."

A look of detached amusement stole over Hunt's features. "And just why should I jeopardize my grandfather's chance at a prize bronc?"

Shallie had hoped to convince him without playing her trump card. "For the same reason that I'm not going to report you to the PRCA for riding in an unsanctioned rodeo. Because we want to help each other out." She held her breath, hoping she hadn't overplayed her hand.

Hunt's taunting smile faded. "You'd really report me, wouldn't you? Being the best really means that much to you, doesn't it?"

Shallie's voice was level when she answered, "It does."

For a long moment Hunt seesawed between angry disbelief and amusement. Amusement finally won out. "All right, if there's one thing in this world I should understand it's wanting to excel. You've got yourself a bronc rider."

The evening air was cool and soft with the scents and moisture blown by the breezes from the wide Colorado

River, which wound through the McIver property. A high, full moon dusted the swaying grass and dappled the gnarled live oak trees with silver shadows. The lights had been switched off in the arena and the bunkhouse beyond was already dark. The air was thick with the croaking of frogs and the busy whir of crickets. But no human sound other than the crunch of their own footsteps broke the stillness. The corral was at the bottom of the hill from the ranch house. All the horses were motionless, sleeping on their feet, except for one. His restless, snowy head surged above the others.

"That's him," Shallie whispered, though there was no one near enough to have heard her voice.

"You're a good judge of horseflesh," Hunt allowed. "I had my eye on him myself. Best of the lot."

Hunt's compliment stirred a warm rush of pleasure that Shallie hastily put aside.

Hunt stopped at his brown pickup truck and pulled his bareback rigging out of the back. He strode with a loose-limbed grace over to the arena and started to turn on the lights.

"No," Shallie hissed in the darkness. "No lights."

"Are you out of your mind?" Hunt demanded. "You want me to ride a wild horse in the dark?"

"Somebody will see if you turn the lights on. Your grandfather can't know about this." A note of desperation crept into Shallie's voice as she envisioned her prize slipping away from her before she'd ever had a chance at it.

"All right. No lights." He grabbed a rope and set off for the corral. "Come on and help me catch this hooved treasure you have *your* heart and *my* life set on."

Shallie followed him. Hunt played out a large, looping lasso as they walked. At the gate he swung his leg over the top timber and straddled it. At their approach, the horses had begun to stir. They began to seethe as Hunt sent a couple of experimental tosses of the rope snaking over their heads. Led by the roan, they churned about the corral. Hunt played out the loop and swung it over his head, a whirring halo. As the roan approached, Hunt let the lasso fly. It cut the night air like a native spear and landed on the roan's head like a slightly askew fedora covering his ears and one eye. The roan balked and would have thrown off the loop but Hunt, with a practiced flick of his wrist, snaked the lasso up and over the horse's muzzle, landing it securely around his neck.

Feeling the hemp tighten around his throatlatch, the roan panicked, rearing up on his hind legs. Hunt gave him plenty of rope, then dropped down behind the gate. Feeling no pressure on its neck, the horse calmed down and Hunt started to reel him in like a nine-hundred-pound fish. Hunt played the roan, using instinct and finesse rather than brawn. When the bronc resisted, Hunt let out some slack. When he became more pliant, Hunt urged him close with a firm but gentle pressure on the rope. Little by little, he drew the animal to him.

"Get a handful of grain," Hunt ordered Shallie when the bronc was almost close enough to touch.

Shallie scampered off toward the barn and quickly found the grain bin. She dived into it with both hands. Back at the corral she offered the treat to the horse. He whinnied nervously at their closeness. But he wasn't a wild horse—one totally unused to the sight and scent of man—just a horse that man couldn't succeed in breaking. The smell of the molasses-laced grain mix was more than he could resist. He buried his muzzle deep in Shallie's up-stretched hands. That was what Hunt had been waiting for. With an unearthly swiftness he tightened his hold on the animal, taking a grip close to its throatlatch where he could control its movement.

With the bronc firmly in tow, Shallie slid back the gate latch and let it swing open. Hunt led the suddenly tractable horse from the herd into the arena. Shallie scrambled up on the chute gate, raising the iron-barred entrance while Hunt led him inside. Once the grating had slammed down behind the bronc, penning him in, Hunt reached for his rigging. A nervous muscle twitched in rebellion on the roan's back as he positioned the leather device. Shallie held her breath and reached through the planks of the chute to grab the latigo, the long leather strap holding the cinch band to the rigging. She prayed he wasn't a chute fighter, a horse that reared up in the box. Bronc riders feared them more than the hardest bucking horse. Their scariest horror stories were about the horses with a propensity for mashing a man between their bodies and the timbers of a bucking chute. Shallie had long ago sworn that she would never keep a horse with even the slightest tendency toward chute fighting in her string.

"Pull it tight." Shallie hauled in the slack, as Hunt held the rigging so that the front edge rested just above the point where the bronc's neck joined the backbone. She cinched it down tightly.

Hunt placed a foot on either side of the chute so that he straddled the space above the roan's back. He bent over and placed a gentle hand on the animal's sides. "He's holding his breath." With a whinnying snort, the horse expelled the air. "Okay," Hunt ordered. "Pull it in some more."

Shallie yanked up on the rigging strap. "How's that?"

"Good." He straightened up and swung his arms to loosen them. Climbing onto an unknown horse was not a bronc rider's favorite occupation. He liked to know everything he could about an animal—how he bucked, which way, and how hard. Trying out a maverick at midnight was an experience guaranteed to start a bareback rider's adrenaline pumping. Shallie, remembering Hunt's taped ribs and the rumors about his numerous other injuries, suddenly wished she hadn't made such a rash request. Out in the darkness, with no one nearby to deflect the flying hooves of a fear-maddened horse, it began to seem not only selfish but dangerous.

"Hunt," she whispered.

A look of annoyance crossed his face. She had broken his concentration, the psychic link he was forging with the roan. Like a boxer stepping into a spotlit ring, a trial lawyer into a packed courtroom, a surgeon into a hushed operating theater, Hunt was in his element. He was a study in focused intensity.

"What?" His question was testy.

"Don't go through with it. I'm sorry I asked you to do this. It was a stupid thing to ask."

His annoyance deepened. He looked from her to the horse beneath him. "No, you're right, I can sense it. This horse has some lessons in him that no man has ever learned before. I want to learn them." With that, Hunt's face settled again into a hard mask of concentration.

Seeing it, Shallie had no doubt about what had made Hunt a champion. The force of his determination hung in the air thick and tangible enough to taste and smell. Shallie could feel it just as she felt the searing heat of the hottest sun or the wind-driven rain of the fiercest storm. It was the heat generated by the force of Hunt's will that welded him to the animals he rode. It was what transformed the spectacle of rodeo into something more, something timeless—the most primitive, yet enduring of dramas, the one man has been playing out since he first rose from primordial beings to challenge the other species of the earth for supremacy. What Shallie wanted or didn't want at that moment no longer had any meaning for Hunt. He had a horse to ride.

His rosined glove squeaked as he jerked it down on his hand, catching the narrow leather strap at its top between his front teeth and pulling it tight. The gloved hand reached down to find the exact point where leather and flesh both conspired to give him the best possible grip.

"Get the gate."

Shallie jumped down and ran around to the front of the chute. She grabbed the rope attached to the gate and looked up at Hunt. The mental energy he had produced had taken on a physical life of its own. It coursed into his broad shoulders, his sinewy right arm. It brought the well-defined muscles of his back to quivering life. The energy flowed down into the firm hills of his buttocks, the columns of muscle that were his legs. It streamed through his body, pumping every bit of tissue with the same iron determination that locked his brain. He eased down on the bronc's back.

The startled roan twitched. The sting of fear trapped Shallie's breath. She had no proof yet that the horse wouldn't rear up, crushing Hunt beneath its muscled bulk. The horse kicked an angry hoof into the creaking planks of the chute, then settled down, allowing Hunt to claim the position that would best allow him to control the animal between his legs. He turned his toes out, locking his ankles, his spurs aimed directly at the bronc's shoulders. Then, with the practiced precision of a conductor raising his baton, Hunt nodded his head.

"Let's see this horse."

Shallie yanked on the rope in her hand and the gate snapped open. In the same instant Hunt threw his free hand high and the bronc broke into the arena. All the animal's pent-up rage was directed toward one objective: ridding itself of the man on its back. Shallie caught a glimpse of the horse's eyes and her pulse pounded faster. They flashed with a fiery light far brighter than that reflected from the moon. They recalled to Shallie's mind the rage-darkened eyes of stallions painted by El Greco. The roan lunged to the center of the arena, making one heart-stopping buck so high that it seemed he thought he could escape along the platinum avenue paved by the moon. For a fraction of a second, horse and rider hung in the air, suspended in a moonbeam's glow. It was as if Pegasus lived again, called back to earth by a man with a spirit to equal the mythical greatness of his own. Shallie felt the ground shudder when he landed. Hunt took the jolt with a rollicking cry of exultation that pierced the night. Shallie felt as if she were witnessing a savage ritual in which man and beast mingled their natures.

The roan leaped for the moon again, fishtailing its body with a wicked shimmy. Hunt clung to the blue-dappled back anticipating each move and matching it. The hooves pounded down again, pointed like a diver's hands outstretched to pierce the water. Shallie half expected the earth to part beneath the animal's onslaught. It didn't. Hunt absorbed the impact, letting it ripple fluidly through him. Tales of the greatest bronc riders in rodeo's hundred-year history flipped through Shallie's mind. She could find none to equal what she was seeing. Hunt combined raw physical strength and technical mastery with a kind of artistry Shallie had seen all too rarely in the arena.

Then, with no warning, the crafty roan changed tactics and tore out in a dead run heading straight for a section of fence shadowed by the concrete bleachers.

"Jump," Shallie screamed. Hunt was one move ahead of both Shallie and the horse. He turned the rigging loose and rolled off the runaway horse's back, landing with a catlike grace on the plowed dirt of the arena.

The instant the hated weight fell from his back, the roan stopped dead. His goal accomplished, he became the picture of docility. Hunt sprang to his feet, ripped his riding glove from his hand, and tossed it into the air with a wild whoop. Shallie ran to him. The moonlight bounced off his face, reflecting an expression of the purest joy she had ever seen.

As they met in the middle of the arena, Hunt swept her off of her feet and whirled her around, his strong hands spanning her waist. Like survivors of a shipwreck or winners of a sweepstakes they were joined by the magnitude of the experience they had just shared. Hunt put her down and sucked in a deep lungful of air.

"That is *some* horse." He spoke each word distinctly.

Shallie laughed, infected by the joy radiating from a man who had just put in the performance of a lifetime. "You rode Pegasus," she marveled.

"Pegasus?"

"I'm calling him Pegasus," she explained, as if it were a foregone conclusion that the horse would be hers. "I've been saving the name for him."

His hands still around her waist, he gazed into her upturned face while she congratulated him with her eyes, her smile. It seemed like nothing more than the logical extension of their shared joy when he pulled her to him. Her hands slid shyly up along his arms to the smooth bulges of muscle. She felt his power pulse beneath her fingertips. The glow from his accomplishment bathed them both in a golden radiance. He smelled the way his wild, whooping cry of exultation had sounded. Their bodies met at the two points where her erect nipples probed the shield of flesh that was his chest. The feel of his chest against the sensitive points of her breasts both disturbed and disarmed

Shallie. Before she herself was even fully aware of it, Hunt saw and responded to the longing that shone from her face.

Lightly, tentatively, his mouth grazed hers. Her breath sounded with a ragged catch in her throat. It was the signal that triggered the release of Hunt's passion. He gathered her to himself, crushing her lips with his, pressing her body against his. His thatch of springy curls tickled the palms of Shallie's hands as she raked her fingers through it.

Shallie clung to him. Never had a kiss affected her this way. She felt as if her legs wouldn't hold her, as if her very bones had melted in the white-hot flame that smoldered in her belly, fanning waves of dizzying heat through her. It had been so long since she'd felt a man's body burning against her, making her aware of the softness of her own flesh.

Since rodeo had become her life, rodeo cowboys were the only men she met and the only men she absolutely could not allow herself to become involved with. That was the surest way she could imagine to become a standing joke with the men behind the chutes. She'd heard their crude jibes often enough to know that no bedroom conquest was sacred. She had no intention of ever allowing herself to be used as the butt of such locker-room jesting.

As if reinforcing her resolution, Pegasus whinnied

in the shadowed corner of the arena. She pressed away from Hunt.

"We'd better get him back in the corral." Her voice sounded as wobbly as she felt. Hunt's arms around her were as secure as the bars of a prison. For a long moment he didn't unlock them.

Then, "You're right. That outlaw nearly jerked my arm out of its socket. If I don't soak it I'm going to feel like something that was ridden hard and hung up wet by tomorrow, and I'll have to let you teach all those young studs coming for the rodeo school how to ride broncs."

When Shallie's prize was safely corralled, Hunt asked, "Shall we drink to your find?"

Shallie hesitated, afraid to speak. What was a simple invitation to Hunt represented much more to her. She wasn't certain exactly what she felt for Hunt McIver, just that he stirred emotions in her which no man had ever touched before and that more time in his company would only intensify those dangerous feelings.

While she was still grappling for an answer, Hunt took her hand in his. Shallie let him lead her up the hill to the dark stone house at its summit.

Chapter 6

A maze of oak-lined paths led Shallie and Hunt past the fifty-year-old house's main entrance to a separate apartment. Inside, it reflected a character far different from that of the main house. The low-slung sectional furnishings in a rough-woven charcoal fabric were stylishly modern. A thick pewter-gray carpet covered the wide expanse of the living room. A picture window opened into the night, offering a view of the shimmering boulevard that the wide Colorado River cut across the McIver property. Glass-fronted shelves of richly grained rosewood lined one wall, displaying a selection of decanters and crystal ware. Hunt stepped toward it, sliding a door open and pulling out a bottle of Courvoisier brandy and two snifters.

"Not bad for a rodeo cowboy," Shallie teased as they sank into the plush sofa.

"Rodeo paid for all of this in only the most indirect

of ways. I'm sure you're well aware that a man, even when he's riding well and winning, can still put out more money in entry fees, airplane tickets, and hotel rooms than he actually wins in a year. No, the only real money in bronc riding comes from endorsements, commercials."

Shallie studied Hunt's heavily lashed eyes, his high-planed cheeks, the sensuously brooding mouth, and began to make a hazy connection between those features and the face on countless ads for everything from jeans to light beer. She knew anyone else in rodeo would have recognized him immediately, but it was just a measure of how far removed she was from the sport's more glamorous side that it had taken her this long to connect Hunt with the cowboy on all those ads. Ordinarily such a realization would have made her feel awkward and inadequate, but the exhilaration from the moment they had just shared in that moonlit arena seemed to wrap them in a charmed circle that warded off Shallie's insecurities. It also emboldened her enough to state:

"There's something I don't understand."

"What's that?" Hunt prompted her, leaning back into a corner of the sofa as if taking command of the piece of furniture.

"You said earlier that you'd been having a run of bad luck on the circuit."

Hunt's answer was a tautly spoken understatement. "You might say that."

"How can that be? You just put the best ride on a horse I've ever seen and you did it in an unlit arena on a bronc you knew nothing about." Shallie's enthusiasm carried her away as she mentally relived the ride.

Hunt chuckled, joining her in the memory. "It was a pretty fair ride."

"Fair ride?" Shallie echoed his self-deprecating words. "It was even better than your ride on Zeus, which was the best bronc ride I'd ever seen until you topped it tonight."

"Aren't you starting to see a pattern?" Hunt's voice tightened with mild sarcasm. "I can ride when there aren't a few thousand people breathing down my neck. It's been this way ever since I acquired this." He held out his hand, back side up, to reveal the angry knot of scar tissue at the base of his middle finger.

"My memento of the National Finals two years ago. I was there to claim the championship that should have been mine. I'd led in the standings by a wide margin all year long. But I drew a nasty, chute-fighting horse who smashed my hand. Split it open like an overripe melon." Hunt squeezed out the last two words. He paused to massage the keratinous mass on the back of his hand, gazing at it as if it were the crystal ball that had foretold the seasons of defeat which followed it. Hunt balled the injured hand into a fist and drove it into the palm of his other hand.

"Like any other cowboy in rodeo I've broken about

everything the human body has to offer. But this—the hand—that was different. My link to the animal was broken. I suppose I tried to start riding again too soon, before the nerves and tendons had had a chance to heal. It was the big show in Albuquerque. I'd never missed that rodeo, always managed to score well.

"I was still stinging from the humiliation of leaving the National Finals in an ambulance and wanted to come back with a vengeance. I still don't know what happened, but when I got into the chute again in front of a crowd, my hand just wouldn't stay locked around the rigging. That failure, the feel of my hand being torn loose, combined with the sound of the crowd roaring in my ears, dug into some deep part of me. The part I ride from. Now, whenever I feel those hungry eyes digging into me, I . . ." The words trailed off as Hunt sat looking at the hand that had betrayed him.

A dozen clichés, expressions of sympathy, of understanding, ran through Shallie's mind. She discarded them all. They rang too false in the face of Hunt's genuine anguish.

"I don't know why I'm telling you all this," Hunt said before the words of sympathy he couldn't bear to hear began. That wasn't why he'd spoken. "I guess it's because you seem to feel for rodeo what I do. On the surface it's stupid for me to keep pushing myself, to keep risking my life in the ring. I make all the money I could ever want from commercials and putting on rodeo schools and a few other ventures. But—"

He paused and Shallie was sure he wouldn't go on, but his words, too long dammed up, burst forth. "I know I can still ride. I don't care about winning another championship buckle. That wouldn't prove a thing to me. But I know that I've still got some rides in me that are better than anything I've done. That knowledge just keeps gnawing at me."

"I know you've got them in you too." Shallie's words were a flat statement of fact scrubbed clean of sympathy or pity. Things she knew Hunt didn't want.

"Enough of this maudlin horseshit," he declared abruptly, as if suddenly realizing how much of himself he'd revealed, and embarrassed to find himself so exposed. He drained away his brandy in one gulp and stood up. "If I don't get in that whirlpool right now, I'm going to seize up like an overheated engine." He headed down the hallway, stopping only to pull a flimsy garment from the closet. "Here, try this on and come and soak with me."

He disappeared down the hall, leaving Shallie holding a skimpy tank suit. From the end of the hall came the sound of rushing water.

Like a flock of pigeons, all of Shallie's insecurities and uncertainties came home to roost. Who wore this suit last? she wondered staring at the flimsy bit of Lycra. An overwhelming desire to cut and run swamped her. An equally strong desire, however, held her rooted to the spot. She thought of Pegasus and remembered that they really hadn't sealed their deal. She needed Hunt's assurance that the horse would truly be hers.

So, telling herself that it was for the blue roan, she stepped into the dressing room, choosing to ignore the troubling evidence which indicated that a force stronger even than her desire to carve out a career in rodeo compelled her to stay. After she'd slipped on the suit, she grabbed a thick towel hanging from a rack on the aromatic cedar wall and wrapped herself in it.

"Come on in," Hunt called out from the thick fog that shrouded the tiled room. Shallie hesitated at the door she'd cracked open. The suit Hunt had tossed her way seemed to accentuate her body more than cover it. "Don't worry," he added, "I'm decent."

Shallie stepped inside. Hunt was lounging at the far end of the oval-shaped pool. His chest was half-submerged beneath the burbling water. His arms, strikingly tan against the pale blue of the tile, were flung out on either side following the curve of the pool. Steam had turned his thick, dark hair into a corona of curls. Beneath the surging water, Shallie could make out the tiny black triangle of a man's bathing suit.

She closed the door behind her and hung her towel on one of the hooks bored into the tiled walls. When she turned around, Hunt's eyes were fastened on her, taking in the low scoop of the tank suit's neckline, the way her breasts were pressed together by the tight stretch material. How they swelled over the neckline, meeting in a deep cleft above it. His gaze trailed to the indentation of her waist, the slim mounds of her narrow hips.

Shallie put an exploratory toe into the water. A spray of bubbles massaged the sensitive sole. The sensation was too delicious to resist. She stepped down the tiled steps and took a seat. Like a thousand talented masseuses, the pressurized spray of bubbles beat against the tight coil of muscles in her neck. Shallie slid farther down, closing her eyes and letting the relaxing warmth work its magic on her tense body.

"This is heavenly," she sighed.

"Yes." Hunt's voice was close. "It is exquisite, isn't it?"

She lifted her dark lashes. Hunt was beside her. When their eyes met, Shallie could neither flinch from the desire sharpening Hunt's gaze nor hide her own. His hand darted through the water to stroke Shallie's outstretched thigh beside him. She delighted in the feel of his hand against her flesh, glad for the long, lean muscles that years of riding had developed in her legs.

Shallie followed the scarred hand back up along the forearm with its powerful swell of muscle, source of the strength needed to control a bucking horse. Back to the rounded knolls of his chest. Down to the developed muscles rippling across his taut stomach.

The pool turned into a bubbling caldron around Shallie as Hunt's hand slid down her spine and pulled her to him. His lips found a spot in the hollow of her neck, which seemed to be charged with an electricity that raced through her at his touch. She reached out to explore the ribs that had been hidden behind bandages the first time she'd glimpsed them. They seemed too strong, too insulated by muscle to have ever been injured.

"You're so tiny. So perfect." Hunt's words were an insensate mutter in her ear as he scooped her closer. With one hand he peeled the wet suit from her shoulder, covering the tender whiteness beneath with his hungry lips. When he pulled the strap completely away, Shallie felt her breast bathed by the warmth of the effervescing water. That warmth was intensified by the hot, liquid feel of Hunt's mouth sliding down to capture the peak of her breast glistening above the water and tempting his tongue.

Shallie felt she was drowning. That if she slipped even a fraction of an inch more, she would be lost beneath the churning waters, beneath her own churning emotions. She wanted Hunt McIver. She couldn't deny her response to him. If only he were any other man on earth, in any other profession. The soft slither of his tongue at her breast erased even that hesitation. She wanted him. But there was something she wanted even more. Something she wouldn't jeopardize for even this achingly intense pleasure.

"Hunt." She couldn't disguise the husky arousal in her voice. He turned his head, slowly, unwilling, toward her. "You won't tell Jake? About Pegasus, I mean."

The cords at the back of Hunt's neck went rigid. He squinted as if he'd been sliced by a stab of physical pain. "I thought we'd already established that."

It was hard for Shallie to believe that such chilly words could come from a mouth she knew to be meltingly warm.

"Or did you feel that you were ensuring my silence by coming here?"

"No, no. Of course not," Shallie stammered, realizing with a sickening lurch that her protests sounded tinnily artificial. "I . . ." She searched for an explanation, but Hunt was already leaving. His back, so firmly pliant, so alive beneath her fingers only moments before, now seemed to be sculpted from unyielding, unforgiving stone. Shallie thumbed the freed strap back up over her shoulder and followed him. A puddle of cooling water pooled at her feet as she stood silently behind Hunt, wishing for a way to erase her ill-timed words. Finally it was he who spoke.

"I've seen too much of what women will do to get what they want. I'm not interested in seeing any more of it. Go on and get dressed and I'll walk you back to the main house."

Shallie swallowed the lump of remorse forming in her throat and answered with all the pride she could muster, "That won't be necessary. I can find my way by myself." To herself she added, *I've been doing just that for two years now.*

"That's probably better. The guest suite is at the end of the hall to your right as you go in the main entrance." With that, Hunt McIver left. Damn him, damn him, damn him. The curse beat through Shallie's brain as she walked the twisting path back to the front of the rambling ranch house. It alternated with another one in which she cursed herself for her colossally ill-timed request. In the end she decided it was for the best. She had too much at stake to risk it for one night of passion. That bit of cold logic, however, did little to warm Shallie as she faced the truth that had been brewing beneath the lid she'd clamped on her emotions—she loved Hunt McIver. As quickly as the revelation flashed across Shallie's mind, she stamped it down, burying it beneath a mountain of arguments against the folly of caring for a rodeo cowboy.

Lonely streaks of gray were cracking the night sky before she finally fell into a shallow trough of sleep.

Chapter 7

Before the sun was even fully up the next morning, the sound of pickups grinding to a halt out by the arena woke Shallie from her short night of sleep. In the early light she appraised the living quarters she'd been too despondent to notice the previous night. Her bed could have slept a family of five. It floated on a thick carpet of the lightest apple green, a shade that was complemented by a patterned wallpaper. Antique oval mirrors, airy landscapes, and delicately carved furniture gave the room a light, feminine touch.

She crossed the downy carpet and pulled back the drape cloaking a window that looked down on the arena. A van with the Circle M brand painted on its side was pulling up beside the bucking chutes. The doors slid open and it disgorged a load of young men all wearing the uniform of the rodeo cowboy—neatly pressed Wrangler jeans, which crumpled slightly where they broke over dusty, scuffed boots. Their conservatively tailored Western shirts always covered an athlete's lean, hard body. Next to a potbelly, the only other thing never seen on a real rodeo cowboy was a gaudy hat of the urban-cowboy variety, topped with the pheasant feathers and beer-can-tab bands that type favored. The hats Shallie saw that morning were the simple ones she was used to seeing in arenas across the country, embellished only with the plainest of black or brown bands. The one bit of decoration that all the young men wore was the silver buckles that said they'd been the best in some county rodeo or they'd won a high school or college championship. At their feet were piles of spurs, riggings, ropes, gloves, rosin, and liniment. The last item was the one that all of them would be needing after a day at Hunt McIver's rodeo school.

As Shallie stared, the gathering of young cowboys jerked to an informal kind of attention. Conversations ceased and all the heads swiveled in the same direction. Hunt McIver strode in. Before Shallie could forbid herself to feel it, a pain pierced the empty spot beneath her heart.

There was a slight stiffness in Hunt's loose-limbed walk and a grim set to his expression. The black mood that had descended the night before still hovered about him like a storm cloud. For a moment Shallie thought she saw in Hunt's features the same disappointment that was weighing her down. She quickly chided herself for her wishful thinking. If there was any disappointment on Hunt McIver's face, it was merely the kind any rodeo cowboy would wear if he'd been denied another female conquest.

Half running, half skipping to keep pace with Hunt's long stride was the cowboy Shallie had seen the night before taking notes on the horses being bucked out.

Judging from his height (about five foot six) and his physique (powerfully developed shoulders and chest), Shallie guessed that the young cowboy was probably a bull rider. Hunt stopped and faced the young, stocky cowboy. His hand, the same hand that had caressed her with such soft promise only hours ago, cut through the warm, humid air with a series of swift signs. The short cowboy nodded and answered with his own signs.

He's deaf, Shallie realized.

The deaf cowboy pulled a crumpled sheet of paper from his back pocket and handed it to Hunt. Hunt studied the paper, then called out something that did not carry to Shallie's station at the window. She guessed he was reading off a list of names, because the clump of cowboys began breaking up into smaller groups.

One group was shorter and stockier than any of the others. Bull riders, Shallie surmised. Her guess was confirmed when they picked up plaited bull ropes hung with large clanging bells and followed a man whom she recognized as a three-time world champion in that event.

Another contingent, with loops of rope coiled around

97

their chests, broke off to follow a big buckle winner in the calf-roping event. They headed toward a large, fenced-in area with a pen full of calves at one end.

When a group gathered that included no man under six feet or two hundred pounds, Shallie knew the steer wrestlers were gathering. The iron men of rodeo, their event involved jumping off a horse galloping at thirty miles an hour onto the neck of a charging steer, then wrestling the animal to the ground. This group moved away to a practice ring where the steers Shallie had hauled down from the Double L waited. The thought of the steers reminded her of what Hunt had called her "hooved treasure."

Her gaze swung to the corral of auction horses. Pegasus was still there, even more spirited today, as if last night's ride had been but a glimpse of what his destiny held. The memory of that ride flamed anew as she looked toward Hunt. The mastery he had displayed the previous night showed in his every gesture, in the easy way he commanded the young cowboys' rapt attention. Shallie stomped down the lump of regret that was beginning to fill the empty space beneath her ribs.

She scolded herself for the futile emotion. Maybe later there would be time in her life for a man, for love. Perhaps not one like Hunt McIver. Shallie knew from painful experience that there weren't many of his caliber, but she sternly reined in her thoughts as if she were handling a headstrong horse. This was neither the time nor the place for self-pity. From far down the hall a rasp of a voice echoed.

"I don't give a good goddamn *what* that wimp of a doctor said, I'm not drinking any damned decaffeinated coffee. So get that pot out of my sight."

It sounded like Jake McIver was in fine fettle. Good, Shallie thought. She wanted to conduct her business with him and be gone as quickly as possible. The prospect of confronting Hunt again caused a noticeable quiver in Shallie's pulse. She pulled on a fresh pair of jeans, then pulled them off just as swiftly. If Jake McIver was partial to feminine pulchritude, she reasoned, there was no reason to handicap herself by dressing like a field hand. Instead she chose a tailored pair of slacks of navy gabardine, which slid over her hips, flattering her lean curves and leggy figure. Her top was of an aqua knit cut in a classically simple style, with no frills at its boatneck to detract from the graceful sweep of Shallie's fine-boned throat and neck.

As she was fluffing the gentle waves back into her palomino golden hair, she noticed a spot of high color on each cheek. They deepened as she recalled the image of Hunt, dripping wet, wearing nothing but the scantiest triangle of tissue-thin material. She slammed the brush down, angry at herself for dwelling on what could never be. She had to concentrate, to marshal her strength to ensure that she accomplished what had to be—her ownership of Pegasus.

"Well, good morning, Shalimar Larkin," Jake McIver called out from the breakfast nook where he and a very sleepy-looking Trish were seated. "I cannot believe my eyes. In the space of one short night you have been transformed from a pretty to a beautiful girl. How on earth did you accomplish that, girl?"

Shallie pasted a sweet smile on her face in lieu of an answer.

A white-uniformed cook was muttering in the corner of the kitchen as she plugged in one percolator and dumped the contents of another down the drain. The kitchen was built along the same mammoth proportions as the rest of the house. The breakfast nook extended off one end. It was surrounded by glass on three sides, opening onto a vista either of pasture filled with cantering yearlings or of a wooded area with the Colorado River weaving through it. The view closer in was just as delightful—dozens of hummingbird feeders hung from the eaves, each one patronized by three or four of the minute birds. Their iridescent colors flashed in the morning sunlight.

"Pretty little things, aren't they?" Jake asked, as if he were personally responsible for designing each one.

"They're lovely," Shallie said, happy to reflect the pleasure the old man took in his darting treasures. Trish looked sourly from the birds to Shallie.

"Good morning," Shallie greeted her.

Trish's answer was an indistinguishable grunt, which Shallie didn't care to decipher. Even in her semicomatose state, however, she was stunning. Looking at her flawless makeup and artfully arranged raven tresses, Shallie was doubly glad she hadn't opted for the stable-boy look that morning.

"Sadie," Jake bawled to the pinch-faced woman in the kitchen, "fetch Miss Larkin a cup of coffee. *Real* coffee, not that *de*caffeinated mess you were trying to poison me with."

As Shallie joined the couple at the table, she mentally played out a number of possible openings she might use to turn the conversation toward selling Pegasus. She knew she mustn't appear too anxious or McIver would suspect something.

"Tell me, Shallie." McIver leaned back, folding his arms over his chest. "Just how much do you and old Walter plan on beating me out of for that mangy bunch of steers you brought down?"

"Mangy!" Shallie echoed in mock alarm, picking up on McIver's bantering style. "Those are prime beeves, every one of them. Just ask those doggers out there. They'll tell you how prime they are, unless they're too wet behind the ears to know a good steer when they jump on its neck."

Jake chuckled. "You're a feisty one, aren't you, Miss Shalimar Larkin. I love to see that fiery red in your cheeks. Go on ahead and name your price. If you're Larkin stock, I know it will be a fair one."

Shallie hesitated a long moment, guilt pricking at her. In one swoop she pushed it aside and plunged onward. "Two hundred and fifty dollars a head."

"Two-fifty a head? Don't cheat yourself, girl. I'd have given you twice that."

You old swindler, Shallie thought, *you should have given me three times that price*. What she said aloud was, "Plus my pick of those horses you've got out in the corral."

"Whoa, now. We haven't bucked out all of those broncs yet. When we do we'll put the lot of them up for auction and you can have your pick of the litter."

"I want my pick before the auction and before you buck out any more horses or the deal's off, and you can pay regular market price for those steers."

McIver's eyebrows jumped a fraction of an inch. "Now I don't know about that. We've got some prime bucking stock out there."

"You've got a sorry bunch of plowhorses and you know it."

"So why are you so interested in them?" McIver asked, cocking his head slightly to one side as if trying to see around Shallie to catch a glimpse of her motives.

"If you'd seen what the Double L has been bucking out lately you wouldn't have to ask that question. We're desperate for good riding stock." The humbling admission deflected McIver's suspicion. He hadn't seen any of the new stock that Shallie had acquired, but McIver knew of the Double L's reputation as a company that catered to ropers and neglected the rough stock riders.

"You know what, Shallie? I like you. You're too damned pretty to be a stock contractor."

The compliment seemed to rouse Trish from her lethargy. She pursed her lips, displeased that any other woman should be the object of a compliment while she was present.

"Stock contractors all need to smoke cigars and have big ole bellies like me." He patted the small swell of flesh that barely rippled above his belt and let out a burst of raucous laughter, startling the hummingbirds outside the window.

"But I do like you, so you got yourself a deal. Go on down to the corral and pick yourself out a bronc."

Shallie knew that he thought he'd fleeced her. Odds were that not one of the horses he had were worth even one of the steers she'd brought down. It calmed her conscience to know that Jake McIver was willing to take the equivalent of a dozen steers for what was more than likely a worthless bucking horse.

"What do you think about the deal I just cut with Shalimar?" Jake demanded. Shallie whirled around to find Hunt looming over her.

"What deal's that?" His voice was as flat and feature-less as a West Texas highway.

"I'm going to let this little lady have her pick of any of those auction broncs. What do you think of that? Have we got a Midnight down there I don't know about?"

Shallie felt her stomach tighten. Would Hunt give her away?

"What are the chances of that happening?" Jake asked.

"Pretty damned slim." Hunt's face was an expression-less deadpan as he added, "Guess Shallie's a gambler."

The grin splitting Jake's face faded and he leaned in close to Shallie. "Now, don't you forget to tell Walter that this trade was strictly your idea, you hear?"

"I will," Shallie promised. His request confirmed her suspicion that Jake McIver believed he was cheating her.

Looking as if he'd just smelled something unpleas-ant, Hunt took the coffee mug Sadie extended to him and stomped out of the house.

"What's gotten into him?" Jake asked after the door slammed shut behind his retreating grandson.

Shallie shrugged, not trusting herself to speak. She took several deep breaths and was able to go on. "I'd bet-ter go and pick out my horse. I need to get on the road."

"No hurry," Jake insisted. "Stay as long as you like. We like having company, don't we, Trish?"

"Yes, of course." The model-perfect woman seemed

to have come fully awake with Hunt's arrival. She gave Shallie a smile that stopped far short of her eyes.

"Day after tomorrow, we're having a big do here. Everybody who's anybody in rodeo will be flying in." McIver reeled off a list of names. Shallie recognized most of them. With McIver's next words she realized what they all had in common. "The party was Trish's idea, she made up the guest list. I just happened to know all the boys."

And they all just "happened" to be on the committee that elected a Rodeo Sweetheart each year. Shallie looked at the young beauty and understood why she would be involved with a man old enough to be her grandfather. The Rodeo Sweetheart title invariably led to a host of commercial offers and, in one or two cases, a career in films and television. If anyone had the clout to get a Rodeo Sweetheart elected, it was Mr. Rodeo, Jake McIver.

"Thanks," Shallie said feebly, getting to her feet and heading for the door, "but my uncle will be needing me."

The air was hot and humid. The ranch looked endlessly lush in the bright morning light, but its beauty was lost on Shallie as she made her way down to the corral.

"This is the position you want to be in when that chute gate swings open." Hunt's deep, rich voice floated up. He was perched atop a bale of hay, his spurs dug into it. A group of wide-eyed young cowboys were scattered worshipfully at his feet. Shallie, unable to meet the accusations in his eyes, glanced away hurriedly when he looked her way.

As if the animal were a magic talisman against the desperate unhappiness threatening to crush down upon her, Shallie sought out Pegasus. The sight of the roan cheered her. He was worth whatever she had sacrificed to obtain him, and now he was hers.

She found Wade in the barn and steeled herself to the task of directing the odious man. What she really longed for was a quiet corner somewhere in which to sob her heart out. Instead she was caught switching from one ill-fitting mask to another. With Jake McIver she'd played the good old girl; now she had to be the stern boss with a surly employee.

"Wade." Grudgingly, the hand directed his attention toward her. "There's a blue dappled roan out in the corral. Could you load him up? We're taking him back with us." Instead of snapping to, Wade leaned languidly against a post and continued to silently eye Shallie. She did not enjoy the experience of having his reptilian gaze slither over her.

"Wade, did you understand what I said? I want to be on the road in fifteen minutes."

"Fifteen minutes, eh? Doesn't give you much time to say good-bye to the bronc-riding stud out there, does it, *Miss* Larkin?" There was a mocking emphasis on the word "Miss." A dark, menacing undercurrent ran through his entire statement.

Shallie suddenly became aware of how far the barn was from the other buildings.

"Don't look all shocked and innocent. I saw you two out there last night. Wouldn't even turn on a light, would you? Think I couldn't tell what you was doing? I saw how you followed him up to his bed." Hoskins's lips curled downward. The sullen mask of indifference he usually wore fell away with that sneer. Shallie saw the bitter, twisted man beneath and the hatred and cruelty that drove him. A thrum of fear beat through her as she realized how dangerously off balance he was.

"Oh, you're right and proper with the working hands, ain't you, Miss Rodeo Contractor? But you start peeling off them drawers just like any of them other rodeo bunnies when a big buckle walks by."

Shallie had heard more than enough. She crested the wave of fear rising in her belly and headed for the barn's one open door.

"Hold it right there, little missy," he commanded, his face contorted with a rage as hideous as his words had been. "I said, hold it!" When Shallie again ignored his command, Hoskins lunged forward, grabbing her forearm. "I told you not to be playing the fancy lady with me no more." His acrid breath carried his words in a stench of frustrated fury that blew hot on Shallie's neck.

"Take your hands off of me, Wade Hoskins, you make me sick."

"You appear to have a hearing problem, Hoskins." Hunt appeared silhouetted in the barn door. In the next instant he was beside Shallie, his hand breaking Hoskins's grip as if the man's fingers were so many dried twigs.

"Get your gear and clear out," he commanded. "Walk to the highway. From there you can hitch a ride. Now move!" Hunt reinforced his order with a boot toe to Hoskins's posterior that sent him flying. The trembling man scrambled along on all fours until he could struggle to his feet and flee the barn. Hunt turned to Shallie, making certain she wasn't hurt.

"Told you I didn't think much of your hired help."

Relief and nervousness forced a high-pitched giggle from Shallie's throat. Before it was half out, a wracking sob overtook it. Hunt pulled her to his chest in a comforting embrace, patting her slender back until the hiccuping sobs had stopped.

"I watched you head this way," he explained in a low, calming voice, "and I followed you down to say goodbye. Apologize. I don't know what. I just knew that I couldn't let you leave without . . ." His words trailed off and he tried again. "I was angry last night. Furious. It wasn't until this morning that I cooled down enough to ask myself honestly how I would have acted if I'd wanted something as much as you wanted that horse."

Shallie controlled herself enough to interject, "It wasn't the way you thought."

"It's all right," Hunt soothed, and somehow with her tears rolling down his strong chest, it *was* all right.

"Hey," he said as her sobs subsided, "I've got a bronc-riding class to teach. Come on and watch. When it's over I'll arrange to get you and your rig back home."

Shallie nodded, grateful to have someone else take over and arrange things for a change. The feeling was luxurious and she clung to Hunt's chest enjoying it to the fullest. The security of that moment was shattered, though, when Hunt, as if observing to no one in particular, said, "You did get what you wanted, though, didn't you? I mean, Pegasus *is* yours."

Shallie looked up and read everything she needed to know about the implications of his statement in his eyes—that she had come to his apartment with a calculated plan to barter her body for the blue roan. He peered at her with a wary, hooded skepticism. A dozen protests rang through her mind, but they all would have served only to reinforce his innuendo. Though not spoken, they still flashed through her eyes, making the gold flecks buried in their brown depths glint with anger.

"You arrogant son of a—"

Hunt silenced her insulting words by stealing the breath she needed to pronounce them with the crush of his lips. Shallie felt her footing slip away from under her. It was replaced by the iron supports of Hunt's arms folding around her. His lips did not question or hesitate; they demanded and took what they wanted. Shallie was defenseless against their authority. His tongue claimed her mouth, plundering its soft, hidden recesses. An army of sensations laid siege to her emotions, conquering them and quelling any resistance she might have put up.

Hunt was a masterful invader. The taste of many sweet past victories was on his lips, along with the knowledge that he would know how to savor the present one. Though far less experienced, Shallie was still aware that the battle had not been entirely one-sided, when she heard Hunt's breath broken into gasping bursts. His hands drew her face, her lips, more fully to his own as if he were driven by a deep hungering need of them.

At the sound of the exaggerated shuffling of feet, Shallie pulled away abruptly. The deaf cowboy stood behind them. His freckles were lost in the reddened face he directed toward the ground, where he was digging nervous circles in the dirt with his boot toe.

Hunt turned to him and cut the air with a few choppy signals.

The boy answered, barely looking up from under the brim of his outsized hat.

"Petey." Hunt pronounced the boy's name while simultaneously signing. "This is Shallie Larkin. Shallie, this is Petey Andrews, my prize helper and all-around *compañero*."

As Hunt translated the words he had spoken, Shallie managed to quell her ire enough to smile at the boy in response to Hunt's introduction.

"Petey tells me the natives are getting restless. Come watch if you like, or sit in the house and talk with Trish. Either way you won't be leaving until the school's done. I'll need every hand I've got for it."

"Well, pardon me for the inconvenience, *Mister* McIver," Shallie exploded. "But if it weren't for your manipulations I'd be happily on my way back to Mountain View at this moment."

"Don't forget," Hunt said, clearly more entertained than offended by her outburst, "that if it weren't for my 'manipulations' you'd be far from doing anything 'happily' right now. You'd still be in the clutches of that piece of slime you used to call a hired hand."

Before she could launch another volley of protests, Hunt was gone.

The thought of spending time with Trish was odious enough to force Shallie into opting for the other alternative Hunt had presented. So, she followed him outside and took a seat in one of the pickup trucks parked at the periphery of Hunt's open-air class.

"Son," Hunt addressed a lanky young man in a plaid shirt and glasses, "if this is all you think you're worth"—he held up a shoddily made rigging—"don't even bother to climb into that arena because I don't want to have to drag you out." The owner of the inferior piece of equipment bowed his head in embarrassment.

Shallie knew that the boy's momentary shame was a small price to pay for a piece of advice that could very well save his life. Hunt pulled a rigging out of his own bag and handed it to the young cowboy, then continued to inspect the others. When he'd deemed them all well prepared, he signaled to Petey, who drove eight high-spirited broncs into the chutes. Dust and the clanging of the metal chute gates clogged the air. The once eager students grew quiet and watchful as they sized up the horses they would soon be tested by.

"Look at them real good, boys," Hunt warned. "Because not a single one of those animals realizes that this is just a class. To them each one of you is the toughest, meanest rider to ever put metal to horsehide and that's exactly how they're going to treat you. They don't know that you're students. They won't be holding back because you're just learning. This is for real for them so it better be just as real for you too." Hunt's tone grew intent as he tried to impress upon his listeners just how serious rodeo was.

"Now what I want each and every one of you to do is climb on board and clamp your riding hand down on that rigging. Then, with your free hand, I want you to reach up and grab yourself a great big handful of sky and hang on.

Because that's rodeo, boys. You may lose that rigging, but you'll always have the sky."

His students stared at Hunt, silenced by what was the closest they'd ever hear to a lyrical description of rodeo. Hunt pointed a finger at the lanky kid in glasses.

"Halstrom."

The young man jumped to his feet. "Yessir?"

"Halstrom, you were looking pretty good on that bale of hay we used for spurring practice. You think you're ready to put it to something a little livelier?"

"You bet," he answered.

Only Shallie noticed how the gangly youth wiped moist palms on his bright green chaps. His bravado was false, but then that was the only kind that was truly real in rodeo. Any man who settled down on the back of a horse that was flaming with murderous intent and said he wasn't scared either didn't know enough to respect the animal or had a few vital connections missing in the self-preservation department.

"Okay, take chute one."

Halstrom scrambled up the gate while Hunt assigned the others to their mounts. Halstrom's long face was lost in the deep shadow cast by his hat brim. Petey helped him to rig up, then swung down to wait at the gate. The bespectacled cowboy was in good form as he burst out of the chute, practically leaning against the horse's rump when it bucked its hindquarters high in the air. Shallie marveled at how Halstrom was transformed on the back of a bronc, completely losing the awkward lankiness he had on solid ground. But one good spin tossed him into the air.

"You didn't want it enough, did you, Halstrom?" Hunt called down from his perch on the catwalk.

Halstrom answered with an angry grab at his hat, lying crumpled in the dirt.

"I didn't hear you, Halstrom. If you'd wanted it badly enough, you would have ridden. Isn't that right?"

"Yessir," Halstrom barked.

"You'll do better next time, won't you, Halstrom?"

"I damned well will." The boy's response was a furious promise. It pleased Hunt, who turned away with a grin, shouting to the others to be ready for their rides. "Get mad," he yelled as if repeating a chant. "Be aggressive. Show me what you can do. Show the world. Bear down. Want it. Get it."

The next student out of the chutes, a cowboy named Wildes, was already benefiting from Hunt's hard-bitten message. There was an unyielding set to his jaw that defied the animal beneath to jerk the rigging from his hand. He rode to the eight-second buzzer, then came ambling back to the chutes, a cocky, self-satisfied strut to his walk.

"Think you're pretty hot, don't you, Wildes?" Hunt called down, freezing him in midstride. "Well, you goose-egged. Scored a big zero for that ride you're so proud of."

"Wha-a-a . . ." Wildes stammered.

"You didn't mark him out."

"Yes. I—" he started to protest, but Hunt cut him off.

"You might have *thought* you did. It might even have *felt* like you did. But your spurs were *not* over the points of that horse's shoulders when his front feet hit the ground on that first jump out of the chute. And if they aren't there, Wildes, up high where the judges can see them, you've just lost your entry fee. No matter what kind of spectacular ride you make after that first jump, it's all over. You might just as well have stayed home."

Shallie wished she could tell the dejected young man just how lucky he was to have someone who cared enough to tell him what Hunt had just told him. She'd seen too many rodeo cowboys throw away their hard-earned money because they'd never had that lesson drilled into them.

The rides continued, with Hunt finding an occasional point to compliment but more often jumping down with both feet on the stupid and not-so-stupid mistakes the novices made. If anything, he was even harder on the boys who made the fewest mistakes, who displayed the most potential. With these few, like Halstrom, he concentrated on reinforcing their "try," a rodeo term that translates loosely into "motivation." An elusive quality that couldn't be replaced by strength or technical expertise, it was the one essential ingredient in the making of a champion.

"You've got to know your horse," Hunt lectured, while Petey loaded up the next round of horses. "Find out everything you can about the animal you've drawn. Ask. Any cowboy who's ridden him, or seen him ridden, will tell you everything they know about him, just like you'll tell any cowboy who asks *you* everything you know about any mount you've ever drawn. Psych that bronc out. Touch him. Smell him. Get as close physically and mentally to that animal as you can."

Shallie doubted that there was a single person other than herself who truly understood what Hunt was saying. They couldn't, because there was a wall between them and every horse they'd ever encountered in their life, a wall she knew wasn't there for Hunt. She had seen the way he approached a horse, the way he rode. For those few seconds, he was linked to his mount by the high, wild streak that neither education, money, nor prestige had been able to tame. That was his edge, his gift. And there was no way he could transfer it to anyone else through words.

By noon only a couple of the best of Hunt's students were still eagerly climbing the chute gates when Petey loaded a fresh section of horses. Most of the students were crumpled beneath the tiny pool of shade cast by their large hats, their exhausted faces streaked by trickles of sweat running through thick layers of dust. A few would be sidelined for the rest of the day with sprained ankles and twisted wrists. Some were already making plans to escape at the earliest moment, having decided that there must be easier ways in the world to earn a little respect. All were walking gingerly, the insides of their thighs having been skinned down to raw patches of flesh.

When even Halstrom groaned at the question "Who'll take chute one?" Hunt called a lunch break.

The two long tables in the main dining hall each seated two dozen, and every chair was filled by the time Sadie and her helpers began carrying in the food. The steaming bowls were heaped with brisket, which had been slowly cooking over a low fire of tangy mesquite wood for nearly a day—plus fresh vegetables from Circle M's own plots, home-baked yeast rolls, corn on the cob, and enough iced tea to float a rowboat.

Shallie, sitting at an inconspicuous spot as far from Hunt as she could manage, was astounded by the ferocity with which forty-eight hungry young men could eat. She'd barely cut into the tender meat on her plate before half a dozen voices were calling out for various dishes to be passed around a second time. Once the single-minded clanging of utensils against crockery leveled off, the clamor of voices began, each one rising to be heard above the others. The camaraderie sweeping the room encompassed Shallie as well.

"Couldn't believe it when I bucked off that first horse this morning," the lanky fellow to her left observed. Shallie recognized the class star, Halstrom, and commiserated with him.

"Mr. McIver's tough," he went on, "but he sure as heck got me mad enough to stick on every horse after that first one."

"You certainly did," Shallie agreed, suppressing a chuckle at the proud swell of accomplishment in his voice.

Halstrom stopped and openly inspected Shallie from behind his thick glasses. Finally the light of recognition dawned on his face. "Hey, you're with the Double L, aren't you? I've seen you working a few shows."

"I own the Double L with my uncle," Shallie answered.

"You do?" Halstrom asked in amazement. "A lady contractor? That's a new one on me. But what the heck, as long as you keep bringing stock as good as the Double L brings, it's fine with me."

Shallie grinned. Maybe there was hope for the upcoming generation of rodeo cowboys.

"Hey, guys," Halstrom called out to his buddies. "This here's the half owner of the Double L. A lady stock contractor."

For a few seconds the conversation and clanking of silverware ceased while the cowboys appraised the strange specimen presented to them. From the next table came a comment.

"This ain't no bull. I drew a Double L horse at a show in Hereford. Zeus I think was the name. Anyway, that is the rankest animal I ever tried to stay on." Other voices joined in. "Best roping calves around." "Always a good weight and they run true."

All around her, talk ran thick with the morning's pumped-up energy. Snippets of tales of victories won and only nearly missed reached her ears. As her gaze swung from one sun- and windburned face to another, Shallie could think of no other gathering in the world where she'd be more pleased to be accepted. Then, from across the room, Hunt's eyes caught and held hers.

Even at that distance, Shallie felt his magnetism disarm her. There was a mocking challenge in his look that made her squirm and look away. Mechanically, she put a forkful of food into her mouth. It could have been sawdust as she chewed drily through the now tasteless lump. Under his scrutiny, even the most automatic process required the utmost concentration. Every motion of her jaw was a forced effort. She glanced up. Hunt's attention had been claimed by a student. Shallie began breathing again.

This is ridiculous, she thought. *Exactly what gives*

him the power to turn me into a frightened rabbit caught out in the open by a fox? As she sawed furiously through a piece of brisket, Shallie decided she would leave as soon as the meal had ended. There was no law that said she couldn't drive the rig back herself.

After lunch she grabbed her overnight bag and headed out to the corral to load up Pegasus. Her first shock was finding that the horse was gone. The second was discovering the Double L semi had disappeared as well. She threw her bag on the barren ground and ran back up to the house. Hunt and a few students were lingering over coffee.

"Mr. McIver." It cost her an effort to keep her voice calm. "May I have a word with you?"

"Why certainly, Miss Larkin. It would be my pleasure."

"I assume you can tell me where my truck and my horse are." Shallie planted her hands firmly on her hips, reinforcing the no-nonsense tone of her question.

"Right at this moment, I'd say they are probably about sixty miles northwest of Austin. I sent Petey to take them both on back up to the Double L, and the way that maniac likes to haul a . . . ah, cover ground, I'd have to say that he's at least that far along."

"You sent Petey home with *my* truck and *my* horse and without *me*?"

"Sure. You'll be needing a good hand to fill in until

you find someone to replace that weasel Hoskins, and Petey was itching to see some new country, so—"

"So, you just sent him on his way without so much as a word to me. Technically what we're talking about here is theft, horse and truck."

"I suppose you're right. Technically, that is." His light, mocking tone infuriated Shallie as much as his packing her horse and truck off.

"Just how am I supposed to get home?"

"They have airplanes where you come from?" he continued to tease. "Don't worry. I've made a first-class reservation for you on the late flight to Albuquerque. At Circle M's expense, of course. I even called your uncle to tell him when to pick you up at the airport." Turning away from her, as if they had nothing further to discuss, Hunt called to the students, "Let's ride some broncs, boys."

Chapter 8

T*he afternoon ground by in* a turgid haze. Accustomed to working from the moment the sun crept over the Sandia Mountains to the moment she dropped, exhausted, into bed, Shallie was like a wild animal penned in a beautifully upholstered cage. The enforced idleness grated on her nerves. She picked up one magazine after another, only to toss each one aside unread. The instant she left her thoughts unoccupied, however, they returned with a maddening persistence to the moment when Hunt's lips had pressed against her own. Then, as if she could outrun those troubling memories and the disturbing effect they had on her, Shallie would begin to pace. She followed a monotonous circuit that always took her back to the window that faced down on the arena.

As she marched past the window, her resolution crumbled and she glanced out. A cowboy with a video camera clung to the fence. As each rider emerged, the cameraman carefully taped his performance. Hunt hovered over it all, gesticulating wildly as he coached his students.

The long, slow hours speeded up as Shallie's thoughts were drawn to the forceful man. She knew that on one level he evoked in her a very basic, uncomplicated response. He was a potently sensual man and obviously used to women reacting to him. But Shallie sensed another, deeper level and suspected that her attraction to Hunt emanated from it.

So what, she snapped at herself, storming away from the window. What did it matter *how* many levels, dimensions, and facets Hunt encompassed? They were all contained within an identity forbidden to her: rodeo cowboy. She jerked the curtains shut and lay down. Though sleep wouldn't come, Shallie willed herself to rest for several hours.

The sun was closing in over the tops of the oaks when she again gave in to the impulse to take up her vigil by the window. As she watched, Trish emerged from the main house and strolled down to the classes still in progress. She was wearing a low-cut knit top and a pair of skinny jeans tight as sausage casings. As she sauntered up to the arena, all action halted as heads swiveled to follow the exaggerated flick of her hips. An icy coil of jealousy unwound deep in Shallie's stomach when she saw Hunt join the pack tracking Trish's approach.

Why shouldn't Hunt be attracted to her? Shallie asked herself. Trish was everything that she wasn't—elegant, ladylike, beautiful, and sexy. Shallie looked down at her work-worn hands studded with blisters and calluses and remembered Trish's slim, well-manicured hands.

A sudden, sharp rap at the door startled Shallie, tearing her from the depressing comparison.

"Dinner in half an hour on the patio, miss," Sadie announced in her peevish voice.

The last thing she felt up to was an intimate soirée with Trish and her matched set of McIver amours. Shallie decided that a good soak was just what she required to brace her psychically for the encounter.

She went to the bathroom and turned both brass knobs on full blast. A roar of water spewed into the sunken, marble-swirled tub. She rummaged through the cabinets and discovered an ample supply of bath oil. Obviously a number of female guests had passed through the Circle M. She chose a foaming sandalwood-scented variety and poured it under the gush of water. The scented steam penetrated far into her dust-dried membranes and brought them back to life. Shallie emptied her mind of the confusing swirl of conflicts clouding it and simply luxuriated in the warm, wet buoyancy. By the time she'd finished, Shallie's skin was glowing with a delicate apricot sheen and she felt almost up to facing Hunt.

The dinner was as light and elegant as the luncheon

menu had been homespun and filling. A bowl of crushed ice topped by jumbo shrimp boiled to a pink lushness dominated the table set up on the patio. Flickering lanterns cast a soft light. The pool in the background was lit from underneath and glowed like a shimmering sapphire. On its surface floated huge magnolia blooms plucked from the nearby trees. Their sweet odor perfumed the gentle air.

"Pretty fancy spread, eh?" Jake McIver's voice cracked out of the darkness, startling Shallie. "Hunt ordered it up. That boy developed some mighty exotic tastes back there at that Eastern school." The haughty swell of Trish's laughter made Shallie uneasy, as if she were the butt of some joke she knew nothing of.

"Come on, pull up a chair. Hunt didn't have all this shrimp flown in from the coast so that we all could stand around staring at it." The three of them gathered around the table set with the finest china and stemware. A dry white wine gleamed in the glass at Shallie's place. There were platters of the thinnest prosciutto ham rolled around crisp wedges of honeydew melon, and an assortment of other hors d'oeuvres were brought in. Shallie nibbled at them, glorying in the array of fresh, unadorned flavors. But she couldn't entirely relax and enjoy the delicacies because she started at every sound, expecting Hunt to enter at any moment.

The sound of a recording of a Chopin piano étude

blended seamlessly with the night sounds of the crickets and owls. It was one of Shallie's favorites. She had liked classical music ever since studying piano as a little girl, but the Country and Western–dominated world of rodeo gave her scant opportunity for indulging her taste.

"I hope you don't mind my choice in music." Hunt's voice emerged from the darkness.

"When has what I minded ever mattered a whit to you?" Jake responded crankily. "Only damned cowboy I ever heard of listened to that classical stuff."

"Just because a man rides broncs," Hunt countered, "doesn't necessarily mean that all he can enjoy is Johnny Cash and Toby Keith." Hunt's hand entered the circle of light cast by the lantern. He pulled out the empty chair beside Shallie and sat down. She flicked a sidelong glance in his direction as the light fell upon his face. He seemed to fairly beam with a healthy, scrubbed vitality. It shone from his face in the tan that had been deeply burnished by his day in the sun.

On her other side she watched Jake McIver's expression change from one of puzzled intentness to outraged anger. He stiffened, his chin jutting forward.

"That's Maggie's piece, isn't it?" he exploded.

"Is it?" Hunt retorted archly.

"You know damned well it is. I told you I never wanted to hear that piece of music played in this house." Jake grabbed the remote control and clicked off the Chopin.

The contrast between the amplified sound and the night silence was sudden and jarring. As it fell over the party, Shallie wondered just who Maggie was. Her speculations were interrupted by Trish.

"Those junior rodeo riders just love you, don't they, Hunt?" Her compliment seemed simperingly obvious to Shallie.

"They're a good group," Hunt answered without elaboration.

"They're going to be a lot better after they've had the benefit of your expertise," Trish cooed.

Shallie wanted to gag, but she knew that flattery, combined with the kind of sultry look Trish was shooting at Hunt from the depths of her smoky eyes, had strangely predictable effects on most men. Shallie comforted herself with the thought that she'd be gone soon and the trio seated around her could return to whatever perverse games they played to keep themselves amused.

"Expertise?" Jake hooted, emerging from his sulk. "I wouldn't call the season Hunt had last year, or the year before for that matter, the work of an expert. Where did you come out in the standings, Hunt? Or don't they bother with classification that far down the line? What surprises me is that he could hornswoggle anyone into coming to his rodeo school."

Knowing the depths of Hunt's feelings about rodeo, Shallie considered Jake's comment almost cruel. But if

Hunt was offended by it, he didn't reveal it. "You're one hundred percent right, Jake. I didn't make the standings the past two years. But I led them for four years before that, and there are a few people who have memories that can stretch back farther than a few months."

"Well, you better not stretch them too far or we'll end up having all the old has-beens hobbling out on their canes, with their hearing aids turned way up so that they can teach the young whippersnappers how it was done in their day. Maybe I'll get out there tomorrow and show them how Jake McIver used to twist a bronc in the old days." Jake cackled with delight at the image.

Trish looked from one McIver to the other with an animal-like avidity, hoping for even more emotional warfare. Shallie thought she would have made the perfect spectator at a Roman circus.

"Or how Junior McIver used to ride." Hunt's comment caused the old man's mood to darken with the rapidity of a summer squall.

Shallie was mystified. But the name "Junior McIver" did ring a bell somewhere in her distant memory. Then it came back to her: Junior McIver, son of Jake, father of Hunt, a onetime bronc-riding buckle winner. She couldn't remember, though, what had ever happened to him.

"That's right," Jake agreed grimly. "It's never hurt the Circle M to have a champion in the family. A champion who's still on top, at any rate. The has-beens are fine for teaching rodeo schools, but they sure as hell don't help bring in the big-money contracts."

"Listen, old man." Hunt's voice was dangerously low. "I don't get into that arena to provide free advertising for the Circle M." He turned sharply away from his grandfather. "Shallie, we'd better get on the road. You wouldn't want to miss your flight."

Relieved to have an escape from the tension-filled atmosphere, Shallie quickly rose to her feet.

"Now, don't run off like that," Jake protested. "The boy knows I was only kidding. Only having some fun with him."

Shallie froze, caught between the two men's conflicting wishes. Hunt put an arm around her and guided her toward the door.

"We really do have to go now. It's a long drive to the airport and Shallie has expressed her strong desire to leave."

Shallie muttered her thanks to Jake McIver for his hospitality and promised to give his best to her uncle.

"And remember to tell him it was you who came up with that little trade we made," he called after her.

Outside, Shallie felt as if she could breathe again after the constriction of the emotionally charged scene on the patio. Hunt held open the door of his forest-green Porsche for her. The bag she had thrown down when she discovered the semi missing was safely tucked in the back. For a long time the only sound was the powerful hum of the well-tuned engine. When Circle M was just a speck of light in the rearview mirror, Hunt spoke.

"You're probably wondering why I put up with him."

Shallie didn't answer, but she very definitely was reviewing several possibilities. Hunt's acceptance of his grandfather's verbal abuse was inconsistent with everything else she sensed about his character. He had too much pride, too much dignity to tolerate it unless there was a good reason. Shallie remembered the glances Trish and Hunt had exchanged, and one strong possible reason entered her mind. An even stronger one popped up to complement it: If Hunt could swallow his pride long enough, he stood to inherit all of Circle M. What a cozy setup that would be for him and Trish. All these thoughts flickered across the screen of Shallie's consciousness in less than the time it took Hunt to draw two breaths and continue.

"I've been tempted to leave. But I couldn't, not now. My grandfather is a difficult man but I think I understand him better than anyone else alive."

Shallie heard a grudging admiration in Hunt's appraisal. Hesitantly, she asked, "Where is your father now?"

"Dead." Hunt dropped the word. "Drank himself into an early grave. I suppose that's one way to escape from my grandfather, but not one that ever appealed to me. Anyway, after he left, pretty early on in my life, it fell to me to maintain the McIver dynasty of champions." The laugh that accompanied his last statement was dry and brittle.

Shallie wanted to ask more questions, but she felt she'd already overstepped some sensitive limits. *I'm better off not knowing,* she told herself, *and not having anything further to do with the world of the McIver men.* Clinging to that thought, she settled back in the leather-upholstered seat and resolutely turned her attention to the shadowy silhouettes passing by her window. As they approached Austin, the silhouettes became more clearly defined by the city lights.

"We're passing over the Colorado River now," Hunt informed her. A thick ribbon of water slid through the heart of the town. The reflections of multicolored lights danced across its surface like water sprites at play.

"And that's the Capitol Building."

To her left a domed structure cut a massive, ghostly figure spotlit in the night sky.

Shallie struggled to keep her attention on Hunt's guided tour, but the true object of her interest lay much closer. Hunt McIver was what she wanted to know more about.

"Quite impressive," she commented limply as they circled the University of Texas, her spirits inexplicably sinking as they hurtled through the night, drawing ever closer to the moment of parting. *It's for the best.* She drummed that thought through her mind like a drill chant for unruly soldiers. *The quicker I remove myself from Hunt McIver and all reminders of him, the better.*

At the airport, Hunt pulled smoothly up in front of the terminal and turned off the engine. He turned to Shallie, started to speak, then stopped. Instead he glanced away and rapped his fist against the leather-wrapped steering wheel as if dismissing the thought he had started to communicate. He retrieved her bag from the back and stepped out. The moment was lost, and he would soon dismiss her as easily as the unspoken thought. Shallie pulled a shaky breath into her lungs, fighting a sadness of a magnitude she had no reasonable explanation for. While she fumbled with the craftily designed door handle, Hunt opened it and she joined him on the walkway.

"Don't bother coming in," she said. "You might get ticketed."

A brief nod served as Hunt's answer.

Shallie drew herself up, trying to shake off the sudden torpor that weighed her down. "Thank you for everything," she said, briskly sticking her hand out for a quick, businesslike shake.

Hunt took her outstretched hand in both of his. "Not a handshake," he murmured as if her gesture had pained him. His lips descended with no further warning. The movement had the effect upon Shallie of watching slow-motion footage of a building being blown up so that it crumbles inward. By the time his mouth was on hers, the demolition of the facade she had constructed was complete. The truth she had attempted to wall in was laid bare. She could not escape it with comforting lies about how it was best that she would never truly know Hunt McIver.

"Hunt, I—"

"I know, Shallie," he finished her confession for her. "You can't leave."

Shallie, never one to second-guess decisions that came from her instincts, slid back into the Porsche. She was determined not to look back and not to lie to herself anymore. No matter how foolish, how irrational, or what the eventual cost might be, she wanted Hunt McIver, whatever the price. She pulled her cell phone out and called her uncle to tell him she'd be in on the first flight in the morning.

As they pulled up to the canopied entrance in front of the Driskill Hotel in downtown Austin, an older man in a uniform heavy with gold braid sprung gimpily forward to take the wheel of the Porsche.

"Hunt, I thought I recognized your car." The parking valet greeted Hunt, taking the keys from him and sweeping the door open, then hurrying over to Shallie's side to help her from the car.

"How have you been, J.T.?" Hunt inquired of the older man.

"Can't complain. How about you? You over your run of bad luck yet?"

"Can't say, J.T. I hope so. Guess we'll find out in Albuquerque next month. That's the first show this year I'm entered in. Doctors have been keeping me out of the chutes. They tell me I shouldn't ride at all this season. But if I don't get back in there this year, I never will."

"I'll be cheering for you."

"The way I've been riding, I'll need it."

"No you won't." J.T. shook his head to emphasize his statement. "You have the magic. Just like your daddy and your granddaddy had it. I've seen all the great ones ride, but none of them had it like you. No, you don't need my cheering, or anyone else's. Just ride your horses the way I know you can."

"Thanks, J.T. I'll be trying to do just that."

"Who was he?" Shallie asked after the car pulled away.

"John Thomas Whitfield. Pretty fair saddle bronc rider in his day, from what I hear. Sad to see him end up this way, but there aren't any pension plans in rodeo."

At the desk Hunt was again greeted by name. "Good evening, Mr. McIver. I trust your grandfather is well."

"He is," Hunt replied to the clerk. Shallie shrugged off the uncomfortable feeling that Hunt was no stranger to this, and probably a large number of other hotels. And that he hadn't frequented them alone. Shallie surveyed the lobby as Hunt filled in registration forms. Crystal beaded chandeliers, wallpaper of an intricately brocaded salmon silk, marble floors, and brass fixtures all spoke of the stately hotel's long history as host to cattle barons, oil magnates, and presidents. When Hunt held out his hand, Shallie took it and followed him up the curving marble staircase.

"This is where LBJ conducted a lot of the wheeling and dealing that landed him in the White House," Hunt explained as the door to their suite was unlocked. He dismissed the bellboy, burdened only with Shallie's overnight bag, with a generous tip.

The two-bedroom suite was sumptuously appointed in antiques. Memorabilia from the Johnson years hung on the wall. Shallie tried to focus her attention on the pictures of the quintessentially Texan president, but all she was really aware of was Hunt closing the door behind them, of his gaze flicking over her like an art connoisseur standing back from a masterpiece so as to better take in the sweep of its genius. The moment lengthened and Shallie grew uncomfortable. Then his eyes caught hers and her uneasiness melted away. She joined him in exchanging what amounted to a visual caress. Her eyes lingered over the sensual curve of his mouth, the sweep of his dark lashes, the expanse of his chest. Down to the gold Finals buckle strapped over his flat belly.

He came toward her like a sheik who has scrutinized all the female slaves at the market and made his choice.

"Shallie, I—"

Her hand went to his lips, silencing him. She couldn't bear to have him think that she wanted to hear the easy lies that would justify their being together. "We have tonight. Just this one night together. I don't want or expect anything else from you."

His lips bore down upon hers. It was as if the passion they'd both restrained since last night had been swollen by denial. She met his urgency, feeling it flicker between them as his tongue sought possession of the soft, dark burrow where her own waited to twine around his in an ecstasy of greeting, welcoming him to the intimate exploration.

Shallie felt the thunder of his heartbeat against her breast. She inhaled his clean, masculine smell, heard the gasp of his breath against her ear as his mouth found the shivery spot at her neck. Shallie's own breath came quickly as her hands sought out the hills and valleys of his back. She clung to them, a mountain climber scaling granite that had the slightest bit of give. The muscles of his thighs, pressed hard against her own, had not even a hint of pliancy. Shallie gave herself over to the luxurious sensations of Hunt's male richness. She tugged at his shirt, pulling it free from the waistband of his jeans. She had already unsnapped the lowest of the buttons before Hunt's hand slid over hers.

"Wait," he urged huskily. "If I'm only to be allowed one night with you, I want it to be one neither of us is soon to forget." With that he turned to the buttons on her blouse and pulled the first one loose from its anchor, kissing the spot where her pulse throbbed beneath the thin gold chain she wore around her neck. His lips trailed soft kisses that hesitated to both taste and smell the honeyed flesh he bared. At the expanded neckline of her blouse, he nuzzled softly, his tongue darting beyond the borders formed by her sheer clothing.

His hands slid up beneath the aching swells of her breasts and met at the button at their cleft. With a torturing slowness he freed the button and slid the blouse over Shallie's shoulders. His mouth returned to the swollen mound below, pressing it upward toward his hungering mouth with a pressure so intoxicating that Shallie felt herself strain against the gossamer fabric of her brassiere. As if to tantalize her beyond endurance, Hunt's tongue traced around the periphery of the lacy undergarment. Then it was gone and his tongue was at the electric center of her breast. It probed with a gentle savagery that sent tingling waves racing out to obliterate thoughts, regrets, hesitations, leaving only the immediacy of the moment. Shallie's lips parted. Her head lolled dreamily back on her shoulders as she surrendered to Hunt's expert ministrations.

The remaining buttons were undone and the blouse and bra floated down, falling from her wrists. Shallie was weak from the sensual onslaught and still it continued to mount in intensity. His hand slid down over the tiny ridges of her ribs, unfastening her jeans. He knelt at her feet and gripped the base of her boot while Shallie pulled her foot out. Both jeans and boots crumpled to the floor like a deflating beach toy.

Shallie gloried in what she read in Hunt's stormy eyes as they passed over her body. Her skin was a creamy white where the sun hadn't burnished it. Her long legs accounted for a disproportionate share of her height. She had never before been made so aware of her desirability. Hunt's awed, almost reverential gaze was like an act of homage. He stepped back.

"*Now* you may undress me."

Shallie approached him slowly, as if moving through a thick cloud of desire. Her hands reached up to undo his buttons. As she did so her breasts grazed the silken wiriness of his chest. His blood throbbed in a heated torrent, making the jugular vein at his neck pulse to his desire's maddened rhythm. Shoals of muscle rippled beneath the pampa of springy hair. Shallie buried her face in its heady, musky odor. Her hands stole downward to the heavy gold buckle at his waist. Then the zipper. The buckle clunked softly against the richly carpeted floor. She felt like a sculptor who had just unveiled her most perfect piece.

She knelt in front of him as he had knelt in front of her, and tugged his boots free. Then her sculpture came to life. He stepped out of the puddle of clothing at his feet and bent toward her. His arms were as firm as any statue's. When they scooped her up, she was encircled by a ring of warm steel. Still holding her, he pulled down the spread with one hand and laid her against the cool, clean sheet. She nestled in the freshly laundered burrow, every inch of her slender body caressed by the ironed cotton.

Hunt slid in beside her and rolled her onto her side to face him. Only the most sensitive tips of their bodies intersected. She felt the mat of hair on his chest. It was a meeting that sent flaming demands for more pounding through both of them. Hunt pulled her closer. Their voracious bodies called out for still more. His hands pressed her even closer. Shallie's softer flesh conformed to his hard contours, melting and swirling about Hunt's firmness in a lapping tide of need. Still she wanted, needed, to engulf him even more completely. Her mouth shaped itself to Hunt's tongue. Hunt understood the request Shallie hadn't even been aware she'd made.

Her legs slid apart beneath him and he entered her.

"Hunt." She whispered his name in the moment when his flesh became a part of hers. But the name that had resonated like a shriek in her ears was a whisper lost to Hunt's.

The blood sang in his ears, stirred by the exquisitely maddening feel of the liquid warmth encasing him. As much as he wanted the sensation to continue forever, urged on by Shallie, Hunt was driven to the swift, sure strokes that would end it. Shallie's shuddery gasps signaled both her own and the culmination of his pleasure. Still clinging to one another, they were sucked into a swirling black void of sleep.

Shallie jerked awake what she thought was moments later, surprised that she'd fallen into such a deep sleep. Beside her, Hunt's chest rose and fell beneath the covers. She remembered calling out his name. It didn't require any effort of memory to recall what she had come so close to telling him; the words had dominated her consciousness since the moment he'd kissed her at the airport and she'd stopped evading the truth.

"I love you." She whispered it so softly that the regular cadence of Hunt's breathing wasn't interrupted for even a second. What she had spoken was the truth. It had been burned even more deeply into her soul by the heat of their shared passion. She studied his supremely masculine face. It wore an expression that reflected how utterly at ease Hunt McIver was with a satisfied female body lying beside him. What they had shared had been a pinnacle for Shallie, something she had never known before, nor ever again hoped to experience.

If Hunt's masterful knowledge of lovemaking hadn't already tipped her off, the blissfully nonchalant look he wore as he slept would have told Shallie that what had passed between them had been pretty standard fare for Hunt McIver. Thank God she hadn't blurted out her deepest, most tender feelings. She had to accept what she'd had with Hunt for exactly what it had been—an intensely pleasurable experience that would never happen again.

Chapter 9

"S hallie." *The sound of his* own voice brought Hunt fully awake. He reached a hand out and contacted only a rumpled expanse of sheet. "Shallie?" He sat up, struggling to orient himself after what he was sure had been only a few minutes of hard sleep.

"I'm here, Hunt." Shallie stood in front of the mirror, the morning light streaming in to turn the curls she was fluffing up into a golden cloud floating around her face. Even more surprising than the obvious fact that it was morning, meaning that he must have slept for hours rather than minutes, was the sight of Shallie fully dressed, her pert behind once again encased in those awful jeans.

"What are you doing with your clothes on, woman?" he demanded with mock anger. "Come over here."

But Shallie didn't move. "I called the desk. It's already 5:30. If you're going to have time to take me to the airport and get back to the ranch before your rodeo school starts, you'd better be getting dressed yourself."

She turned crisply away without seeing the rapid series of emotions—surprise, disappointment, resignation, and finally anger—which flickered across Hunt's face. As he rolled out from under the covers and padded to the bathroom, the two of them could have been strangers stuck by accident in the same hotel room.

Once more, Shallie tried to convince herself that it was better this way. It was better that she had been the one to pull away first, rather than wait for Hunt to remind her that she had a plane to catch and he had a rodeo school to teach. She couldn't have stood that. It *was* better this way.

Shallie was repeating the words that had become her chant to ward off the inevitable pain as the Albuquerque-bound plane bore her high over the arid expanses of West Texas. She looked out of her window without seeing the clouds floating regally below. Her senses were turned inward, where she once again experienced Hunt McIver.

She tried to divorce herself from the turmoil of pain and longing that rose in her by concentrating on what she was certain Jake McIver's grandson was feeling at that moment—nothing. Undoubtedly old Jake had taught his grandson well that women were nothing more than bright, shiny ornaments, like the kind you hauled out at

Christmas, then packed away or threw out when they'd served their decorative function. Certainly Hunt must have been infused with the old man's philosophy or he wouldn't have been able to coexist with him for all these years.

Her struggle against a confusion of emotions ended the moment she saw her uncle's gentle face amidst those waiting to pick up passengers at the Albuquerque Sunport. But he was not wearing his usual expression of bemused tranquillity. He was clearly upset and Shallie was pretty sure she could guess why.

"How could you have let Jake McIver swindle you so bad?" He didn't allow Shallie time to answer his opening question. Instead he plunged ahead with his own explanations. "Oh, it wasn't your fault. That old horse thief could sell a milking machine to a dairy farmer and take his cows for a down payment. When that Petey fellow told me, or rather wrote me, what had happened, I knew I should have gone. If only my damned old knees—"

"Uncle Walter . . . Uncle Walter." It took two tries before Shallie could break into her uncle's headlong frenzy of self-recrimination. "I wasn't swindled. It was Jake McIver who got the rough end of this deal." Shallie felt like Jack coming home with a handful of beans and trying to convince his mother that they were magic.

"Shallie, honey, I know you're as good a judge of horseflesh as anyone in stock contracting, but even if you bought another Midnight he'd hardly be worth the difference between what you got for those steers and what they're worth. Besides, Petey tells me the horse hasn't even been bucked out yet. You bought a pig in a poke."

"If I did, Uncle Walter, it'll be the first pig ever to compete in the National Finals."

Walter Larkin, his face speckled red both from the sun and his agitated state, fell silent. "How can you be so sure of that?" he asked warily.

"Because I *have* seen Pegasus ridden."

"'Pegasus,' is it? So this is the horse you've been holding that name in reserve for, eh?" He cocked his head sideways, still not convinced but somewhat mollified.

"Just trust me, Uncle Walter," Shallie pleaded, "until you see him ridden. Or rather until you see someone *attempt* to ride him."

A ferocious spring dust storm was blowing outside. It drove sand and grit into every exposed pore as they made their way across the airport parking lot. Shallie forced herself to stay with her uncle, walking at his halting pace. They slammed the pickup truck doors, relieved to be sheltered from the blasting winds.

They drove down Central Avenue, passing turquoise-jewelry outlets, motels named for Indian spirits, and X-rated bookstores. Low-slung cars sporting tiny steering wheels of welded chain and upholstered in crushed velvet splendor prowled the street. Above the tackiness of Albuquerque's main street loomed the eternals in Shallie's life—the granite blue Sandia Mountains and the boundless sky.

As they covered the miles between Albuquerque and the Double L, against her will Shallie's thoughts drifted back to the Circle M. Such a short amount of time had passed there, yet what an upheaval it had created in her life. She was so absorbed that she didn't notice that Uncle Walter was uncharacteristically quiet. He had to clear his throat twice to capture her attention.

"Petey, he . . . uh . . . well, he told me what happened with Hoskins." He spat the name out as if it had a vile taste. "I wanted to flay that man alive when I found out he'd laid a hand on you. I never should have sent the two of you off together."

Shallie watched her sweet old bachelor uncle color with anger and embarrassment. "Petey also told me about McIver's little bronc rider charade. I owe that young man a debt of gratitude. Makes me shudder to think what might have happened if he hadn't come along." Anxious to change the subject, he went on. "That Petey is about the best hand we've ever had working the place. And, without that Hoskins around, even Cahill is starting to put in a full day's work."

Her uncle's voice blended in with the scenery as he recited the contracts that had come in while she'd been gone. What grain rations he had the horses on. Which of the bucking bulls he'd decided to breed. The new rodeo clown he'd heard of. They ascended smoothly into the Sandias along a wide, sweeping highway past a sign indicating the turnoff for a nearby ski area and continued on until they crested the mountains and descended into the high plains that were home for the Double L. The gritty wind was still blowing when they pulled up outside the ramshackle adobe house. Shallie thought longingly of the soft breezes along the Colorado River. She quickly shooed the traitorous thoughts from her mind. She had more important matters to occupy her.

Shallie spent the rest of the day, with Petey at her side, working through the Double L's string of bucking horses, doctoring the high-strung animals for all the myriad ailments that horseflesh is heir to. Petey was a bright and able helper, so eager to be useful that he seemed to anticipate Shallie's every need, handing her the pressurized can of antiseptic powder or a syringe of antitetanus vaccine before she even requested them. It was a delightful experience after working with the sullen Hoskins.

By the time they dragged wearily into the house that evening, Walter already had a hot meal on the table waiting for them. Shallie was famished and silence reigned as she and Petey concentrated on the steaming bowls.

"It's funny." Shallie laughed after taking the edge off her hunger. "After a day like we just put in pampering those nags, to think about the so-called animal lovers who are so worried that rodeo stock is mistreated."

"It is a little crazy," Uncle Walter agreed. "Most of those horses would have ended up at the glue factory if it hadn't been for rodeo. Instead they get a lifetime of good pasture and grain with maybe five minutes of work a year."

"Right," Shallie agreed. "And that 'work' is doing what they love best—throwing cowboys into the dirt."

Though Petey smiled along with Shallie and her uncle, Shallie felt she'd unintentionally excluded him and reached for the notepad that had been the vehicle for their communication all day.

"Petey," she wrote in her strong, forthright hand, "were you raised on a ranch?"

The ruddy-cheeked boy nodded his head in a vigorous "yes." Taking the paper and pen, he wrote, "Got the switch a thousand times for riding my daddy's milking cows."

"A true rodeo cowboy," Shallie wrote, laughing along with Petey. "How did you end up at the Circle M?" Shallie wished she could have thought of a topic of conversation unrelated to Hunt McIver, but she couldn't come up with one.

"Went to rodeo school there. Want to be a bull rider. Didn't have tuition. Hunt let me work it off." Petey, a veteran note writer, cut out as many superfluous words as he could pare away.

"You ride bulls?" Her initial assessment of Petey's physique had been accurate.

Petey nodded his head wearily as if he'd answered the same question a thousand times. "YES!" he wrote, grinding the pen into the paper. "Hunt only one who believes a deaf cowboy can ride in rodeos. PRCA won't give me permit. Afraid I'll ride forever if I can't hear the eight-second buzzer." Petey's short burst of laughter sounded as if it had come from an amused robot.

"Hunt's the best," Petey scribbled on. "When I showed up at his school last year, he learned sign language so he could tell me what bull-riding teacher was saying. Helps me all the time. Lets me ride his bulls. Everybody else thinks deaf means cripple. Not Hunt."

Shallie had difficulty reconciling a Hunt McIver who would learn sign language to help out a deaf bull rider with the compassionless sort of man it would take to live with Jake McIver. But Shallie knew that there were two standards of behavior in rodeo, one for women, in which nothing other than the conquest mattered. And another one for men. Within the second, deep friendship and awesome acts of loyalty blossomed. Lucky for Petey he was covered by that standard. Besides, Shallie decided, it probably puffed up Hunt's ego to have such an appealing fellow idolize him.

The next hour passed quickly, with Petey scratching out his life story as fast as he could get the words down.

His powerful need to communicate made Shallie suspect that, gifted with speech, Petey would have been among the most garrulous of people. He told about growing up on a small ranch in West Texas where "tarantulas big as poodle dogs" would creep across the sunbaked highways, about his three older sisters who had "babied" him to death, how he'd ridden in every podunk rodeo in his half of the state and won at bull riding in most of them.

Hunt McIver's rodeo school had become his goal three years ago and he'd worked toward it ever since. It was a stepping stone to an even bigger goal—becoming a PRCA member. And that's how he had wound up on Hunt's doorstep, broke and dying to ride every bull on the place.

Shallie was admiring the irrepressible zest for life that shone on Petey's face when her uncle's landline rang. Her uncle rose shakily on creaking knees.

"I'll get it. It's probably Morgan Hendrix about those roping calves he wants to borrow."

Not until she'd heard the phone ring did Shallie admit to the hope she'd been harboring all day—that, in spite of the fact that he didn't have her cell number, Hunt would call. That somehow her instincts about him were wrong. She watched her uncle's slow progress toward the living room and strained to hear his words as he spoke into the receiver. When he didn't turn and call out, "Shallie, it's for you," she slumped into her chair. That slight motion

151

and general deflation that accompanied it were not lost on Petey.

"Not Hunt?" he wrote.

Shallie felt exposed, her stupid adolescent crush laid bare for all to see. Of course, it probably wasn't the first time that Petey had seen a female acting like a moony cow over his employer. She pursed her lips and shook her head, not wanting to reveal any more than could be divined from a tight nod.

Uncle Walter returned to the dining room, scratching a spot above his ear. "That's puzzling."

"What's that?" Shallie asked, forcing herself to act interested.

"That was Hunt McIver."

"What did he want?" Shallie managed to ask the question with an unconcerned coolness while squelching the question burning on her lips—*Why didn't he ask for me?*

"Seems Jake's got the contract, as usual, to put on the rodeo in Albuquerque next month and they don't have enough roping calves to fill it. So Hunt wants us to haul up a load of calves and one bucking horse. Pegasus. He wants us to bring that horse you just traded them for. Now, isn't that curious?"

Shallie didn't answer. Her uncle was already absorbed in transmitting Hunt's message and his greetings to Petey. Suddenly the small house seemed close and overheated. She grabbed her parka from a peg by the front door.

"Going to check the stock," she called out behind her as she shut the door. The air, calm now and with just the slightest cool reminder of winter, was a relief. A ruff of clouds hugged the Sandias. The brittle husks of chamisa plants, their gay yellow flowers long since turned to dust, rattled drily in the wind. A breeze ruffled the pasture full of dark-headed blue grama grass.

Shallie stalked off toward the barn, the hurried beat of her boots across the pebbled drive matching the accelerated beat of her thoughts. Did Hunt want to see her again?

In the barn she peeked into Pegasus's stall and confronted the real reason Hunt had called. If ever there was an animal to challenge a bronc rider, to call forth his best, it was Pegasus. As much as cowboys feared and cursed a rank horse, they prayed with an equal fervor that they would draw one. Only on a mount with "try" to match their own, did they have a chance of marking a money-winning score. And no horse had more of that elusive quality than Pegasus.

The roan, his blue dappling like a saddle of melting snowflakes on his white back, rolled a magnificently disdainful eye toward his visitor and whinnied softly. He looked as haughty and proud, as untamable, as he had that first night in the Texas moonlight. Shallie struggled against the thought but couldn't keep herself from making an equation between the invincible animal and Hunt's own adventuring spirit. The very quality that made them the best, the most desirable, was exactly what rendered them so totally unsuitable for ordinary life.

"It's a curse," she whispered to the horse. A thoroughly uninterested Pegasus went on chomping hay.

Chapter 10

Shallie *looked over her shoulder* into the full-length mirror. The tailored black gabardine slacks fit perfectly, emphasizing the pert curve of her buttocks, then falling straight down the length of her slender legs to the tops of her boots. A cowl-necked top of soft lilac jersey was tucked into the waistband, which she'd cinched closed with the Contractor of the Year buckle presented to her the previous spring by the Little Britches Rodeo Association, in appreciation for the fine quality stock she'd supplied their competitions. Her freshly washed hair shone with a fragrant golden patina. A delicate plum gloss slicked her lips. She was just settling her new teal-blue Resistol hat on her head when she tore it off. The pants and top followed.

How ridiculously obvious! she berated herself. *For years I've worn jeans and old boots to rodeos. Now, suddenly, after one meaningless night with Hunt McIver,*

I start primping like I'm going to be walking down a ramp with a tiara on my head, holding an armful of roses instead of herding steers. She reminded herself again that one solid month had passed without so much as a postcard. It had been a month in which all her chilliest assessments of Hunt McIver had been borne out.

"What's the holdup, Shallie?" her uncle called out. "The steers and that horse of yours are loaded up and waiting. Performance starts at eight. That only gives us a couple hours to get out there and set up."

Before he had a chance to finish, Shallie burst through the door, wearing her standard uniform of jeans and a leather jacket. She'd even scrubbed off the lip gloss. "Let's go," she glowered, her annoyance with herself peppering her words.

The rodeo coliseum was a huge turquoise oval. As they approached it, Petey nudged Shallie, pointing to a huge banner that flapped over the entrance. It read "Welcome Rodeo Fans" and featured a movie screen–sized close-up of Hunt squinting into a setting sun beneath a Jameson hat, the sponsor of the ad. His eyes were narrowed to smoldering slits, glittering a crystalline blue against the mahogany of his tan. His mouth was set in a hard line that suggested sensuousness, a hint of cruelty, and absolute dominance over all he surveyed. The effect was heartstopping, in spite of the fact that Shallie fully realized

Hunt had been posed, lighted, and coached to produce that precise reaction. The exuberant smile faded from Petey's mute lips when he saw the scowl on Shallie's.

They pulled around to the far side of the coliseum, where the stock pens were located, and began unloading.

"Go on and take that horse of yours around to the bucking chutes," her uncle told Shallie. "Petey and I'll get the calves sorted and penned."

Shallie felt like an escaped criminal on the run as she made her way inside the coliseum leading Pegasus. From the moment she entered the brightly lit arena, Shallie felt she was being watched, that Hunt's eyes were tracking her every move. She could sense his presence. The inevitability of their meeting both tantalized and terrified her. Only the familiar animal smells comforted her as she approached the chutes.

"Hey, Shallie, how's it going?" Soft-spoken greetings welcomed her from cowboys who had come to know and accept her as Walt Larkin's "little niece." She slipped past the barrier that prevented anyone who was not a member of the exclusive rodeo fraternity from entering the area behind the chutes, where the cowboys prepared for their events.

"Heard you was bringing the calves tonight," said a beefy man with arms as long as a gorilla's. "Glad to see it's true."

"Thanks, Ty." Shallie smiled at the calf roper.

157

"Ty Weatherby!" Her uncle's voice echoed down the concrete corridor leading into the arena. Petey trailed behind him. Shallie stepped away as the men shook hands and pounded each other's upper arms. A crowd of ropers gathered to visit with their favorite contractor, Walter Larkin. It cheered Shallie to see her uncle brighten in the company of his old roping buddies.

"Shalimar Larkin." Shallie stiffened. There was only one man who used her full name. "You pretty little thing, who's that ugly fellow with you?" Jake McIver's voice ricocheted off the arena walls.

"Jake McIver. How have you been?" Her uncle pumped McIver's hand.

"Pretty fair. How about yourself? How's half of the best head-and-heels team to ever get down the road doing?"

"Can't complain, other than a bad deal some slick horse trader pulled on my niece."

McIver held up his hands as if to defend himself. "Now, I told Shallie to tell you that that trade was strictly her idea. She talked me into it."

"Don't worry, Jake," Walter said, his smile belying the teasing anger in his voice, "Shallie told me."

"Walter, I'd like you to meet Miss Trish Stephans." Trish stepped forward, preceded by a thick jasmine-scented cloud. "Trish, I believe you and Shallie know each other already."

"How have you been?" Shallie asked.

"Never better, actually," Trish answered, looking at Jake with a gleam in her eye. "As a matter of fact, you might say that this is one of the best nights of my life."

Shallie decided not to rise to the bait and inquire about her cryptic comment.

"You better run along, Sugar," Jake advised, kissing her on the cheek. Trish whirled and left.

"How about joining me in my box?" McIver asked expansively. "We'll have a better view than Slick Bridgers up there." McIver gestured toward the rodeo announcer, a Western dandy dressed in a shimmering lime-green suit, accented by white boots and tie, perched on a platform above the bucking chutes. "And," McIver added with a twinkle, "if you'd care to join me, I can offer you an abundance of liquid refreshment."

Ordinarily Shallie would have refused the invitation, preferring to be a part of the drama behind the chutes. But not tonight. Tonight she wanted to hide as far from the center of action as possible, because that is precisely where Hunt would be. Fortunately she and her uncle didn't have to work tonight. Once they had deposited the stock Hunt had requested, Circle M's professional crew took over.

Shallie settled into the plush private box and took advantage of the rare opportunity to really observe the folksy pageantry of a professional rodeo. An Indian man entered, his black hair pulled back and wrapped tightly with a red bandanna, followed by his wife, a squat woman in a purple velveteen blouse and voluminous print skirt. Chunks of turquoise studded their silver bracelets, belts, and squash-blossom necklaces.

The couple was trailed by a gaggle of junior high girls giggling behind the outsized combs they held to their mouths. The girls were the object of some intense scrutiny from a gang of teenage boys wearing crumpled straw hats and T-shirts cut off just below their armpits.

The clink of glass caught Shallie's attention and she turned to see Jake and her uncle hoisting a toast. Slick Bridgers announced the Grand Entry. The whirling tapestry of gleaming horses and costumed riders was doubly spectacular from the vantage point afforded by a private box.

"And now, ladies and gentlemen"—Slick Bridgers called for attention as dozens of riders pulled their mounts aside to form one long entryway—"it gives me great pleasure to present to you this year's Rodeo Sweetheart." The lights dimmed and a spotlight focused on the cleared pathway. Slick Bridgers continued his introduction. "Each year at this time we have the privilege of announcing the winner of this most coveted title. The holder of the Rodeo Sweetheart title is selected by a committee composed of contractors, contestants, sponsors, and rodeo aficionados. The committee makes its choice on the basis of beauty, personality, and rodeo spirit.

"And here she is, America's Rodeo Sweetheart, Trish Stephans."

Shallie felt her stomach drop as Trish rode into the spotlight on a glistening palomino. She was dressed from head to toe, hat to boots, in black velvet. The crowd broke into an appreciative roar of applause. At the same moment Jake McIver unloosed a deep, rolling belly laugh, as if he'd just pulled off the practical joke of a lifetime. Trish looked like a fairy princess mounted on her golden steed.

How perfect she and Hunt would be together, Shallie thought bitterly. Now that Trish had gotten what she'd wanted from McIver Senior—the introductions to the people who had given her her crown—she could indulge herself by going after McIver Junior. They would be rodeo's sweetheart couple, a matched pair of dark beauties.

Shallie squirmed under the onslaught of jealousy, an emotion she had little previous knowledge of. As Trish rounded the arena and rode off, the spotlight abruptly swung upward, blinding Shallie.

"Welcome, won't you please," Slick Bridgers requested, "the contractor for this year's ten-day performance of the Albuquerque rodeo, Mr. Rodeo himself, Jake McIver." Jake stood and bowed.

"Jake," the announcer continued, "is like the coach of the opposing team. He's brought in all the fine stock which will be roped and ridden by the many cowboys who have entered."

Jake leaned over and pulled Walter and Shallie up out of their seats. "We have Walter Larkin and his niece Shallie to thank for the fine roping calves being used tonight." A cheer went up from the many old friends Walter had made over his long years with rodeo. It was swelled by the cheers from the new friends Shallie had added to their numbers.

She sank back into her chair, grateful for the return of darkness and anonymity. Well, Hunt would certainly know where she was now. Which only meant that it would hurt that much worse when he didn't come to her.

The lights came back on and Shallie saw that all the broncs had been loaded. Pegasus was in chute five. Her horse looked like an aristocrat among peasants, trying to remain aloof and take no notice of the commoners around him.

She recognized a few of the cowboys rigging up. She'd never seen any of them in person before, since their world of professional rodeo and Shallie's of amateur rarely intersected. But their faces were familiar from *Pro Rodeo Sports News*. Jesse Southerland, the man who'd taken the bareback-riding title from Hunt, was limbering up his tightly wound body. He was known for his feline quickness, his sharp features reflecting a twitchy alertness.

A spot of flaming auburn hair told Shallie that the

current Rookie of the Year, Emile Boulier, would be competing as well. The red-haired cowboy from Canada had made many friends during his first year on the circuit, and Shallie could understand why, watching him share a joke and a smile with another cowboy.

But neither man was the reason Shallie was scanning each face behind the chutes. When she didn't find the high-planed face she sought, Shallie decided that Hunt's fears about riding in front of a crowd had overwhelmed him. Then she noticed a cluster of young women wearing designer jeans, fur jackets, hats with elaborate bands, and boots made from a variety of exotic species waiting by the entryway behind the chutes. Buckle bunnies, Shallie thought, amused by her first glimpse of professional rodeo groupies. They were more attractive and much more slickly turned out than their country cousins whom she'd encountered at amateur rodeos. Shallie imagined, though, that they all had the same motivation for sneaking back behind the chutes— to meet a rodeo hero. Their ultimate goal was a buckle, a championship buckle bestowed by the champion himself. That was their prize and badge of distinction. How they acquired it was their business.

Shallie smiled, thinking of the girls' misguided drive for adventure and hoping that they'd find genuine outlets for it someday. But her smile withered when she saw the outlet the buckle bunnies *had* found—Hunt McIver.

With what struck Shallie as merely a show of gentlemanly courtesy, Hunt, his rigging bag slung over his shoulder, pushed patiently past the coquettes in jeans. He swung up on the planks behind Pegasus's chute. Excitement surged through Shallie at the prospect that Hunt and the blue roan were to meet again. It flickered out as Hunt moved down the catwalk to chute six. He hadn't drawn Pegasus after all.

Jake McIver's attention as well had been drawn to the blue roan. "Hey, that's not my horse in chute five."

"Well, it used to be," Walter remarked drily. "That's the horse you traded Shallie for. Hunt asked me to bring it. Made a special request."

Jake McIver settled back in his chair, a disgruntled expression creasing his features.

"Worried, Jake?" Walter asked with a chuckle. "Think that horse you took those dogging steers for might not brighten Circle M's reputation?"

Shallie ignored her uncle's good-natured needling, knowing that both men were in for a surprise. Shallie felt her uncle grow a bit tenser with each rider. She knew he was anticipating the humiliation to come if Pegasus wasn't everything she'd promised. She could understand his anxiety. Being bested in a horse trade hurt, but to be bested by Jake McIver was pure misery.

"In chute five," Slick Bridgers called in a singsong fashion, "a horse called Pegasus. Emile Boulier, a cowboy from way up north, will be trying to ride the winged horse. Emile is our Rookie of the Year and has earned a reputation as a tough, tough bronc rider. So, old Pegasus probably won't be flying too high tonight."

Don't listen to him, Shallie mentally urged the blue roan. *Show everyone that you deserve your name.* She scooted to the edge of her seat and studied Boulier's expression as he settled onto Pegasus's blue-mottled back. He had the iron-hard look that habitual winners wore. Shallie tried to sense what Pegasus was feeling. It was his first time in an arena, his first time under the bright lights and scrutiny of thousands of people. He might stall out. Emile Boulier might subdue him. The magic Shallie had seen in the moonlight might not work beneath a concrete dome. Then the gate flew open and Pegasus bolted into the arena with a mad flying leap.

The magic was there all right.

Boulier's hat flew off, as if a giant hand had jerked it from his red head when Pegasus's hooves hit the earth. The instant after he contacted dirt for the first time, Pegasus launched himself into a shattering series of arcs that had the crowd gasping in disbelief. The arena lights flashed in Pegasus's eyes. He caught the reflections and hurled them back as bolts of lightning.

Boulier was good, there was no doubt of that. He clung to Pegasus's back like a saddle burr, riding with a powerful, rolling style. For a second it seemed Pegasus recognized his command and was bowing to it. But with a cleverness even Shallie hadn't counted on, Pegasus tucked into a spinning buck that pivoted around a tight circle. Centrifugal force unseated Boulier and he slid off his rigging. Pegasus made one more jump for a moon he couldn't see, and the Canadian cowboy was hurled to the ground. The moment the man with gall enough to attempt to inflict his dominance on him was gone, Pegasus once more became the regally unconcerned equine aristocrat. Boulier got to his feet and watched as Petey, who was working as a pickup man, herded Pegasus away. The cowboy shook his red head in admiration at the horse's performance.

Shallie leaned back in her seat, exhaling the breath she'd been holding. Uncle Walter pounded her back, pulling her to him for a crushing bear hug. "We're going to the National Finals," he whooped. "We've finally got a chance. Damn, I wish John was here."

"You rooked me!" Jake McIver exploded.

"Rooked you?" Walter echoed. "Don't forget, Jake, that's the same horse you were embarrassed to have as part of your string just a minute ago."

Shallie almost expected McIver to throw both her and her uncle out of his box. He seemed dangerously intent upon something. Finally, he burst out, "I can't remember the last time anyone got the better of me in a horse trade. And I've traded with the biggest crooks going. Just goes to show, you're never too old to learn."

Shallie was relieved that McIver had decided to dismiss the whole affair as an expensive lesson. She would not like to have been the object of Jake McIver's wrath. On the other hand, she doubted that he would enjoy publicizing the fact that anyone, much less a woman, had outtraded him.

Hunt was already settling down onto the back of his mount when Shallie returned her attention to the arena. His expression bothered her. It was too tight, too controlled. He looked as if he believed that with such rigidity he could imprison the haunting specter of past rides, when a cheering crowd had turned suddenly cool and silent.

Relax, Shallie wanted to shout across the coliseum. *Forget about the crowd. Remember that moonlit ride. Remember* . . . but Hunt's horse, a big bay, was already lunging into the arena. Hunt's spurs were planted high, right where he'd instructed his students to place them, well over the bronc's shoulders. The horse was a solid, steady bucker and Hunt put a solid, steady ride on him. It was a commendable performance, one most bronc riders would give their favorite riding glove to produce. But it lacked the fire and verve even of Hunt's performance as the Mystery Rider at that first rodeo.

The buzzer sounded and Petey rode alongside his boss. Hunt reached out and grabbed Petey's waist, levering himself off the horse's back. In one fluid motion, he rolled across the back of Petey's horse and dropped safely on the other side.

"All right, ladies and gentlemen, we just saw the first ride of the season for Hunt McIver, a four-time world champion in the bareback, who's been having a spell of bad luck lately. The judges tell me that Hunt has scored a very respectable seventy-nine for that ride."

There was a smattering of unenthusiastic applause. Hunt's face was drawn in disgust as tightly as if he'd bucked off.

"A seventy-nine!" Jake McIver spat out the score. "He won't even stay in the money with a puny score like that, much less burn up the glory trail to the National Finals."

Shallie felt her internal temperature rise by several degrees. "You know, Jake," she blurted out, unable to restrain the angry torrent, "I gave you credit for knowing people, but you must not know the first thing about your grandson if you think he rides for money *or* glory."

"Oh?" Jake questioned, one eyebrow shooting up quizzically. "Maybe you'd better tell me why else a man risks his neck on the back of a bronc then."

"No," Shallie answered, more to herself than to Jake McIver's question. "I think I'd better tell Hunt." She was the only one who'd seen him ride Pegasus, seen him turn bronc riding into an art that transcended both man and beast. She alone—not the buckle bunnies, not the agents, not the fickle fans, not even Trish Stephans. Only she had the key that might help him unlock again the strongbox of his potential. As she made her way down the concrete ramp leading to the bucking chutes, she heard the crowd go wild in a frenzy of applause.

"What a way to start off our second section of bronc riding," Slick Bridgers shrilled. "That was some ride just put on by last year's bareback champion, Jesse Southerland. An eighty-four! Looks like we'll be seeing Jesse in Las Vegas again this year."

"Congratulations, Jesse. Good ride." Hunt's deep voice rose above the din behind the chutes. As Shallie turned the corner, his broad back was to her and he was extending his hand to Jesse Southerland. Trish, still resplendent in her black velvet outfit, clung to Hunt's arm.

A mean and wary look haunted Southerland's hatchet-shaped face. He cautiously extended his hand as if fearing that Hunt intended to crush it. "Thanks, Mc-Iver." He dropped Hunt's hand after a perfunctory shake and quickly turned away.

Trish, however, grabbed the victorious Southerland before he could leave. "And congratulations from me too," she gushed, in a voice a couple of octaves higher than her normal range. Instead of a handshake, Trish embraced Southerland and kissed him squarely on the mouth. She stepped back, groping for Hunt's arm. Southerland leered his appreciation. Shallie was turning to retreat when Trish's artificially high voice trilled out.

"Shallie, have you come to congratulate Jesse on his wonderful ride too?"

Slowly Hunt turned toward her. Bands of steel seemed to be tightening around Shallie's chest, making it hard for her to breathe. "Hello, Shallie." His greeting was both cool and warmly intimate, as though there were no one else around.

"Hello, Hunt." For Shallie, in that moment, there *was* no one else around. Minutes, hours, days passed in the fraction of a second that their eyes met. Then she became aware again of Jesse Southerland and Trish. Trish was beaming expectantly at her. Shallie knew she had to deliver the words expected of her.

"Congratulations, Jesse. And Trish. You must be very proud."

"Oh, I am," Trish said enthusiastically, with more high-voltage animation than she'd ever displayed around Shallie before. "But it's not really pride in myself. It's pride in all of rodeo and all the wonderful people who have chosen me to represent their sport."

The words rang as false as a teenage beauty queen's acceptance speech. They had the canned quality of a spiel that had been rehearsed many times in front of a mirror. Still, an exuberant glow surrounded Trish like an aura. Her skin was flushed with excitement and Shallie had to admit that she was a rare beauty. As Trish snuggled closer to Hunt, Shallie's heart sank. She wanted to run away but reminded herself that she hadn't come to make any bids for Hunt McIver's attentions, nor had she come out of the kind of false love of rodeo which Trish had just mouthed. Hers was genuine and it compelled her to speak.

"Hunt"—she forced herself to address him—"may I speak with you for a moment?"

"Go on ahead, we're all friends here," Trish cooed. "Aren't we, Jesse?"

Southerland's lips slid back in a hungry grin in answer to Trish's flirtatious question.

Shallie made a silent appeal to Hunt. He acknowledged it. "I was just getting ready to throw my gear into my truck. Come on out with me."

"I'll be waiting right here for you, Hunt," Trish called after them. "Maybe Jesse will be nice enough to keep me company."

"I'll see you in Jake's box," Hunt called over his shoulder as they made their way up the ramp. "Why don't you go on up and show him the crown he won for you?" Trish didn't answer. She already had her arm twined through Southerland's.

Coming from the clamor inside, the night was still and cool. Behind them was the track where races were run each fall during the state fair. Beyond that were the Sandias, cold blue sentries guarding the horizon.

"What was it you needed to talk with me about?" Hunt's question was crisp, as if nothing other than a commercial transaction between two contractors had ever taken place between them. In her mind, Shallie knew that nothing of any more significance to Hunt *had* happened. It was her own heart, however, that she couldn't convince otherwise.

"The way you rode tonight—"

"I know," Hunt interrupted. "Jake could have done better and he probably told you as much. At least I didn't bail out or get bucked off."

"But you didn't ride the way you could have either. I know that and so do you. You rode with your head and your hand. That night I saw you on Pegasus, you rode with your heart. You were so in touch with him that he couldn't have made a move that would have surprised you. You were ahead of him on every jump. That's the way you should be riding, Hunt. Forget the crowd. Forget your reputation. Do what you tell your students to, tune in to the horse."

The leather rigging landed in the back of Hunt's pickup with a thud. For a long moment they listened to the sound of Slick Bridgers's voice and the cheers of the crowd echoing out across the parking lot. Shallie sensed that she'd affected Hunt, probably angered him. It didn't matter. She'd had to tell him, not for his sake so much as for the sake of rodeo, to ensure that the sport was all it could ever be. She didn't regret her words.

Hunt leaned against the truck, sorting out his feelings.

"No one has ever told me what you just have, has ever bothered, or dared, to be that honest with me."

That part was easy and clear-cut to Hunt. Her words had rung in his head with the same clarity as the most honest of his own thoughts. The part that was confused was how he wanted to react. He kept remembering how she had tasted, her lips warm against his. How her arms had felt wrapping around his neck when she was beneath him, quivering with the pleasure they'd shared. As strongly as he wanted to feel her against him again, he wanted to push her from him. To repel the memory of her strange coldness that morning at the Driskill Hotel.

Hunt was unfamiliar with confusion. His life usually followed a fairly direct line between desire and fulfillment. He thought about the buckle bunnies who'd accosted him earlier, about the fresh young faces looking for the most meager hint of attention from him and willing to barter their bodies to get it. Perhaps there had been too many exchanges like that in his life, one too many mornings when he couldn't get his pants on and clear out fast enough. Maybe that was why, when he'd awoken that morning wanting nothing more in the world than to hold her, her coldness had bitten so deeply. She had such a strong will in such a small, soft body. He'd known other wills encased in bodies equally alluring. The smartest course for him to take, Hunt decided reluctantly, would be to thank her for her advice and leave.

Shallie sensed Hunt preparing to speak. She edged away, expecting him to blast her for butting into his affairs and presuming to tell him how to ride broncs.

"Thanks for caring enough to tell me that. You're absolutely right."

Shallie looked up, her bottom lip dropping in surprise.

It was the tiny quiver of her lip that undid Hunt's resolve. It drew his own lips down, pulling them to that thin sliver of vulnerability. Shallie was as surprised as Hunt that their lips would ever find one another again. But beyond that instant of surprise, no further thoughts registered in either mind.

"Let's get out of here." Hunt held the door open and Shallie slid in. He drove without direction until he found a long stretch of highway that rose steadily uphill. At its crest, they looked out and found the lights of Albuquerque like diamonds strewn at their feet.

He turned off the motor and silence blanketed them both. Shallie watched the winking pinpoints of light and listened to Hunt's steady, even breathing. A gust of wind howled up the long valley and rattled the truck.

"I've always loved rodeo," Hunt began, as though voicing the preamble to a larger statement, then he stopped.

"I have too." Shallie urged him on with her agreement. "At least as long as I've known it existed."

"I could tell that. A lot of women love rodeo for the week it's in town and they can dress up in the Western clothes they keep stored in a box for the rest of the year. And some women love rodeo until they can snatch a man out of it, then they wish the sport had never been invented."

"My mother was like that," Shallie breathed. "But that syndrome works both ways. There are a lot of men who say they love rodeo and say they really admire a woman making a go of it in the sport. But that admiration cools off fast when they realize that she's not going to be staying home to cook dinner when there's a show two states away." Shallie's natural honesty seemed to call forth that same quality in Hunt.

"It must be hard for outsiders to understand rodeo fever when they haven't got it pounding in their blood. Sometimes I don't understand it myself. I look in the mirror and wonder why I do it. I'm over thirty. The young bloods, the 'baby hots,' coming up now are seventeen, eighteen. I'm an old man on the circuit. Why can't I just rest on my laurels? I suppose I've been doing just that for the past two years and for most of this season as well. Here it is, the beginning of June. Southerland and Boulier have been hitting it hard since January, flying to every rodeo in the country, racking up points, and Albuquerque is my first this year. Part of the reason is Jake. I don't like the idea of him working rodeos anymore. So, I've been doing more contracting than rodeoing."

Hunt fell silent, but Shallie could feel the weight of unspoken words hanging between them. As if he'd paused to gather strength, Hunt burst out, "I know I've still got it. Hearing you say it just makes me all the more sure of it. I feel like this could be my last year to prove whether or not I really have what I think I do in me. But there's Jake . . ." His voice trailed off. He reached out for Shallie, as if she were the answer he was seeking, and pulled her to him.

It was like being enfolded in a warm, downy nest, a nest heavy with Hunt's intoxicating scent. She slid her hand up to the smooth skin of his neck. His pulse surged beneath her fingers. The tuft of chest hair which escaped over the top of his shirt collar tickled her cheek. Hunt's arms wrapped more tightly around her. He stroked the soft downy feathering of her cheek as she snuggled more tightly against his chest. His hand trailed down, playing over the delicate bones of her neck and throat. It cradled her chin, lifting her head up, tilting it higher until she was inhaling the breath warmed by his lungs.

"Shallie." His lips were so close to hers that she could feel them forming her name. It echoed and reechoed in her ears as she strained to find a thousand nuances in the way he'd pronounced that one word, "Shallie."

His lips flicked over hers. Shallie's eyes closed and the sparkle of Albuquerque's lights flashed in her own head, an explosion of sensation as Hunt's tongue painted a galaxy of starlight across her mouth. She felt his cheek-bones beneath her fingers, the butterfly fluttering of his eyelashes. His breath came in ragged bursts as his mouth pressed down on hers, demanding that she yield it to him. Then, as if waking from a perplexing dream, Hunt shook his head.

"No. Not here. Not like this."

Shallie understood and was pleased by his restraint, glad that it had exceeded her own. "Yes, we'd better get back. Rodeo's probably over by now. Petey will be needing some help loading the stock."

Hunt started the motor. He reached out for Shallie's hand and pulled it into his jacket pocket to keep his company. Then they drove down into a constellation of twinkling lights.

Chapter 11

"S*low down, Petey.*" **Hunt leaned** forward and grabbed Petey's wildly gesticulating hands until the young man was able to calm himself and begin again. When he'd finished, Hunt made a few quick signs in return, then grabbed Shallie's arm and pulled her along after him as he sprinted up the arena ramp.

"Hunt, what's wrong?"

"It's Jake. Petey wasn't too specific, but he thinks something is wrong with the old man."

They rushed up the flight of stairs while the announcer called out a score in the bull riding, the last event of the evening. At the private box, they found Jake, his jacket open, his face flushed, sprawled out across his chair. Walter was outside, running water into a paper cup.

"Jake." Hunt dropped to his knees beside his grandfather. "What is it? What's wrong?"

"Nuh . . ." he started to answer, his voice alarmingly

weak. He cleared his throat as if something had been stuck in it and began again. "Nothing. Not a damned thing," he bellowed with a forced heartiness. "I'm just a bit tired. That's what I told Petey and Walter when they started yammering about getting a doctor. Isn't an old man entitled to get tired once in a while?" He sipped the water Walter offered him.

A heavy shadow of concern lay across Hunt's face. "Are you sure, Jake? You don't look well."

"How the *hell* am I supposed to look at seventy-seven years of age? You're not going to look so hot either when you're my age. Help me up. I'm going back to the hotel, then hopping the first flight I can get out of here. I'm too damned old to be traipsing around the country."

"I'm coming with you." Hunt took the old man's arm, helping him to his feet. As soon as he was upright, Jake shook off Hunt's helping hand.

"Like hell you are," he sputtered. "You've already paid your entry fees and you've got another ride coming up in this rodeo. Just because you're riding like a sissy in knee britches is no reason for you to take the first excuse that comes along for you to duck out. Who knows? You just might start riding like a McIver again if you keep at it."

Hunt's jaw tightened and he stepped stiffly away. Shallie was amazed again by McIver's monumental insensitivity. With Petey and Walter helping him, he hobbled off. Shallie glanced over at Hunt, searching for a clue to his reaction to his grandfather's harsh words, but his eyes were an impenetrable navy blue. They grew even darker as he stated flatly, "This is the last rodeo Jake is going to ramrod." There was no rancor in his words, only a bald statement of fact. For several long moments his face remained clouded by the shadow of deep thought and worry. It brightened abruptly.

"Shallie, I have a proposal to make." He looked eagerly into her face while he ordered his freewheeling thoughts. "If this had happened before tonight, I would have dropped out of rodeo completely to devote my full attention to running the Circle M. But after our talk this evening and with Jake's, ah, 'encouragement,' I've decided that I'm going to start rodeoing again, hard. But if I don't have someone to produce the rodeos we're already holding contracts on, I can guarantee that Jake, no matter what condition he's in, will be out there doing it himself." He paused to let his words sink in, hoping they would lead Shallie to the same conclusion he himself had reached.

He took a deep breath and dived in again. "So, what I'm proposing is this—you and your uncle take over all of Circle M's contracts for the rest of the season."

"What?" Shallie tried to make sense of his offer. Circle M was one of the top three rodeo production outfits in the country. They had close to a million dollars in stock and equipment and contracts for the biggest professional rodeos in the nation.

"Think of the advantages," Hunt urged. "You can merge Double L stock with what we have and work it under our PRCA contract. That way you'd have a chance to give Pegasus the exposure he needs to have a shot at the Finals."

Shallie had dreamed that the blue roan would carry Double L's brand to the National Finals. But she'd imagined that if it happened at all, it would be a struggle of many years.

"What would your grandfather say?"

"Leave that to me. I'll make him realize that his health is more important than a rodeo company. Besides, he's already learned that you can operate with the best of them. What do you say? I can start calling around tonight to set everything up, if you agree."

Shallie glanced around, wishing her uncle hadn't left. Hunt's offer was a bit like seeing her own future pass before her, speeded up by time-lapse photography. He was offering the prize she would have spent much of the rest of her life working toward. She tried to think of reasons not to accept it but couldn't. The Double L had no contracts to honor and a fat handful of overdue bills to pay.

"Yes," she burst out, as soon as her head had stopped spinning. "Of course! If your grandfather and my uncle agree, what's to stop us?"

"Good." For Hunt the matter was settled. "I'd better get back to the hotel to check on Jake and get in touch with all the places where we have contracts—Fort Worth, Scottsdale, Houston, Tucson, Phoenix, Prescott, El Paso, and a few others I'll have to look up."

The list dazzled Shallie. Circle M had contracts for all the biggest shows in the Southwest, the ones with the biggest purses and best competitors. And Pegasus would be at every one of them. Shallie figured that the bulk of the bucking stock would come from the Circle M. Double L could fill in with much of the roping stock, but Pegasus would be an unvarying member of the troupe. The list drummed through her mind—Fort Worth, Scottsdale, Houston. Houston! The enormity of what she was presuming to undertake hit her as she considered that particular rodeo. Was she *really* planning on jumping from putting on rodeos in the dinky, slapdash wooden arenas of small ranching communities, to producing an extravaganza in the Houston Astrodome? A quiver of panic shimmied through her stomach. It was impossible!

"You can do it." Hunt's words were a soft counterpoint to her pessimistic thoughts. He opened his arms and she fell gladly into the warm embrace, absorbing its strength and confidence. Wrapped in his arms, she felt she *was* up to the scope of the task that had been laid before her like a gift from the gods.

"I'll help as much as I can," Hunt promised. "And Petey will be with you. He's practically run the Circle M for the past couple of years anyway. And Jake can still handle all the contract bidding and negotiation. I just don't want him wearing himself out actually running any more rodeos." His voice was firm, and Shallie knew that if she didn't accept his offer, he'd find someone who would. She backed away and faced him squarely.

"Tell your grandfather to relax, because between me and Walter, his worrying days are over. We'll put on the best rodeos that Circle M ever produced." Shallie realized that there was more than a hint of bluster in her words, but hearing them still cheered her. She knew that a bedrock of truth supported them—she *could* produce rodeos as good as any Jake McIver had ever put on.

"Okay, from here on out, things are going to start moving pretty fast," Hunt cautioned.

"I'm ready." Shallie had to reach below the insecurity churning through her, to a deeper level of confidence that would make her promise reality. "You'd better get over to the hotel," she advised. "I'll stay and help Petey sort out the stock."

Hunt looked at her. Shallie felt he was on the verge of saying something, something she wanted very much to hear. But a curtain abruptly fell, cloaking whatever sentiments he'd been about to reveal.

"Fine." He pronounced his judgment crisply. "I'll book you and your uncle suites at the hotel. We'll meet tomorrow morning. I'll be on the phone for the rest of the night making arrangements for you to take over operations."

Shallie tried to detect a glimmer of regret in his voice at having to be occupied during the time they might have spent together. She couldn't find one. Hunt's boot heels tapped out the farewell he hadn't spoken. Shallie listened to the lonely tune until it was lost in the crashing symphony pounded out by hordes of departing rodeo fans.

"Come back again tomorrow night, folks," Slick Bridgers invited the crowd. "And bring your friends. The rodeo will be in town for nine more action-packed nights."

Down in the arena, Petey was flapping his arms to drive a Brahman bull into the holding pen. She joined him and spent the next few hours feeding the stock and bedding them down for the night. It was long after midnight before she had the chance to discuss Hunt's proposal with her uncle.

He considered it in silence for a moment, nodded his head, and spoke. "If we team up with the Circle M, I might have a chance of getting away from these New Mexico mountain winters. They're hard on the knees."

"So, it's all right with you?" Shallie asked breathlessly.

"Might as well give it a whirl. I don't see where we could possibly stand to lose."

Shallie hugged her uncle, relishing the thought of being Hunt's partner. Technically she supposed that she and her uncle would be partners with Jake McIver, but it was Hunt she intended to consult about any problems that arose and she already foresaw a number which would require their working together—closely.

Excitement kept sleep at bay that night. By the time sunlight seeped in through the heavy curtains of the hotel room, she was raring to start her first day as a professional rodeo contractor.

A crimson and orange sunrise was lighting the eastern sky as Shallie knocked on Hunt's door.

"It's open," a groggy voice bellowed. Shallie turned the knob and stepped inside. Hunt poked his head out from under the barrier of covers he'd constructed around himself.

"Shallie." The belligerence of his earlier greeting was gone, replaced by a surprised delight. "I thought you were one of the crew. You're up awfully early."

"Actually I never made it to sleep. I was too excited. I'll go and wait somewhere until you're ready to get up."

"No you don't." Hunt sat up, his chest bare beneath the covers. He extended his arms toward her. "You owe me a morning of cuddling."

For a moment, Shallie hesitated, but only for a moment before she went to Hunt's arms. He swept her under the covers in a rollicking bear hug, tickling her and nuzzling her neck until Shallie screamed for mercy.

"I can't breathe," she said between gasping fits of laughter.

"Lucky for you, madam," Hunt informed her in a somber voice, "I have been trained for just such emergencies. Only one thing can save you now, expertly administered artificial respiration."

Shallie's laughing fit dissolved as Hunt's lips moved over hers. They held her captive as his hands sought out the buttons on her blouse, the zipper on her jeans. Hunt's bed was a cozy burrow warmed by a night of heat from his body and redolent of his clean, musky smell.

The twining of their bodies was as joyously free as their playful teasing. In her jubilant mood, Shallie was unable to hold any part of herself in reserve, as she had their first time together. Hunt responded, instinctively giving of himself as generously as Shallie did. He was by turns tender, in response to Shallie's baring more and more of her most vulnerable self, and passionate as the tenderness kindled Shallie's desire. For the first time Shallie allowed herself to envision a future that might include Hunt McIver.

She held nothing back, giving herself to Hunt as a woman gives to the man she loves. She felt her love returned in the gentle touch of his hand along her rib cage, the softness of his kisses along the tiny curls ringing the nape of her neck. No, she told herself, these caresses cannot be counterfeited, the feelings behind them faked. Those intuitions intensified her pleasure, bringing it to a level she had never before experienced. Hunt shared it with her. Shallie felt she'd been stripped to her bones, cleansed, and rebuilt.

"Shallie Larkin." Hunt lay on one elbow above her, staring into her face as though seeing it for the first time. "Why didn't we do this that first morning we were together? Why were you up and dressed and ready to run out of my life that morning?"

Shallie searched his face, doubt prodding her, making her analyze it for the proof she needed. Proof that she could entrust her most fragile sentiments to this man. She found it in his eyes. But was she fooling herself? Was she wanting a warmth, a caring, perhaps even something more, to be there simply because she wanted it so desperately? No, she couldn't be mistaken. He *did* care, at least a little.

Her answer came out sounding like a timid little girl's. "I was scared."

"Scared? Darling, what could you have been scared of?"

"You?"

Hunt placed a questioning finger in the center of his chest. Shallie nodded. "You. Your reputation. Looking like a fool. Like I expected more than you were ready to give."

Mild annoyance formed tiny lines on his forehead. "Why couldn't you have given me a chance to decide what I was ready to give?"

"I don't know, I guess—"

A pounding at the door interrupted Shallie's explanation, an explanation she hadn't completely sorted out yet, even in her own head.

"You awake, Hunt?"

"Yeah," Hunt answered with a weary sigh. "What do you need, Johnnie?"

"Slack's going to start in fifteen minutes," the Circle M hand reported, referring to the overflow of contestants who had to be winnowed down during an early morning competition. "I can't find your grandfather. Are you going to run it?"

"No. My grandfather went back to the ranch. You've got a new boss, Johnnie. Name's Shallie Larkin. She'll be arriving in a few minutes. Get down to the arena and meet her there."

"Her?" the voice from the other side of the door asked plaintively.

"Your hearing seems to be working real fine this morning, Johnnie," Hunt answered. When the sound of boot heels shuffling down the hall announced Johnnie's departure, Hunt turned to Shallie and warned her, "Don't think that this means our conversation is over. We've got quite a few things to straighten out before we can . . ." He stopped.

Shallie realized she'd been holding her breath, anticipating the words he might have spoken. Instead he retraced the verbal route he'd taken and ended up by saying simply, "We've got a few things to straighten out, that's all."

Then his voice whisked into a brisk cadence. "You feel up to running a rodeo today?"

"It looks like there will be some disappointed slack ropers if I don't."

"That's the spirit. I set up most everything over the phone last night. Here"—he stretched forward and pulled a long list off the writing desk next to the bed—"this is the Circle M schedule for the rest of the season. There will probably be some late additions, but this is a fairly complete list with names and numbers of all the committee people sponsoring the rodeo in each town—local media sources, contract acts, the clowns, riding groups, announcers, who to call for feed, the best vets in each city. It's all there, and what isn't written down you'll find inside Petey's head."

An uncomfortable premonition began to take shape in Shallie's mind. "Slow down. You're acting like you're going to be dumping all of this on me right now. Aren't you going to be helping me out for the rest of the time you're here?"

"Sure I am. But since that amounts to about another five minutes before I have to hop a plane for Red Lodge, Montana, I figured we'd better get moving."

Shallie was too stunned to force out the words forming on her lips.

"Look," Hunt explained, "I don't have to ride again here until the last day of the show. That's more than a week away. After your pep talk last night, I realized I couldn't just vegetate here while every other bronc rider in the country was hitting three or four shows, racking up points for the Finals." Hunt bounded out of bed and began stuffing his rigging and a few pairs of rumpled jeans into his gear bag.

"I'll be back at the end of the week."

"B-b-b-but—" Shallie sputtered, too full of questions to know where to begin.

"Oh yes, I almost forgot. You're coming with me to the awards banquet the last night of the show. I'll be in town early enough to take you shopping. I can't wait to get you peeled out of those damned jeans." He laughed, and the door closed just as the boot Shallie tossed in mock fury landed against it. She bounced out of bed to watch Hunt, his bag slung over his shoulder, spring jauntily across the parking lot.

Take care of yourself. I love you, she yearned to call after him. But it was too soon, still too soon. She let the curtain drop back into place and pirouetted around the room, a demented doll in a windup music box, dancing to the crazy tune humming through her veins.

Chapter 12

When Shallie arrived, her uncle was already in the arena, organizing the ropers into heats and breaking the calves into different groups so that each man would get the animal he'd drawn. The ropers astride their horses were either yawning or fidgeting with their lassos. Shallie stopped to take in the scene before her. Already brimming with happiness, she was further warmed by the sight of her uncle. The opportunity to run a full-scale pro rodeo had worked on him like a tonic. He hardly seemed to need his cane as he moved among the mounted ropers.

"All right, Bedichek," Walter announced to a young roper, "you're up." Bedichek backed his horse into the open-ended wooden box next to the chute holding the calf he'd drawn. Both man and animal faced the center of the empty arena.

The roper nodded his head, signaling that he was ready. The barrier in front of the calf dropped and the animal scampered out like a frightened cat. A few fractions of a second later, Bedichek's barrier dropped and he spurred his horse after the runaway calf, whirling a loop of rope over his head. The loop sang through the air, neatly catching the calf. Bedichek swung out of the saddle, hitting the earth at a running gallop.

The superbly trained filly he rode continued to fill her end of the event by backing up, so that the rope stayed taut until her rider reached the calf and threw it to the ground. Then Bedichek ripped a leather cord from where he'd tucked it into his belt and tied three of the calf's legs.

"Eight point seven seconds," Walter Larkin announced. "Heck of a good run, Bedichek."

Shallie entered. "Go on and grab a cup of coffee," she said to her uncle, taking the clipboard from his hand. "I'll run this for a while." As he left, Shallie turned to the men wearing jackets emblazoned with the Circle M who were ranged along the chute railings.

"Who's doing the untying?" she asked, motioning toward the calf bound in the center of the arena. The chute helpers gaped at her as if she'd addressed them in Swahili. Finally a grizzled cowboy spoke up.

"You must be Sallie Larkin." She recognized his voice. He was Johnnie, the hand who had come to Hunt's hotel room door that morning.

"That's Shallie," she corrected him gently, holding out her hand. "And you must be Johnnie."

Johnnie took her hand and announced to the others, "Meet our new boss, boys. Hunt says she's in charge now." The invocation of Hunt's name worked a quick magic and, with no further discussion, two of the hands hopped down from the railing and raced to untie the roped calf.

Hiding her delight that there was to be no confrontation about her authority, Shallie looked down at the clipboard. "Wilkinson, you're up. Pierson's on deck. James, you're in the hole." The ropers jockeyed their horses around to occupy the lineup Shallie had dictated.

The rest of the day speeded by, gobbled up by the thousand and one tasks required to maneuver man and animal into the right place at the right time to ensure that a rodeo would take place. Through them all, Shallie remained buoyed by the elation which had carried her since she'd shared Hunt's bed that morning. Her ebullience bubbled through everything she did and spilled over onto everyone she spoke with. It bewitched the normally grumpy rodeo secretary who kept the records and made her amenable to Shallie's requests. It caused the cowboy who came to her complaining that the calf he'd drawn "must have been blind or drunk" to end up laughing along with Shallie at the ridiculousness of his charges. It even helped her to charm the prima donnas of rodeo—the barrel racers—out of their accusation that the cloverleaf pattern course they ran their horses through had been a few inches off the night before.

Shallie skipped from crisis to crisis, resolving them all as easily as if she'd been producing big-time pro rodeos for years. Her workload steadily increased as the hour of the evening performance approached. As the crowds began passing under Hunt's giant face welcoming them to the rodeo, Shallie was matching riders with the broncs they'd drawn.

Jesse Southerland's name was third on the list. He strolled in minutes later, with Trish Stephans draped over his arm. But Shallie was too busy to do more than note their arrival. By the time the final chords of the National Anthem faded away, Shallie had to have all the bronc riders and their mounts sorted out and ready to go. As a gifted vocalist sang an a cappella version of the "Star Spangled Banner," she enjoyed her last quiet moment of the evening. From then until the end of the rodeo, Shallie would yell her throat raw.

"Let's ride 'em," she prodded those bronc riders who were slow to nod for their horses to be turned into the arena. Southerland was ready and waiting when it came his turn. Shallie didn't watch his ride but knew it had been an outstanding one from the crowd's cheers and Slick Bridgers's feverish announcement, "Jesse Southerland has taken another giant step toward a second bronc-riding championship tonight! The judges have just awarded him a ninety-one for that spectacular ride."

Southerland gathered up his gear and strutted out of the arena with Trish attached to his arm. While most cowboys were careful to downplay their accomplishments, Southerland allowed his to puff him up like a bantam rooster.

"Who's ready to ride a horse?" Shallie called out, chuckling under her breath at the cocky figure the departing Southerland cut. With amazing good cheer, Shallie moved the contestants along so that they were right on schedule at the rodeo's halfway mark.

The lights dimmed and a flatbed truck carrying a Country and Western singer dressed in a swirl of gold lamé that winked in the pale lilac spotlight rumbled into the center of the arena.

While the crowd enjoyed the halftime entertainment, Shallie lined up the team ropers so that they were ready to go the instant the singer had finished.

Finally Shallie was shouting, "Bull riders, are you ready?" to the men in the last event. Bull riding had been designated the world's most dangerous sport by the Sportswriters of America, and the fear-whitened faces of some of the contestants showed that they fully appreciated that rating.

Shallie almost smiled at the bull riders' characteristic limbering-up postures, which made them resemble crazed chickens pecking for food. Her smile died, however, as she remembered the two basic lessons about bull riding. One. The rider weighed about 150 pounds. A bull could weigh up to one ton, 2,000 pounds. Two. While even the bucking horses would try to avoid a man, a bull would hunt him down and try to trample a fallen rider. They would charge a horse as well, which was why Shallie waited until her mounted pickup men had cleared the arena before she started the final event. They were replaced by a pair of clowns. Superb athletes beneath their greasepaint and fright wigs, their job was to distract the bulls from thrown riders long enough for the cowboy to have a chance to scramble over the arena fence. When the clowns were in place, she signaled for the bull riding to begin.

The first rider jolted into the arena, spinning on the back of a one-ton top that not only whirled but levitated as well. Shallie always tensed up during the bull riding. Perhaps because all that was needed was a glove, a rope, and an entry fee and any anonymous farm boy could become a bull rider. This meant that the contestants were younger, less expert, and more apt to be injured. But tonight the clowns, offering themselves and their antics to the enraged beasts, performed well, and all the riders were in one piece when they unbuckled their chaps.

Shallie breathed a sigh of relief when the last one was safely behind the chutes. Slick Bridgers again wished the crowd a good night and urged them to come back tomorrow and to bring their friends. The smallest pang of envy pricked Shallie as she watched the crowd file out. For them the evening was over, while she and her crew had several hours of hard work ahead before they could call it a night.

Last night's lack of sleep was catching up with her. She stifled a yawn against the back of her hand and pulled on her work gloves.

Two hours later, she was spreading hay for the horses with a pitchfork when Johnnie, the chute helper, approached her.

"'Scuse me, Miss Larkin." He addressed her with a respect that made her feel eighty years old.

"Just call me Shallie," she said with a laugh.

"You've got a phone call. Up in the secretary's office."

"Thanks," she answered, handing him the pitchfork. She pulled off her gloves, tucked them in her back pocket, and headed for the office at a gallop.

"Hunt," she exulted when she heard his voice.

"Damn, girl, I've been calling your cell all day."

"Sorry, I left it in my jacket."

"How did it go?"

"Terrifically. Not a hitch. Well, actually, I can't say that. There were a few minor ones, but we ironed them out."

"Wouldn't be a rodeo without problems and you wouldn't be a producer if you couldn't solve them."

"Tell me about you. How did it go in Red Lodge?"

"Well, I didn't embarrass myself." Hunt glossed over the question. "How did Southerland do tonight?"

Shallie hesitated, not wanting to tell him about his rival's stellar performance that night. "Scored a ninety-one," she said, abbreviating her answer.

Hunt didn't respond immediately, then, "I've got a lot of catching up to do before I give that son of a buck a run for the big buckle. Look, I'm up in Cody, Wyoming, tomorrow night. Then I'll be headed for Greeley, Colorado, and make it back to Albuquerque for the last day of the run. Have we still got a date for that awards banquet?"

"We most definitely do."

"Good. Keep doing whatever you were doing, I'm sure it was right. I'll see you."

Shallie clung to the phone receiver for a moment. She held on to it just as she wanted to cling to this one perfect moment in her life. She prayed it would last and was beginning to believe that it just might.

She floated through the next eight days on a cloud of exhilarated energy, held aloft by Hunt's nightly phone calls. The only moments of unpleasantness were her daily confrontations with Trish. The newly crowned Rodeo Sweetheart seemed to have been born to play the part of queen and actually bloomed even more lushly in the role like some complex flower which can only blossom in the overheated environment of the hothouse.

"I just heard from Jesse," Trish cooed to Shallie on the ninth day of the Albuquerque rodeo's ten-day run. "He won the bronc riding up in Cody, Wyoming. Isn't that wonderful?" Trish narrowed her glittering eyes, studying Shallie for a reaction.

Shallie tried to figure out what game the woman was playing. She must know that Hunt had ridden in the Cody rodeo. Was Trish sizing her up as a threat, trying to gauge the depth of her emotion for Hunt? Why did she care? Maybe Jesse wasn't enough for her. Perhaps she wanted to keep Hunt on hold while she frolicked with the current champion. Whatever the explanation, Trish Stephans was clearly accustomed to having it all and having it her way.

"But Hunt did come in second," Trish added, digging deeper for Shallie's feelings. "He's really doing pretty well for someone with his handicaps. The torn tendons, I mean."

"Trish, I have a hard time figuring out just what you *do* mean." Shallie had no desire to fuel the rivalry Trish was trying to create between them. Always at the back of Shallie's mind was the fear that Trish could reel Hunt back in whenever she chose, whenever her fancy turned back to him. "How is Jake doing?" Shallie asked.

"How would I know?" Trish said without the slightest hint of concern.

"I just thought you might have called to find out after all that he did for you."

"Did for me!" Trish echoed her words with outraged disbelief. "All he did was introduce me to a few friends. I did the rest for myself. Do you think an introduction would have been worth two hoots if I hadn't had something to back it up with? No one can *do* anything for you, Shallie. You'd better learn that. You've got to be ready to do it all for yourself."

The spiteful look curdling Trish's face revealed more than Shallie cared to see about the ruthless person behind the glamorous facade. Then it was gone, wiped away as quickly as a picture on a television screen can be switched off, when a group of giggling girls came over to ask Trish to autograph their programs. Once again she was the serenely lovely rodeo queen catering to her adoring subjects.

The transformation chilled Shallie. Had Hunt seen beneath her mask of beauty? Shallie left Trish to her fans. Hunt would be back tomorrow, and tonight she had a rodeo to produce.

Chapter 13

L ord, woman," Hunt muttered hoarsely, "I knew you'd look good if I could ever get you peeled out of those damned jeans, but I never counted on you looking quite *this* good." He sank back into a chair provided for the male auxiliaries of the patrons of the exclusive shop he had taken Shallie to. Shallie stood before him, modeling the third creation he had insisted she try on.

Shallie laughed, enjoying every second of the shopping trip she had been shanghaied into. She sucked in her cheeks, pasted a haughty expression on her face, and pirouetted in front of him like a haute couture model. She whirled, paused, and threw a wicked look over her shoulder. "Does zee dress please monsieur?" she asked in the most sultry French accent she could achieve.

"Indeed it does, mam'selle. Could I negotiate a package deal and get the dress *and* the model inside?"

"Pairhaps somezing can be arranged." Shallie pouted before bursting into giggles.

Everything seemed such fun with Hunt. She was silly and carefree around him. Shallie couldn't remember being girlish and giggly like this even when she was a girl. And certainly for the past several years, she'd been far too serious. But around Hunt, she sparkled and effervesced like the headiest of champagnes. It was odd that such a man, so often stern and brooding, should be the one to unloose this side of her. The other effect he had on her—the knee-wobbling surges of physical desire—were much more understandable. He had the same effect on women who only saw his face on those gigantic hat ads. It almost seemed that Shallie needed someone as strong, as confidently masculine as Hunt to free the more delicately feminine side of her nature.

"Most flattering," the sales attendant, a slimly elegant middle-aged woman, announced.

"You couldn't be more right," Hunt agreed. "I love that color." To Shallie he whispered, "And I love the way it shows off your adorable body." He chuckled with mock lasciviousness.

"All right then, wrap it up," he said, handing the sales attendant a credit card. Shallie retreated to the dressing room. Alone, she was able to examine the garment in more detail. She ran her hands over the luxurious fabric, letting herself begin to feel that it was truly hers; Hunt had chosen it for her.

The dress was an emerald-green silk of classic simplicity. Its magic lay in the deep, shimmering color and the way it was draped over Shallie's breasts, falling away from their peaks to be gently drawn in at her waist, then swelling again over her derrière. She'd never owned anything like it and had never imagined she could look the way she did in this dress. She slipped it off, regretting that the spell had to be broken.

"What time is it?" Hunt asked as they drove back to the rodeo grounds. Shallie checked her phone and told him.

"Good," he responded, wheeling the Porsche around. "There's still time." Without another word he glided the smoothly powerful car onto the highway. After a few miles they shook loose the tentacles of the city and turned off on a quiet road that cut across a high mesa heading west. Gradually the earth around them turned a rust red. Mountains bordered the expanse of land they traversed. On one side was a range of volcanic cliffs formed of hardened black lava; on the other were the cobalt-blue Sandia Mountains. They drove through the valley between. They passed the Jemez Indian pueblo, each ramshackle house sporting a *horno*, the beehive-shaped adobe oven used for baking, in the backyard. The road began to climb as they reached the Jemez Mountains. They drove through

Jemez Springs, a mountain retreat. A few miles later, Hunt pulled over and got out of the car.

"Feel like a hike?" He didn't wait for an answer to his question before setting off up the steep mountain. Shallie followed behind, slightly puzzled, but only too glad to accompany Hunt, no matter where he led her. By the time he stopped, she was puffing madly in the high altitude. Once she got her breath, she noticed how still it was in the pine-roofed sanctuary Hunt had led her to. He glanced around, alert as a wild animal.

"Good, there's no one else here. I didn't think there would be this early in the summer." He stripped off his flannel shirt and, leaving Shallie stupefied, ducked behind a thick growth of pine. A minute later she heard a splash and entered the enclosure to find Hunt basking in undisguised bliss in a pool of water. His satisfied grin was half-hidden by the wreath of steam rising from the pool.

"Hot springs," Shallie said needlessly, feeling slightly foolish that she, the native, had failed to guess Hunt's destination.

"Come on in. I can't tell you how good this feels." Shallie hesitated. The thought of undressing in front of Hunt in broad daylight, on the side of a mountain, made her feel as shy as she had that first evening in Hunt's whirlpool.

"All right," Hunt sighed, sinking further into the steaming water, "but you'll never know how exquisite it is to be immersed in warmth at the same time you're looking out onto snowcapped mountains."

Shallie couldn't resist the description and hurriedly shrugged off her clothes. Her rushed movements slowed, then froze when she turned to see Hunt watching her, the sleepy look of contentment gone now from his eyes. In its place was a keen, piercing gaze that carved over her exposed curves with an edge of flint.

"My God, you're beautiful," he whispered.

Shallie dropped her modesty, seeing it through Hunt's eyes for the false pretense it had been. What had made her timid wasn't the thought of Hunt seeing her unclothed in the full light of day, but the fear that what he saw might not please him. Desire had made his words come out in a rasp that underscored his honesty. Shallie finished draping her clothes across a pine limb and started toward him. Her movements were slow, languorous. She knew the pleasure the sight of Hunt's body afforded her, and now that she was sure of her own, she wanted to share the same pleasure with him. His eyes caressed her, feeding her newfound confidence. For the first time in her life, she felt completely at home within her own flesh. Hunt's frank admiration of her high, firm breasts, her taut stomach, and long, muscle-striped legs told Shallie of their allure, their power to arouse desire.

The water that burbled up from a geothermal spring

deep under the earth was as warm on her foot as the blood heating her veins. She stepped into it, the mist parting to allow her entrance. The stillness bore down upon her. For a hundred miles the land rolled away in front of her vision, dead-ending only when it came to the Sandias. Above her there were only the pines arching like spires to direct the eye toward the blue infinity above. There was nothing and no one except her and Hunt McIver.

The heated water lapped up around her knees. It licked at her legs, enveloping her in its delicious warmth. She ducked under the water, tasting its mineral tang on her lips and bobbed up again, her hair slicked back in a shining ribbon against her head. Sunlight caught in the droplets of water on her eyelashes, transforming them into sparkling crystals. Liquid gems collected in the tiny hollows of her collarbone and ran in rivulets between her breasts.

She was less than an arm's length from Hunt and still he had not touched her. Instead he let the water and the heat from his searing examination gently arouse her. And they did. Every inch of Shallie's moist skin tingled with desire, waiting for his touch. Her breasts ached for the feel of his hard chest against them. She knelt before him. The water swirled between her legs, tantalizing her, making her yearn for the fevered press of his body. Still he did not touch her. Yet his eyes never left her.

Slowly, with just the slightest ripple of water to

betray the movement, Hunt's hands moved. They cupped Shallie's breasts from beneath. He held them, the lordly potentate, judging their firmness, their weight. His eyes never broke contact with hers. He watched her face as he trapped her straining nipples between his thumb and forefinger, watched as Shallie's lips parted and her eyelids fluttered closed. Surges of pleasure, delayed by minutes that had seemed like hours, swept through her at the masterful touch of his fingers.

Then Hunt's control was gone as completely as Shallie's. He pulled her to him, their tongues meeting, then entering a feverish duel. The press of his body against hers revealed that he had been as achingly ready as she. Neither one of them could wait a moment longer. He slid her on top of him, her legs straddling his. Shock waves of sensation collided within her as he bent her toward him to take the tip of her breast into his mouth. His hands on her hips raised and lowered her, guiding her expertly into a rhythm that wrought the ultimate in pleasure for them both. The rhythm grew more fierce until it seemed to take control of them, dictating with a relentless need that had to be satisfied. It left them spent and gasping.

"Shallie, my darling." Hunt's words were lost in Shallie's damp curls.

She clung to him, dazed by the ferocity of desire that had risen up and taken her by surprise. Trembling still, she raised her head from the damp mat of Hunt's chest.

Her eyes found his. He was as awed as she by the intensity of their hunger for one another.

"Shallie." He said her name as if it were a statement, the summation of all he'd aspired to in his life. His lips were soft on hers, mere echoes of the lust that had screamed through them both as he kissed away the crystals of water hanging from her lashes.

Hunt rolled over, Shallie secure in his arms, and he began to love her again. The water supported them, transforming their coupling into a weightless ballet in which each was freed of the restraint of gravity. Their only thought was to lavish the other with pleasure.

As they descended the mountain, Hunt's arm wrapped around her shoulders, Shallie felt her legs wobble beneath her like two sticks of licorice. But there was no time for rejuvenation. They both had to be back at the arena.

Chapter 14

Shallie approached the turquoise-colored coliseum with the first prickles of regret beginning to stab through the dreamy haze she'd been in since leaving the hot springs. It was the last performance of the rodeo. She hated to see it end. The past ten days had been enchanted. She tried to make herself believe that there were more in store, but in a deep corner of herself, she believed that life, or at any rate *her* life, wasn't like that. It had been too good, too perfect. You didn't get both the man and the career you dreamed of all in one tidy package.

Once she stepped into the arena, Shallie had no more time for such gloomy ruminations. The next chance she had to pause was during the National Anthem. Throughout it she felt someone's eyes hot on her neck. She glanced over her shoulder. Hunt, standing on the catwalk above his bronc, was smiling at her. Her own smile came in automatic response. She turned quickly away, afraid that anyone who'd seen them would be sure to guess the secret they shared. She groped in her pocket for the list Walter had hastily thrust into her hand as she arrived late, and read the first three names:

> *Hatch Glover—Pegasus*
> *Emile Boulier—Odin*
> *Hunt McIver—Avalanche*

Damn, Shallie muttered—Hunt hadn't drawn Pegasus. Jesse Southerland was far in the lead, with an average of 87.5 from his two rides, while Hunt was going into his second with a mediocre 79. It would have helped if Hunt had drawn Pegasus and ridden the roan the way Shallie had seen him ride.

The first rider out didn't even come close to challenging Southerland's lead. Shallie watched Hatch Glover, a cowboy in his late twenties with a thick, drooping moustache, settle down on Pegasus's back. She felt a hum of pride. Her horse didn't even flinch as the man's weight bore down on him. It was as if he had been trained from birth to be nothing less than the perfect bareback bronc.

"In chute number one, ladies and gentlemen, we have Mr. Hatch Glover from Salinas, California. Hatch is a familiar face to all of you who follow pro rodeo. He's a consistent runner-up at the National Finals in the bareback riding. He was National College Rodeo champion in this event for three years running."

Shallie frowned. She hadn't realized what an impressive reputation the moustachioed cowboy had. Could he best Pegasus? He certainly had the credentials and, from the set of his jaw, it appeared he had the spirit as well. The moustache bobbed down as he nodded for the gate. Pegasus burst out as if blown loose by dynamite. He took two thundering leaps, then seemed to cock his head and decide to change his strategy, almost as if he realized he'd never unloose the strong rider with moon-grazing bucks. So he switched to a snaky, shimmying style of bucking that had Glover running all over his back like spilled pudding. With a jaunty flip of his hindquarters, Pegasus tumbled him into the dust.

There was a burst of scattered applause. Shallie looked behind her to see where it was coming from. The applauders were the handful of true aficionados in the crowd, the ones who actually understood what was happening in the ring. They were clapping for Pegasus! She looked over at the cowboys behind the chute. Every pair of eyes was on her horse.

"Did you see what that damned horse did?" she overheard one stupefied cowboy ask his buddy. "I swear to God that animal changed up his style. I swear he did it on purpose."

"Damn, wish I'd drawn that, what's that horse's name? Pegasus? Wish I'd drawn him. A man could score some points on an animal like that. He must have had all four feet a couple of yards up in the air going out."

"Horse should be in the Olympic high jump. Damn!"

Shallie smiled. These were the men who voted for the stock that went to the National Finals, and they were undeniably impressed.

". . . had a couple of bad years." Shallie's attention was captured by Slick Bridgers's announcement. *Damn him*, she thought. *Why does he have to keep bringing up Hunt's bad years as if they hadn't been preceded by four record-breaking ones?* She sought out Hunt's face. It didn't betray even the tiniest flicker of response to Slick's comment. His eyes, so soft and loving that afternoon, now glittered like a frozen chunk of the North Sea. They had an eerie, abandoned look about them, oblivious to the chaos that churned around Hunt. His features were honed as sharp as obsidian. She thought of how pliant and warm they had been and a surge of raw physical desire shot through her.

"Hunt's going to be riding Avalanche, a bronc who has gone to the National Finals for three years running. There have been rumors that Hunt's getting some of his old licks back. Well, we'll see here tonight how far old Hunt will get down the comeback trail. Avalanche has knocked the licks out of more than one cowboy. That is one tough bronc."

Shallie shut the words out and watched Hunt's lips carve out the words that called for the gate. Shallie followed his eyes. They were focused on something far outside of the arena. Avalanche thundered out of the chute as if he were paying homage to his namesake. He landed with a spine-jarring thud. Shallie felt the shock tear through her, but Hunt's face registered nothing. He could have been riding in a trance. His body, though, was fully alive and tuned in.

Hunt took the next jolt lying back on the horse's hindquarters. He seemed to feed the shock wave back into the animal so that the next buck was even higher and showier. Hunt took it as casually as a kid on a bike riding over a bump in the sidewalk.

"He's doing it," Shallie screamed as the wild, primitive side of Hunt called out to the horse beneath him and brought forth torrents of the same untamed, savage energy. Shallie could feel the electricity running through the crowd. Even those who didn't know enough about rodeo to appreciate what they were seeing realized that it was different and more exciting than what they were accustomed to. The buzzer blared. Hunt slacked off. As if the current had been broken, Avalanche rumbled to a sputtering finale. With one last halfhearted buck he threw the rider who had mastered him into the air. Hunt landed on his feet, his hat still firmly planted on his brow.

The crowd was stunned into silence for a fraction of a second, then the tumult erupted. The only person in the coliseum not stomping his approval was Jesse Southerland. The judges knew and appreciated what Hunt had done and their scores reflected that knowledge. One held up a chalkboard with the figure 48 scrawled on it. The other held up a 49.

"Ninety-seven points!" Slick Bridgers shouted into his microphone. "That is our highest score for the entire run in any of the riding events. Let me get verification from our rodeo secretary. Yes, it's true, that score just put Hunt McIver in the lead, making him our unofficial winner for the bareback riding by half a point."

Shallie shot a triumphant fist into the air in jubilation. An arm swept around, pulling her off to the sideline. The vacant look was gone from Hunt's face. He was one hundred percent there, with her, glowing his victory.

"Hunt, you were wonderful. You rode like I knew you could."

"Yeah, wish Jake had been here to see it. I think he would have been surprised."

Later, behind the chutes, Hunt collected the prize that rodeo cowboys value more than any other, the understated praise of their colleagues.

"Nice ride, Hunt." Emile Boulier's praise was untinged by any taint of jealousy. The other compliments were just as genuine. Shallie had seen that same spirit at every rodeo she'd ever attended, in the way one contestant would tell his hottest rival everything he knew about a horse the competitor was about to ride, in the way riders helped one another rig up in the tense moments before a ride. Maybe the men and women in rodeo weren't bigger-hearted than those in any other sport. Maybe it was just a matter of mutual survival or a ritualized show of magnanimity, but to Shallie it felt like something more, which was why it surprised her that Jesse Southerland didn't offer his congratulations. He stood back glowering at Hunt, Trish by his side. When the newly crowned queen stepped forward in their direction, Jesse yanked her back with a vicious jerk. As he pulled Trish away, her gaze lingered on Hunt. Shallie read the feelings behind it clearly. Jesse had been either a passing fancy or the pawn in a ploy to make Hunt jealous. Either way it was clear that Trish was finished with him. She wanted Hunt again.

"Why don't you go on ahead and start getting ready for the banquet? I'll help Petey run the rest of the show," Hunt whispered. "As if there's anything to run—you've organized it all so well."

Shallie hesitated for a moment, then realized that Hunt was right. All there was left to do was to hurry the contestants and Hunt could hustle cowboys along as well as she.

"Get going," he laughed, swatting her lightly on her bottom. "I'll come by for you at your hotel room."

For once, Shallie had ample time to prepare. She decided she would make the most of it by transforming dressing into a stylized ritual. She started by laying out the cloud-soft silk dress as if she were her own lady-in-waiting. Again she delighted in its rippling smoothness as she pulled it from its tissue-paper wrapping. Then she noticed that there was something else in the box. She drew out a slinky bit of apricot fluff. A teddy, Shallie realized with delight as she identified the exquisite piece of lingerie. She remembered hearing Hunt speaking with the saleswoman while she was dressing. He must have chosen the flimsy garment as an unspoken message to her, a message that Shallie found quite exciting.

She poured several capfuls of bath oil into the flooding stream of water she turned on. Although the air was heavy with the oil's fragrance, it was Hunt's scent still clinging to her that Shallie inhaled as she lowered herself into the steaming water, which plunged her instantly back into the embrace of memories only a few hours old. *I'm obsessed*, Shallie thought as the image of Hunt's naked form rippling beneath the water of the hot springs seeped into her mind. To have her every thought so dominated was unsettling for Shallie, who had for so long been a paragon of control and discipline. She hurried through the rest of her bath at a more characteristically efficient pace.

Shallie wiped a circle in the mirror free of steam. The face that greeted her was a surprise. It was somehow different. Both younger and older at the same time. Her skin glowed with the luminosity only the young possess, yet her eyes had a wiser, more womanly look. Her lips were slightly swollen as if being well kissed had brought them to full flower. She patted herself dry, finding that every point on her body had become a souvenir reminding her of Hunt's touch. She slipped on the teddy. Its apricot color brought out the sunny tones of her skin perfectly. She looked at herself with Hunt's eyes and happily anticipated his pleasure. She would wear nothing else under the dress.

In honor of the occasion, she brought out her rarely used supply of cosmetics. The mascara and liner intensified the color of her eyes to a rich, velvety brown. A terra-cotta blusher and lip gloss supplied a shimmering crown to her own natural luster. She dabbed touches of the bath oil behind her knees and ears and deep in the cleft between her breasts, knowing that the oil would last longer than a cologne and thinking of how sensuous it would become when combined with the body heat that Hunt invariably generated.

Hunt knocked at her door just in time to help her with the buttons at the back of the neck of her dress. His hands lingered as they forced the delicate pearl-shaped buttons through the loop of fabric. Then they slid to her shoulders and pulled her to his chest. He looked over her shoulder at their reflection in the mirror ahead.

The image in the mirror bewitched Shallie. They looked so right together. Shallie was so captivated that she dared to imagine Hunt as her husband helping her with the cozy chore of buttoning her dress.

"You look even better than I dreamed you would," he whispered huskily in her ear. She watched, mesmerized, as his hands slid down the shimmering material to lightly trace the outline of her breasts, her waist, her thighs. "God, you excite me. I wish we didn't have to leave, but we're late as it is."

"I don't have any plans for afterward." Shallie caught his eye in the mirror. "Do you?"

"Why, you little wanton!" He laughed. "Have I corrupted you this thoroughly?"

"Absolutely. You've hooked me on your physical charms." She shot him a playfully sultry glance, knowing even as they both laughed that she had spoken the truth. She was addicted, there was no denying it, but it went much further than mere physical attraction. She wondered how fast and in which direction Hunt McIver would run if he realized just how deeply attached to him she was. Tingles shimmied down her spine. Hunt had taken the brush from her dresser top and was running it with infinite delicacy through her hair.

"I love the way your hair feels. The color. It's like a palomino mane woven from silk." She melted under the caress of the brush.

"This is getting dangerous. We'd better leave now or we won't make it."

Hunt put down the brush. "You're right. There will be plenty of time later on. As much time as we need."

Shallie tried not to let herself read too much into his words, but it was hard. She could no longer imagine a future for herself that did not include Hunt McIver.

Chapter 15

How elegant," *Shallie breathed as* Hunt stepped aside and let her enter the door held by the uniformed doorman at the restaurant where the awards banquet was to be held. "A midnight supper. It's almost like a cast party on Broadway after the last night of a long run."

"That's a fair analogy," Hunt agreed. "We're more like theater people than athletes in the fact that our workday often stops at midnight too. Then we're so keyed up from the evening's excitement that we don't sleep until dawn."

The entire restaurant had been reserved especially for the awards dinner. One glance around the room told Shallie that rodeo had come of age. She recognized the governor of New Mexico and a couple of state senators. A nationally known Indian artist from Taos was chatting with a famous diva who had flown in from New York for the annual run of the Santa Fe opera. In the corner, Shallie spotted her uncle deep in conversation with the widow of one of the state's largest landowners. He glanced up and waved her and Hunt over.

"Miriam," he said, smiling from the woman at his side to Shallie, "I'd like you to meet my niece, Shallie Larkin, and I'm sure you know, or know of, Hunt McIver. Shallie, Hunt, this is Miriam Prescott."

Miriam Prescott met with Shallie's immediate approval. In her midfifties, she had the ruddy vigor that can't be purchased at any exclusive spa; it is only imparted by a lifetime of outdoor work and hard physical activity. Her light-gray eyes seemed to take in everything and filter it with a screen of irrepressible good humor. Miriam Prescott seemed to Shallie to have acquired none of the pretensions that so often accompany wealth. Shallie could easily imagine herself sitting down with Miriam and a cup of coffee and completely losing herself in a good conversation.

Glancing around the room, Shallie observed, "I had no idea rodeo was popular with so many influential and well-known people."

"Oh my heavens, yes," Miriam Prescott countered merrily. "You never know who you'll meet up in those box seats. Frequently there are visitors from the East, like the diva, Merrilee Sellers, who come for a one-time novelty. Then there are real fans like myself, and I know the governor sees as many performances as he can. As a matter of fact, Hunt, he was rendered positively speechless by your ride tonight. We've both seen Avalanche several times before and no one has ever come close to riding him, much less doing as superb a job of it as you did. Don't you agree, Walter?" Miriam's eyes, crinkled by sun and laughter, sought out Walter's, and they laughed like two conspirators.

Shallie's gaiety was cut cold when she noticed Trish Stephans smoldering in a far corner. Trish was so intent upon Hunt that she didn't even notice Shallie staring at her. She reminded Shallie of the way a cat crouches in the long grass, totally motionless except for the twitching of her tail, as she stalked an unsuspecting bird. Jesse was by her side, glowering angrily at the world. A white-jacketed waiter carrying a tray of fluted champagne glasses passed. Jesse lightened his load by two. He stuck one of the glasses in front of Trish. She refused it. Jesse shrugged sullenly, then proceeded to drain both glasses in quick succession. When the waiter passed by again, Jesse swapped the empty glasses for two more full ones. He was not taking his loss well, Shallie thought. No better, certainly, than Trish was taking hers. Of course, Shallie reminded herself, neither defeat was final.

The dinner, served by a platoon of waiters, was every bit as elegant as the surroundings and the company. The diners were finishing up the raspberry glacé and starting on their after-dinner coffee and brandy when the awards ceremony began. Shallie paid little attention, since most of the awards were honorary ones that the money men behind rodeo presented to one another. The majority of contestants had already packed up and were traveling hard to make the next rodeo. She was savoring the intoxicating smell of her brandy when she felt Hunt rise beside her.

"There must have been a mistake." He spoke to the master of ceremonies. Heads swiveled toward him. "I didn't produce this rodeo. That honor belongs to Shallie and Walter Larkin. They did a super job and are going to be doing a lot more." Hunt raised his hands above his head and led the applause as the emcee called Shallie and her uncle forward. At the dais, they were presented with a plaque for, said the head committeeman, "an exceptional job of producing one of the smoothest-running rodeos we've had in years."

Shallie's pride was enhanced by seeing her uncle bear the award back to his seat, his face shining in the reflected beam from Miriam's. *This has to be the most perfect day of my life*, Shallie was thinking again, when she caught a whiff of Old Spice cologne wafting over from the man on the other side of the banquet table.

Without any warning, she was yanked from the present and hurled back across seven years. It was the third of July. She was seventeen years old. Her riding club was having a father-and-daughter playday. She was sitting astride her horse, Toby. Her father was behind her, his Old Spice aftershave clean in her nostrils. They were lined up beside all the other father-and-daughter teams they'd been competing against all day. She'd been so proud that this handsome man, erect in his clean, white shirt and the best horseman there, was her father. When their names had been called for the first-place team, the same sentiment had held her thoughts—*this is the most perfect day of my life.* Late that night her father and uncle had driven away into the darkness for the Fourth of July round of rodeos known as the Cowboy's Christmas. Her father had never come home.

Shallie felt she'd had to pay for every moment of happiness with one of sadness ten times more intense. She'd learned early that the world does not sustain perfection. If it seems too good to be true, it is. The only happiness that lasts is the kind built on hard work.

Shallie clung to the brandy snifter in her hands as if it were physical proof that she was no longer a heartbroken girl, *I'm a woman now*, she screamed to the phantoms that tortured her. In answer, they reminded her of the price she'd paid for caring too much. Lessons learned young are learned well.

"Shallie, what's wrong?"

She looked into Hunt's face and realized that she'd been staring into her brandy as if it were a crystal ball.

"You look as if you've seen a ghost. Are you okay?"

She nodded, trying to shake the shadow of the past

from the present. She finished her brandy and signaled the waiter for another. Its warmth relaxed her and soon she was wrapped in conversation with Miriam Prescott, delighting in all her insider's tales of New Mexico's high and mighty.

"Shallie," her uncle said, "why don't you keep your hotel room for another night. It's too late for you to drive back to the ranch alone. I'll be seeing Miriam home. We can load up the stock tomorrow."

Shallie caught a new sparkle in Miriam Prescott's eyes and, for what might have been the first time in her life, realized what an attractive, virile man her uncle was.

She glimpsed at the wrist of the man opposite her. "It's almost three in the morning!" she exclaimed.

As if he'd been waiting for her cue, Hunt stood. "That's too late for me. May I take you back to the hotel, Shallie?"

Shallie smiled, appreciative of his courtliness and formality in front of her uncle. She stood as Hunt pulled the chair out for her. "Yes, it's been a long ten days." After a round of good-byes, Hunt whisked her outside. Shallie's last glimpse of the gathering focused on Trish. Jesse was slumped down in a chair beside her, but Trish was as predatorily alert as ever, her eyes gleaming an unspoken message to Hunt. Was Hunt aware of Trish's rapacious interest in him? Shallie didn't dare a direct question, so she probed indirectly.

"Jesse Southerland didn't seem too pleased about being beaten," she observed as Hunt held the car door open for her.

"I don't understand why he should be so bothered. He's still way ahead in the standings and I'm not even ranked yet."

"Trish didn't seem to be having a very good time either," Shallie ventured.

"Trish? You can never tell about her."

Shallie wished she'd been facing Hunt when he made his cryptic evaluation. Sitting beside him in the dark car, it was impossible to decipher his meaning. She was afraid she detected a hint of admiration in his voice. Was Trish's jealousy ploy working? Perhaps I've made myself too available, Shallie thought with a stab of remorse. She wondered if she shouldn't leave Hunt with a good-night kiss and a yearning for more. She wished she were more adept at making the kinds of calculations that seemed to come naturally to Trish.

The car pulled to a stop in front of the hotel and Hunt leaned over. "I've been wanting to do this all night," he confessed, his lips finding hers.

All thoughts of strategies and pretenses of aloofness flew from Shallie's mind as her lips returned his kiss with the warmth it had elicited. Hunt would be leaving early the next morning. She had a long list of obligations at other rodeos. It would be weeks, maybe months, before their schedules brought them together again. Hang what Trish would do, Shallie decided. She wanted only to spend every second she could with the man she loved, no matter if they would never spend another together again.

In the hotel room, Hunt drew off the emerald sheath as if he were unwrapping an exquisite present. He stood back to appraise Shallie, her legs long and slender beneath the short bit of apricot lingerie.

"You are one sexy woman," he growled throatily.

The brandy loosened her tongue enough to reveal, "Only with you, Hunt."

"Shallie," he said, his voice suddenly serious, "it's not fair for me to say anything right now, because I'll be leaving in a few hours and I'll be going down the road so hard and so fast that there won't be time for anything but phone calls. But when I'm through this year, there will be all the time we'll ever need. Do you understand what I'm saying?"

Shallie was afraid to answer. Afraid that her slightest breath would blow his words away forever. She nodded. His hand brushed her cheek, sliding back to tangle in her hair. He pulled her head to his chest, burying his face in her hair. "Shallie," he whispered, "you don't know what you mean to me." There was an ache in his voice, which was silenced as his mouth fitted itself to the sinuous curve of her neck.

Her head fell away, exposing the sensitive arch even

further. Hunt's hands slid over the silken material at her waist and rose to caress her breast. He tugged down the shoulder straps. Her hands glided over the snap buttons of his shirt. Impatiently, Hunt shrugged off his clothing and the remainder of hers. His lips pressed her back down onto the bed. He followed.

Shallie felt herself slip away again to that place she had visited only with Hunt, where all thoughts—past, present, future—had no meaning. Sensation became all that mattered. She was ruled by Hunt's smell, his taste, the feel of his chest against hers. Worries, doubts, insecurities, all vanished, swept away by the tidal wave of feeling crashing down on her. She gave herself over to it and swam in a black, weightless sea of desire.

The pounding seemed to come from within her own head, passion's relentless beating. But it didn't stop when she willed it to. It continued until Hunt cursed and, pulling a sheet around himself, went to the door.

"This had better be mighty important," he growled, letting in a streak of daylight as he opened the door.

Shallie couldn't hear the response, but she froze when the pitch of the voice reached her ears. It was Trish and she was crying.

"Are you sure?" Hunt asked.

All Shallie could make out was more sniffling and a few muffled words.

"Dammit to hell," Hunt cursed. He looked around the

room behind him, his gaze ricocheting distractedly from Shallie before he turned back to Trish. "All right. I'll be down. Wait for me by the pickup. You know which one it is." Hunt shut the door gently behind her. "I've got to get over to the grounds," he announced, grabbing up clothes off the floor. "I'll be back as soon as I can. Wait here for me." With that curtly delivered order, he was gone.

Shallie listened to the muted sound of his departure down the long, carpeted hall, then the slamming of two doors and the spatter of gravel as Hunt's truck pulled away. Shallie slumped down in the bed. An icy fist plunged down her throat and settled in her stomach. Hunt had gone away with Trish. That one bare fact echoed and reechoed through the empty room. The streaks of sunlight peeking around the corners of the drapes lengthened but did nothing to warm Shallie. When she finally pulled herself out of the stunned numbness engulfing her and glanced at the clock, it was nearly seven. She estimated that Hunt had been gone for well over two hours. She had to help her uncle load up the stock. Dully, she pulled back the covers and forced her legs over the side of the bed. She pulled on the silk dress and slunk to her own room. She was dressed and packed in less than fifteen minutes.

As she pulled up to the rodeo grounds, she saw Jesse Southerland stagger toward his truck, parked near the stock pens. A trickle of fresh blood ran from his nostril.

Moments later, Hunt came out of the coliseum. Trish was clinging to his arm. Hunt's right eye was nearly swollen shut. The three of them on the deserted parking lot looked like the major characters in some primitive drama. It took Shallie only seconds to know how the script they'd just played out had read: Trish had somehow maneuvered Hunt onto the rodeo grounds. Perhaps she'd fabricated some excuse, perhaps he'd come willingly. Perhaps two factors, deception and Hunt's own undeniable urge, had combined. It didn't matter. Once they were alone, Trish had reclaimed Hunt just as Shallie had feared all along that she would. Then Jesse, the recently scorned lover, had stumbled upon them. The fight that followed was as inevitable as Hunt and Trish's coupling.

The icy fist in Shallie's belly wrapped its fingers around her heart. She cursed herself for having been half a dozen kinds of fool but mostly for being the kind stupid enough to care for a rodeo cowboy. She'd known how it would end and had only herself to blame for the dull throb of pain that was already beginning to crack through the shocked numbness.

Hunt saw her. He shook Trish from his arm and came toward her. With every slap of his boots against the parking lot, his words "Shallie, you don't know what you mean to me" came back at her like a jeering taunt.

"I'm sorry I couldn't get back," he said, as casually as if he'd left her in the middle of a card game or a television program. "We couldn't find Jesse at first. Trish was afraid he was going to try something really desperate. We finally looked here and found him trying to get Pegasus into the chutes and rigged up. It took some physical persuasion to convince him that he was in no condition for a ride."

Shallie stared at Hunt, amazed to see his eyes sparkling as if she were supposed to enjoy his hastily constructed fiction. Behind him, Trish cocked her head, trying to catch more of their conversation. An amused smirk tilted the corners of her mouth. It was the smirk that snapped the thin leash Shallie was holding on her rage.

"You liar," she hissed. "Who do you think I am? Some dumb buckle bunny who's so thrilled to be with the big rodeo stud that she'll believe anything he tells her? Well, I'm not." Anger pumped a rush of blood to her head where it pounded so fiercely in her ears that she could barely hear his feeble lies.

"Shallie, what are you talking about?"

His retort rang hollow and false. She couldn't believe he'd resort to such a cliché.

"You're just like your grandfather, aren't you, Hunt?" Shallie hurled the accusation. "That's why you stay with him, admire him in spite of the abominable way he treats you. You're two of a kind, two whoring tomcats—"

Hunt's hands clamped around her forearms, as if Shallie were some shrill accordion that he could silence with one decisive gesture. "I love that old man." His face had gone a deathly white. "And I won't stand for you or for anyone else—"

"What?" Shallie challenged. "What won't you stand for? To hear anyone speak the truth about him? About you? Because you're cut from the same cloth, Hunt McIver."

His hand snapped back and quivered in the air next to her cheek, poised to strike, to slap at both the mouth and the words that issued from it. With one convulsive gesture, he pushed her from him. In a voice of iron calm, he told her, "We'll be forced together at some rodeos. Don't come anywhere near the chutes when I'm competing. If you need to know anything about the contracts you're working, call Jake or have your uncle call me. We won't speak again. Ever."

"Don't worry. The last thing in the world I want is to see or talk with you." Even as she spoke them, Shallie knew that her venomous words were a lie. As she watched Hunt McIver walk away, Trish molded to his side, she knew it was a lie she would live with the rest of her life.

Chapter 16

Fort Worth. Scottsdale. San Antonio. Tucson. Salinas. Odessa. The rodeo grounds changed from floodlit grandstands to sunbaked bleachers over the next months and so did the names of the towns. Even the weather changed, heating up along with the furious pace that would climax in December at the National Finals. Yet in the face of constant change from one motel room and arena to the next, over long, dusty miles traveled in the cab of a semi loaded with rodeo stock, Shallie felt like an insect imprisoned in amber, locked in a static and unmoving world ruled by pain.

Intellectually she realized that she was living the dream she'd had since first deciding to challenge one of the last great bastions of masculinity and become a rodeo contractor. But emotionally she took no delight in the acceptance and recognition she was achieving. A rodeo didn't pass when the top cowboys and members of the rodeo committee didn't compliment her and Walter on how smoothly the show had run or on what fine stock they'd turned out. Especially Pegasus. Shallie's "pig in a poke" had, in the space of a few months, established himself as a legend on the circuit—the horse that bucked straight and fair and didn't fight in the chute, but absolutely could not be ridden.

At the rodeo in Phoenix, Shallie heard the words of an old hand, a man who had held the bronc-riding title for six years in the late fifties and early sixties, and who had ridden every great horse to come out of a chute during those decades, as he told one of his cronies, "I saw that Pegasus today and I do believe that he is the finest bronc I've ever seen. And that includes Midnight. I drew that danged grave-digging horse back in '59 . . ."

Shallie left the pair to reminisce about mounts ridden before she'd even been born. For a moment her spirits soared, then plummeted just as far when she realized that she would never be able to share that accolade with Hunt. That realization and its effect were like the symptoms of a lingering infection that was cutting Shallie's appetite for life.

She'd climbed to the highest rung on rodeo's ladder. At that height she discovered that the excitement in the arena was outdone only by the perpetual partying which accompanied it. Her new friends and acquaintances were champions she had only read about before: movie stars who liked to rope and be part of the exclusive rodeo fraternity, oil millionaires playing cowboy, agents searching for a face that would epitomize the West and sell their clients' products, and the ever-present swarm of hangers-on—buckle bunnies, photographers, and reporters. Among the last group, Shallie quickly became the year's novelty attraction. She was interviewed and reinterviewed about what it was *really* like to be the only female stock contractor working the professional circuit. She repeated her answers for countless digital recorders and television cameras.

"What about dating?" The Houston talk-show hostess cocked her head toward Shallie while the television camera blinked its red light at her. The woman had obviously patterned herself after Katie Couric, hoping to catch the manner that made people bare their innermost secrets in public. "I mean, all those gorgeous cowboys, isn't that quite a temptation? Or would mixing business and pleasure be bad for business?"

Lady, Shallie thought to herself, *if you only knew just how little I was "tempted."*

"Oh, I don't know," Shallie answered, smiling warmly, "I've noticed some pretty attractive 'temptations' walking around the streets right here in"—Shallie glanced quickly at the station's logo on the camera—"Houston."

The interviewer laughed with calculated warmth.

"But I do know what you mean," Shallie continued.

"And you're right about business. When I'm producing a rodeo there's not a second to spare for appreciating the 'scenery.'"

Another laugh and the show was over. The station's limousine dropped Shallie back at Houston's seventy-thousand-seat Reliant Stadium, where the turf was being rolled up and replaced by truckloads of dirt and sand in preparation for the beginning of the two-week run of the largest rodeo in the world. At the rodeo office, Shallie learned that 360 contestants had entered and would be vying for over two million dollars in prize money in front of more than a million total fans.

"Hey, Shallie, what dink of a horse did I draw?" Shallie turned to see Emile Boulier standing behind her. His easygoing, boyish manner was always a welcome relief. She enjoyed his good-natured kidding and suspected that he had a bit of a crush on her.

"You're up on Zeus tonight and Laredo in the second go-round."

"I can't believe it!" Boulier whooped. "Two good broncs. For once I stand half a chance of scratching a decent score. Unless McIver's here, I might even be good for the all-around money."

Shallie felt the Arctic Zone at the pit of her stomach freeze over again at the mention of Hunt's name. The red-haired cowboy edged past her to scrutinize the list himself.

"Well, bye-bye all-around money," Boulier grumbled. "McIver's entered. That's real unusual. He hasn't come near a rodeo you've contracted since Albuquerque. I figured he was afraid of drawing Pegasus."

Hunt is here. The three words shrieked in her ears. She checked the list. There he was, scheduled to ride the last two days of the rodeo's two-week run.

"At least I won't be the only one losing out on that first-prize money. No one is going to beat McIver. He's been riding like a maniac since Albuquerque. And I mean that for a fact. The man rides like he's about half a bubble off plumb. He just goes wild on a bronc. The funny thing about it is, though, the rest of the time he's so quiet it scares you. He always seems like he's stalking something. Like his mind is on something that's just in back of you or right around the corner. It's spooky."

Stories about Hunt had drifted back to Shallie over the past months. Some said it was an old score he was settling with his grandfather that had put the iron in his spine. Some said Hunt just needed the money badly enough to ride that well. The ones who really knew rodeo, though, and what makes rodeo's heart beat, said he was obsessed. Hunt McIver was determined to put the best ride on a bronc that man had ever made on animal.

"There's just no way to beat McIver. He's on a hot streak that's got us all iced," Boulier lamented. "Even though he missed the first part of the season, he's still won enough to buy himself a ticket to the Finals."

Shallie nodded. Her throat was drawn up tight. She couldn't trust herself to speak. Her mind whirled. *Maybe he's hurting as much as I am.* The thought surfaced from the maelstrom churning through her brain, like a bit of flotsam thrown ashore after a storm. That slender hope grew over the next few days, nurtured by Shallie's wild yearnings. *I must have meant something to him*, she dared to theorize.

By the twelfth day of the Houston show, she believed it. She dressed with extra care, slipping on the blouse she'd searched Houston for. It was a deep emerald green. Hunt was riding that night.

As she was heading for the chutes, her uncle intercepted her. "Jake's here tonight. He'd like us to join him."

Shallie was about to protest, then realized that she would stand a better chance of talking with Hunt in his grandfather's box than she would down by the chutes. Besides, if her hopes had any substance to them at all, he would search her out wherever she was.

The parking lot they crossed was thick with Cadillacs, Mercedes, and the scent of money. Shallie followed her uncle to the stadium's most exclusive club, where Jake McIver sat surrounded by rodeo officials and wealthy hangers-on. A drink was in every hand and the rodeo was flashing in front of them across a closed-circuit television screen.

"Shalimar Larkin, come sit down here next to me and let's watch that grandson of mine whip a few cowboys." His cronies joined in Jake's laughter. He shooed a kewpie doll of a blonde off his lap and waved Shallie over. "You've been doing a hell of a job," he said as she sat down beside him. "Got nothing but good reports." His attention turned to the screen. "Isn't that your horse Pegasus?"

As Shallie looked up, it seemed the roan was about to burst through the screen and lunge right into their faces. He was in his usual unridable form.

"Damn, but you skinned me on that deal, girl." A grudging admiration lurked in Jake's statement.

The door swung open and Shallie froze, hoping and fearing that it might be Hunt, even though logic told her that he had to be down at the chutes preparing for his ride. She turned. It was Miriam Prescott. Her uncle jumped out of his chair to meet her at the door and escort her to the table. It brought Shallie a rare moment of pleasure to see her uncle so obviously in love and having his love returned so completely. Since the Albuquerque show, Walter had finally given in and bought a cell phone so that he could call Miriam from whichever rodeo they were working that week. A couple of times she'd flown out to meet him. It made Shallie both happy and even more lonesome than ever to see the one person closest to her caught in the throes of a mutual romantic entanglement. He was glowing now as Miriam demurely sat beside him and responded to his proud introductions with her usual grace and poise.

When Shallie turned back to the screen, Hunt's face dominated it. He lunged out of the gate with his spurs tucked well above the point of his bronc's shoulders. He was rock steady, his hand glued so solidly to the rigging on the bronc's twisting back that he made it appear as if the riders who had gone before had been kidding when they'd been bucked off. Hunt made bronc riding look like no more than an exercise of will.

"I was hot," Jake McIver intoned. "And his father was hot. But that boy puts us both in the shade."

The eight-second buzzer sounded. Hunt, still in perfect time with the horse's movements, rocketed into the air, landing on his feet. He walked away from the crowd's ovation like a man eager to leave the office at the end of a hard day.

"Will Hunt be joining you?" Shallie heard a tiny crack in her voice and hoped no one else noticed.

"Oh, I doubt it," Jake sighed.

His melancholic tone triggered an onslaught of memories. Shallie saw herself hurling the accusation at Hunt that he was just like his grandfather. Saw his face whiten and remembered the conflict she had perceived earlier when they'd discussed Jake McIver. Human relationships were rarely simple. She'd known that. Why had she ever believed that such a basic rule didn't apply to Hunt and his grandfather?

A second later she was on her feet heading for the chutes. By the time she wound her way through the concrete maze of the vast stadium, past the booths selling bumper stickers reading "Only Cowgirls are Tough Enough to Love Cowboys," and the cotton candy concessions, and the man hawking $860 aardvark-skin boots, the calf roping was half over and the saddle bronc riders had taken over the warm-up area recently vacated by the bareback riders.

Petey was loading saddle broncs into the chutes. She tapped him on the shoulder. He turned and his eyes went to her hands. During the long miles they'd spent together hauling livestock across the country, Petey had taught her the rudiments of sign language.

"Where's Hunt?" she asked with a few flicks of her hand.

"Gone," Petey answered in even fewer.

"Where?"

Petey answered with a shrug and uplifted palms, saying either that he didn't know or didn't care. She glanced around. Two old veterans were crouched down on the ground, their feet in the stirrups of their saddles, stretching the leather loose.

"Yeah," she overheard one of the pair drawl to his

buddy, "that's the way it is with him. He rides a different bronc and a different woman in every town."

His friend laughed, pulling lips back over gums flecked with blackish-brown specks of chewing tobacco.

Who were they talking about? Shallie tried to dismiss her own question. What did it matter *who* they were discussing? It could be most of the cowboys on the circuit. The irony amused her. She'd been so upset about Trish Stephans's and Jake McIver's influence, when all along it was rodeo and the different women in every town she should have been blaming. She'd known that from the start. Let Hunt McIver prove it to her if he was any different.

The next morning's paper showed Shallie just how close she'd come to utterly humiliating herself. The *Houston Chronicle* had a big double-page spread on the rodeo. It included an interview with her, but was dominated by a picture of Hunt with Trish at his side, beaming lovingly into his face. The caption read: "The crown prince and princess of rodeo step out for an evening on the town after last night's performance, highlighted by McIver's showstopping ride."

On the next, the last, day of the rodeo's run, Shallie studiously avoided the bucking chutes. She watched Hunt's second showstopping ride on closed-circuit television. From her seclusion high up in the stadium club she saw him accept both the buckle for winning the bareback riding and Trish's congratulatory kiss. She watched and tried to hate him. She tried, but all Shallie succeeded in doing was conjuring up a whole new platoon of ghosts, each one with a memory to devil her.

Shallie was alone in the club. The usual crew had all left for the invitation-only award ceremony. Walter had agreed to collect their award for producing a smooth, money-making rodeo. She flicked off the set and gathered up her gear. There was a rodeo to put on in El Paso. She left a message for Walter to meet her there. She wanted to be on the road by the time the ceremony was over.

Driving away from Reliant Stadium, Shallie vowed that she wouldn't waste another minute of her life moping over a man she could never have. But even her determination could not keep the black dog of depression from hounding her. The ache that had opened up in that parking lot in Albuquerque throbbed now with a pain that wasn't assuaged by even the tiniest flicker of hope. It was torn open every time she passed a billboard and Hunt peered down at her, or she picked up a newspaper or magazine and saw more pictures of the "crown prince and princess of rodeo."

At El Paso, she discovered she could keep depression at bay in groups. As usual, Walter disappeared at the end of the first show, running off to call Miriam and spend an hour telling her about the rodeo. Since Albuquerque, that had been Shallie's signal to troop back to her motel room. But after Houston she was determined to extinguish all memories of and longings for Hunt. So, when Emile Boulier asked in his endearingly eager, forthright way if she might possibly want to stop by the party later, she agreed.

It was after midnight by the time Shallie had finished with the stock. Emile was waiting to escort her to the rented hall where a famous boot manufacturer was hosting the festivities. The strains of a country waltz floated out to greet them. It was an old Cajun classic, "Jolie Blonde Waltz." Emile brightened as the French words reached his ears.

"May I have this dance, mam'selle?" he joked.

Shallie fought down the stab of sadness piercing her as she remembered that Hunt had made the same joke. But she laughed and fell into the waltz's swaying rhythm. It was a brittle, forced laugh. She hoped Emile wouldn't detect its falseness. The feel of his broad chest against hers was so like Hunt's. If she just shut her eyes, she could believe that Hunt was holding her, that it was Hunt guiding her through the enchanting patterns woven by the music. It was comforting to feel strong arms around her again. She snuggled into them like a bird sheltering against a storm. Arms wrapped more tightly about her and the heart beating above her own picked up its tempo.

"Shallie, I—" The sound of Emile's voice rudely

broke the momentary spell Shallie had allowed herself to fall under. She jerked away from the startled cowboy, stammering apologies.

"I'm sorry, I've been tired lately. I . . ." Her words dribbled off. How could she apologize to one man for using him as a stand-in for another she loved? She drew away from Emile and headed toward the pool of light spilling out of the open door of the hall. An overflow of cowboys, many with their contestant numbers still pinned to their backs, most with a buckle bunny hung on one arm, stood in the pool of light.

"Shallie Larkin," a voice from the crowd called out as she approached the crowded hall. "Never thought I'd catch you mingling with the common folk." It was Jesse Southerland weaving toward her. He stuck a glass in her hand and filled it from the bottle he was carrying, sloshing the amber-colored liquid on her hand as well.

"Goodness," Jesse said in mock alarm, "let me wipe that off for you, Miss Stock Contractor." He gallantly pulled Shallie's hand into his own, then proceeded to lick the spilled whiskey off with his tongue. Shallie pulled her hand away and felt Emile tense beside her. Jesse laughed, both at his prank and Shallie's outrage. Emile stepped forward. Shallie joined in Jesse's laughter, knowing it was the only way to forestall the fight that the two rivals would have welcomed.

"Who did you draw this evening?" she asked Jesse,

already knowing the answer but hoping to defuse the tension.

"Got a dink." Jesse's mind was already miles away from thoughts of fighting as he described the horse's performance. A few more rough stock riders joined them, and they gossiped about bulls and broncs as if they were absent friends. With each drink, Shallie found that the conversation grew more animated, more witty. She enjoyed the attention the cowboys rained on her, leaving the buckle bunnies ignored. Jesse and Emile vied to amuse her. Though she knew that the source of Jesse's interest in her was jealousy, settling a score with Hunt McIver for snatching Trish from him, she didn't care. After a couple of stiff drinks, Shallie no longer cared about anything. It was a wonderful, floaty feeling after all the months of heaviness.

Jesse and Emile began pulling out their most outrageous stories as they competed for Shallie's laughter. Emile told about the time in Canada when he'd convinced three American cowboys that they would have to practice curtseying because the queen was coming to the rodeo that night and they were going to be "presented."

Jesse tried to top Emile with a story about riding backward in a Grand Entry. Emile came back with one even more outrageous. A fuzzy haze prevented Shallie from catching the beginning of Jesse's next story.

". . . to ride the horse nobody could ride." Jesse's

features seemed more pointed than ever as Shallie brought him and his story into focus. "So there I was, all alone in this big, ugly turquoise coliseum. Had the damned nag in the chute and was rigging him up, getting ready to settle down on his back when this huge hand comes down and jerks me off."

Shallie suddenly felt as if she'd missed something very important and struggled to surface from the cozy pool she'd immersed herself in.

"Who? Who are you talking about?" she sputtered frantically.

Jesse eyed her warily. "I said it was the horse that couldn't be ridden. Your damned horse Pegasus." Jesse's anger lay close to the surface and it erupted when Shallie stopped laughing. "I would have ridden him too if Hunt hadn't decided to play the big hero." Jesse slapped a half-filled glass down. All the 100-proof merriment had leaked from his face. He stomped away, looking as angry as he had that morning in Albuquerque.

Suddenly the hall seemed too loud, too crowded. Hunt hadn't been lying! He *had* stopped a drunken Jesse from riding Pegasus. The realization screamed in Shallie's brain. She needed air. Emile followed her outside.

"I think I've had enough for one evening."

Emile insisted on walking her to her room. At her door, he leaned down to kiss her. Shallie turned her cheek.

"I need a friend," she whispered.

"Sure, Shallie," he answered softly. "As long as there's a chance to become something more."

"I can't promise that."

Alone in her room, Shallie shut her eyes, hoping to fall into a stuporous sleep before the implications of Jesse's unwitting confession hit her. She didn't make it. Hunt hadn't been lying, nor had he been fighting Jesse for Trish. He *had* wrestled the disgruntled cowboy off Pegasus and she hadn't believed him. It had been her caustic words that had driven him to Trish. Knowing that she had brought this misery on herself made the pain even more acute.

Chapter 17

Shallie awoke feeling as miserable physically as she did mentally. Still, she dragged through the day, and that evening was back at the hospitality suite with part of the crew of diehards who carried the festivities into the wee hours. It was only after too many drinks and too much forced laughter that she was exhausted enough to fall asleep before regrets and memories could begin their nightly torture. By the end of the El Paso run, Shallie was a regular on the party circuit.

"Don't see much of you in the evenings anymore," her uncle said as they pulled out of El Paso.

"I'm surprised you noticed," Shallie snapped, "as much time as you spend on the phone to Miriam." She instantly regretted her words, knowing they sprang more from envy and a lack of sleep than anything else. "Don't pay any attention to me," she apologized. "These past few months have been a strain on both of us and we still have a long way to go to the Circle M. Then we'll just barely have time to load up the fresh stock and hit the road again."

"Yeah. I'm glad Petey flew back," her uncle added, as relieved as Shallie for the change of subject. "He ought to have most of the stock separated out for us by the time we arrive. It's strange to think that most of Double L's roping stock is down there at the Circle M now. Our old place is pretty much deserted."

Shallie heard the hint of regret in her uncle's voice. "It's still Double L stock, no matter where it is," she comforted him.

"I know. It didn't make any sense having them stuck up in the mountains when most of the shows we've been working are down south." With a sigh, Walter turned his attention to the stack of mail that had accumulated during the show, when there hadn't been time to read any of it. He chuckled softly at a letter.

"From Miriam?" Shallie guessed easily.

"Uh-huh." Walter paused. "Shallie, there's something . . . Miriam and I . . . Well, we . . ." He stopped again, then finally abandoned the effort. "We'll discuss it at the end of the season."

Shallie was fairly sure she knew what her uncle wanted to discuss. Conflicting currents of sadness and joy swept through her. She was pleased that her uncle, after so many solitary years, had found someone to love and care for. But she knew that his marriage to Miriam Prescott would mean the end of the Double L and the end of his rodeo days. The spell of the road had been broken by the even stronger enchantment Miriam Prescott and life with her held.

Her uncle ripped into another envelope. "Shallie." He gripped her hand on the big steering wheel. "Shallie, we did it!"

"Did what?"

"We made the National Finals! Says here that Pegasus and some of our roping calves and dogging steers have been selected to compete in Las Vegas!"

Shallie's elation was curiously subdued. She almost felt as if she'd just paid off a debt, a debt she owed to her father's memory. Only the mental image of Pegasus pitted against the best the sport had to offer excited her. "Hey, that's great."

"I never thought we'd do it. What a way to go out," Walter let his secret out in the midst of his excitement.

"So, you *are* planning to call it quits."

Walter nodded. "That's what I wanted to talk to you about, Shallie. This season has been more exciting than I could have dreamed. It's what I'd always wanted, or thought I always wanted. Until I met Miriam. But now . . . Well, none of it really seems to matter very much without her."

Shallie winced. Her uncle's feelings closely mirrored

253

her own: with no one to share it, rodeo's thrill had vanished for her too.

"I wanted to finish out this season, then Miriam and I planned to get married. I hated breaking the news to you, Shallie. But now that we've made the Finals, I don't feel so bad about it."

"Don't feel bad about anything, Uncle Walter," Shallie insisted. "I'm happy for you. For you *and* Miriam. You deserve each other. Besides, I'm ready myself to leave rodeo. Life on the road ages a person too fast." She slid her hand across the seat to squeeze Walter's.

"These last few years have been good, haven't they, Shallie girl?"

"Wonderful," she agreed. "And the best are still to come." The words tasted of ash and sounded, to her own ears, as false as the smile she wore for her uncle's benefit. Shallie wondered if happiness would ever be anything other than a charade for her.

As she had predicted, there was no time at the Circle M to do much more than unload the trailers and fill them with fresh stock. Walter left in the car while Shallie led Pegasus to a lush pasture. Thick live oaks shaded it and the Colorado River meandered through it. She left the horse to rest and build up his strength for the Finals. The liquid coo of a dove cut through the afternoon stillness. It took Shallie back to her first evening at the Circle M, when she'd walked in the darkness with Hunt listening to that same mournful song. She felt as if that night had been half a century ago when she was still fresh and life was full of possibilities. Now, here she was, less than a year later, dismantling all her dreams even as she attained them.

A horn honked in the distance. Petey was leaning out the window and gesturing for her. When she was close enough, he signed to her, "Hurry up. We're ready to go."

She gave a meager nod and climbed in beside him. As they approached the ranch house, Jake McIver came out and flagged them down. Petey pulled up. The old man leaned in the window and growled at Shallie.

"I can't believe you'd leave without even so much as a howdy-do."

"I'm sorry. We're running so late."

"Well, you'll be running a little later. Come in the house. I want to talk with you."

In the living room, Jake settled himself into the cattle-horn throne in which Shallie had first seen him. "What I had planned on doing was offering to sell out half the business to you," he began bluntly, then stopped to clear his throat. "So, I called up my lawyers and had them go through the papers. Come to find out that Jake McIver is nothing more than a figurehead in this operation and my grandson is the real money man behind it.

Seems Circle M has been floating on the money from his commercials and endorsements and such for several years now, and he had it rigged so that I wouldn't find out. Anyway, I don't have half the operation to offer you. The whole shooting match belongs to Hunt. I suppose he wanted me to go to my grave thinking I was still Mr. Rodeo."

Shallie started to protest, but Jake McIver held up his hand to silence her.

"Don't bother telling me I'm too mean to die or some such nonsense. I'm over seventy-seven years old and I'm *ready* to die. What's to live for? All my friends are gone. Every time I tell a story now, everyone thinks I'm either lying or senile. There's no one left who knows that for every story I can tell there are three more too rough to admit to. No, I won't be sorry to go. Don't regret a thing except, maybe . . ." McIver drew in a deep breath. "Maybe the way things are between Hunt and me."

Regret weighed down McIver's words and Shallie squirmed, thinking of how harshly she had judged the old man. "He loves you very much," she said.

"I suppose he does." McIver sighed. "Suppose he'd have to, to put up with me all these years, then go and spend all his money running this place and never let on I really wasn't the boss. I've been tough on him, though. Might have been too tough. We never talked much. Not about anything important. I just hope he understands."

"He does," Shallie said, thinking of everything Hunt had said to her about his grandfather and cursing herself for letting her insecurities and jealousy cloud the meaning of his words.

"Things went kind of bad between us after Maggie died," Jake mumbled, as if he'd uncorked a flow of words that streamed forth now of their own accord. "What is it now? Twenty years ago this April. Finest woman that ever drew breath. Hunt's grandmother. My wife. My Maggie. Knew I'd never feel that way again." He looked up at Shallie. "You remind me of her."

His comment caught Shallie off guard. He'd been talking as if he were no longer aware she was even in the room, much less in his thoughts.

"Same feisty spirit," he rumbled on. "Not about to let anyone put her on the shelf to be admired and fussed over. Not my Maggie. She was just like you, had to be in the middle of everything. Running it if she could." He chuckled at memories two decades old and still as bright as the day they had been coined by Maggie McIver.

"Hunt's father never in his life felt the way about one woman that I felt about Maggie. Oh, he married Hunt's mother, but not because he wanted to." Jake McIver grew somber as he turned his vision inward to a sad night more than thirty years back, when a scared teenage girl had told Jake and his wife about her condition. "But that's an old story," Jake said, "and I don't want to waste any more of your time with old stories about my son and my mistakes."

Shallie noticed that Jake never spoke his son's name. She guessed from his expression of grief, long ago congealed beneath a mask of endurance, that it still hurt too much to hear the name he'd given to his son.

"To make a long, sad story short, Hunt's mother didn't want to raise a child, so we adopted Hunt and didn't hear too much from my son again." Jake McIver paused.

Shallie could read in his face the pain associated with the memories he'd unearthed. She sensed that beneath his brief outline was a complex story, which would tell most of the tale about the men Jake and Hunt McIver had become. From the way Jake's features were hardening, though, it didn't appear that it was a tale she was ever likely to hear. Then for a brief moment they softened again, exposing the vulnerability and tenderness he had been revealing to Shallie. His voice faltered as he spoke.

"I wonder if Hunt hates me, the way he hates his father, for—"

"Jake, honey, have we got company?"

The voice that cut through Jake's words came from the back part of the house. But Shallie didn't need to see the speaker to know who she was—Trish Stephans.

"You'll tell me when Mr. Childress gets here, won't you, Jake?"

"I will, darlin'," Jake shouted back to her. In a softer

voice he explained to Shallie, "She wants a movie contract. I know a movie producer. He's flying in today."

Shallie nodded her head as if she understood. But she didn't, not really. All she understood was that Trish Stephans was probably the reason Jake was worried that his grandson hated him.

Jake easily discerned her disapproval. "I've always tried to do something for every woman in my life. Trish wanted to be Rodeo Sweetheart, now she wants to be a movie star. I wanted her company. At least for a while that's what I wanted. So we made a trade. Can't see that either one of us have been hurt."

Jake McIver, shorn of his blustery facade, seemed to shrink before her eyes. He was right, she didn't approve, but she could certainly understand. She understood loneliness and the things people did out of loneliness. Shallie crossed the room and put her arms around a tired old man. "He really does love you," she assured him again.

Jake clung to her for a moment. Tears filled his eyes as he looked up at her. "So like my Maggie," he whispered, "so like her." Abruptly he pulled away. "You'd better get moving before some rodeo committeeman calls up to chew my butt because his rodeo is five minutes late getting started."

Shallie straightened up, hesitant to leave.

"I said get going, unless you enjoy watching old men blubber."

"Thanks, Jake," she whispered, "for everything. I'll see you at the Finals."

He waved her away with a show of gruffness, and Shallie pushed open the heavy oak doors of the stone home Jake McIver had built half a century before for the woman he'd never stopped loving.

Chapter 18

The highway was a clean slice through the Nevada desert, barreling straight into the glitter gulches of Las Vegas, home of the National Finals, the world's richest, roughest rodeo. A gigantic cowboy grinned down at Shallie from a billboard, announcing that the nine-day-long Super Bowl of rodeo, in which the top fifteen contestants in each event competed for championships, would begin in two days. But Shallie's mind was on her visit with Jake McIver almost one month ago.

She'd walked out of his home, reflecting on the forces that mold people, shaping them like trees bent before a slow, yet persistent wind. She imagined that right after Maggie died, Jake had probably turned to the first of the women who would trek in an endless parade through his life for a temporary relief from his pain, the same kind of relief she'd found in compulsive socializing. When did temporary measures become permanent fixtures? she wondered. When did they move from propping up a sagging personality to being an integral part of it? Shallie would never know exactly how it had happened with Jake, just that it had.

The last party she had attended was simply to tell Emile, as gently as possible, that she wouldn't be going to any more functions with him. She'd learned from Jake how cruelly unfair it was to let others pay the price of her pain.

Emile had accepted her decision with his usual good grace. She left early to return to what would become a succession of empty rooms where she would face sleepless hours and torturing thoughts of what might have been. But gradually sleep grew less elusive and by the time they rolled into Las Vegas, her natural equilibrium had been reestablished.

The big truck hummed as Petey guided it through the maze of freeways leading to the heart of the city, where the rodeo was to be staged at the mammoth Thomas & Mack Center. Every seat had been sold out long before the first of the big semis nosed into town, carrying the animals who would form the all-star team opposing the best cowboys in the country.

Petey slid the truck in beside a dozen others. A maze of pens made the grounds resemble a feedlot. Shallie hopped out and was approached by a National Finals board member, Chet Williamson, a whip-thin man who still looked fit enough to add another buckle to the collection he'd won as a national finalist during the seventies.

"Shallie Larkin, glad to see you." He took her hand, dismissing an unneeded introduction. Shallie would be the only woman pulling up at the National Finals in a semi loaded with stock.

"Chet Williamson, good to meet you." Shallie returned the warm greeting.

"I'll let our livestock superintendent show you around, but basically we're penning the animals in three categories: Put your least rank stock over there." He pointed to an area at the far end of the maze of steel pens. "Then put your top bucking horses and bulls over there. And right here," he said indicating a complex of pens constructed of a heavier grade, reinforced steel, "are the eliminator pens. Put your unridables in here. We want to have all the stock evened up as much as possible so that all the cowboys are riding stock of approximately the same quality."

The first animal off the truck was her prize, Pegasus. She led her snowflake-kissed treasure straight to the eliminator pen. She knew he wasn't absolutely "unridable." She'd seen it done by one man. But in Pegasus's season on the professional circuit, it had never been officially accomplished. He whinnied as if the excitement that buzzed like static in the air had infected him as well. It pleased Shallie to believe that he realized what an achievement it was for him to be here.

His shaggy winter coat kept him warm in the chill

winter air. Shallie snuggled further into her down parka. Pegasus was a spot of brilliance, shockingly white amidst the mottled browns and grays of the other broncs. Always the aristocrat, Shallie thought to herself. Her musing was cut short when Petey came up to her, his hands flying. He couldn't find the special grain mixture she had developed especially for the horses selected for the Finals. When Shallie couldn't locate it either, she had to borrow a pickup and head out for the nearest feed store in search of the high-protein mix.

Prima donnas, she thought with amusement, knowing that this was just the first of an infinite number of missions she'd be embarking upon over the course of the next week and a half.

When she returned, the grounds were even more cluttered with semis. All around her were the symbols of the best in rodeo contracting. Painted across the eighteen-wheeled trucks, sewed onto the crews of men unloading livestock, and seared into the flesh of the animals themselves were the brands and logos of the producing companies she had read and dreamed of for years. But now that she was actually one of them, sharing the sport's pinnacle, she halfway wished she could leave before the rodeo even got underway.

Hunt would be here, of course. The rampage he'd been on since Albuquerque had continued. In the few months he'd competed, he'd won enough to buy himself the third-place ranking. Emile was second and Jesse Southerland led the bronc riders. Since all of the top fifteen bareback riders would be competing in each of the ten performances, a meeting with Hunt was almost inevitable.

She scooped the grain mixture into the troughs, reflecting on the route she'd taken to the Finals. She realized that luck, and Hunt's intervention, had played a large part in her presence among rodeo's greats. But she also knew that she'd put in as much hard work and caring as any contractor. In that sense, she'd earned her trip to the Finals. And she was going to enjoy it! Her decision strengthened her.

She *could* face Hunt.

"Shallie!" Walter, with Miriam by his side, waved her over. He had spent the few free days after their last rodeo at the Prescott ranch, then he and Miriam had flown in together.

"Come on, girl," he chided her. "All us big-time contractors and some of the contestants are gathering at the hospitality suite."

She waved them on, promising to join them once she'd changed.

In her hotel room, she pulled out the emerald-green dress and held it up as if it were a talisman. *I'll need it,* she thought, slipping the silken sheath on. She added perfume and makeup as if they too were part of the psychic armor she needed for the ordeal of seeing Hunt again. All she wanted was to survive their meeting with as much grace as possible. But deep down inside, she actually wanted much more. Though she wouldn't allow herself to dwell on her futile hopes, she also hadn't been able to extinguish them. As Shallie paused at the door of the hospitality suite, a kind of panic close to stage fright clawed at the pit of her stomach. The clinking of ice cubes in glasses supplied a tinkling counterpoint to the bass rumbling of the predominantly male voices at the gathering. Shallie took several deep breaths and entered.

"Shalimar Larkin!" Jake McIver hailed her. He was encircled by her uncle and Miriam, Petey, and several of the biggest contractors in the business. Though his voice was hearty, weariness strained his face and his eyes were lackluster. Shallie shot him a look of concern. He intercepted it with a wink, which told Shallie that any strain he might be putting on his health was less important to him than maintaining his "Mr. Rodeo" facade.

"Gentlemen, I'd like you to meet a producer good enough to put any one of you out of business tomorrow, Shallie Larkin."

Shallie shook hands all around, but her attention was elsewhere. She scanned the crowded room filled with handsome, athletic men in Western suits, accompanied by wives and girlfriends attractive enough to be shown off at the National Finals. She tilted her chin upward, craning her neck to search the corners of the room for a dark head of curly hair above a pair of high, slashing cheekbones.

Petey nudged her gently and directed her eyes to his hands. They formed the words "He's over there," then pointed to a corner behind Shallie. She instantly began to sense his presence in the form of a warm spot between her shoulders. The heat built until she couldn't stand it any longer. She dared a quick glance over her shoulder.

For the first time in over half a year, they looked at one another. Shallie was stunned by the powerful effect Hunt had upon her. It was as if the past months had distilled everything she had ever felt for him into one heart-stoppingly visceral reaction. The expression he saw, however, was one of shock. In the same instant that Shallie's features began to unfreeze, Hunt turned from her, from the chilly expression that seemed to glaze her features. The smile that finally reached her lips fell upon his stiff back as he deliberately pivoted away.

Shallie whirled around. Her emotional roller-coaster ride could have been measured in fractions of seconds. Only Petey had even noticed it. Commiseration deepened the lines around his eyes. Petey's sympathy was more than Shallie could bear. She fled the suite without pausing to make excuses for her abrupt departure.

Back in her room, she ripped the gaily colored dress off, but she wouldn't allow the tears misting her vision to fall. No. She wouldn't waste another teardrop on Hunt McIver. She'd cried enough for him already. As far as she was concerned, he had died and she had already put in more than her share of mourning.

Shallie was as good as her resolution. At the opening performance the next night, she was back behind the chutes with the fifteen best, and most nervous, bareback riders in the world. At first glance it looked more like a field hospital, with contestants ripping off miles of adhesive tape and unrolling dozens of elastic bandages to bind every imaginable portion of their anatomy. Knees were wrapped, both inside and out of jeans. Shoulders, wrists, elbows, and fingers were encased in sticky white tape. Shallie knew that a lot of the outside reinforcement provided crucial support for torn ligaments and strained muscles. But most of it served only to shore up the mental image each cowboy was brewing of himself as tough and invulnerable, a match for any horse in the chutes.

A camera crew scurried about, filming the proceedings. A female interviewer, desperately overdressed in heels and a skirt, stuck a microphone in front of Shallie and asked what it felt like to be the only woman contractor at the National Finals.

Shallie slid into the "good old girl" persona she used for such occasions. "It feels a whole heck of a lot better than if I wasn't here." She grinned. The crew chuckled appreciatively, knowing the retort would make good footage. Her smile, though, blinked off as abruptly as the camera's light.

She followed the television spotlight as it fell first on Emile, then on Jesse, capturing the top two finalists and probing the rivals for predictions.

"Well, I don't know," Emile answered in his Canadian drawl. "I suppose I have as good a chance as the next fellow of winning. These broncs don't play any favorites, you know. I'm going into this in second place, just a couple hundred dollars back from Jesse Southerland. But I'd say the man to watch is Hunt McIver. With the size of the purse here, if he stays as hot as he's been, he could take home that great big gold buckle."

Southerland was far less gracious. "I'm going into this in the number-one berth and that's exactly how I intend on leaving it. No, I don't consider McIver a threat. We've all seen him choke before and I think he'll do it again."

Southerland was opening his mouth to elaborate further on the trouncing he intended to give Hunt McIver, when the bright light blinked off, leaving him in darkness. The crew hurried after the woman in heels as she made a beeline for the entryway. It didn't surprise Shallie to see Hunt amble in with his usual loose-jointed grace.

She forbid herself to react to his appearance. When her traitorous body refused, she sealed off her mind, ignoring the way her hands went cold and her stomach seemed to sink a foot lower. The camera crew intercepted him before Hunt reached the chutes where Shallie stood on the catwalk running above them.

"Hunt." The female interviewer addressed him as if they were old friends. Hunt's eyebrows jumped an almost imperceptible fraction of an inch at the presumption. He looked around as if searching for an escape and saw Shallie, her lips curled upward in a slight, ironic grin that chilled his soul.

"Hunt, is Trish Stephans going to be in the crowd cheering you on?"

The name rose above the clamor to sting Shallie with a barb she wished she could will herself not to feel. But feel it she did. It drove her to the only method she had for soothing that pain—escape.

"What?" Confusion and irritation cracked Hunt's voice. He wanted to push past this pest of a woman with her high heels sinking into the arena dirt and her stupid questions and find Shallie. Find her and shake her until she rattled. Why had she smiled at him like that? The interviewer clung to him like a gnat.

"Trish Stephans?" the woman persisted, finally capturing Hunt's wandering attention. "Will she be here rooting for you?"

When he looked up again, Shallie was gone. "Ma'am," Hunt said, fighting to keep his voice even, "maybe you haven't noticed, but you're at a rodeo. These are horses here," he said, swinging his hand toward the chutes. "And we're here to ride them. Now, if you've got any questions on *that* subject, I'll think about answering them. Otherwise, will you please get out of my way?"

The woman stepped aside, her eyes widening in disbelief at encountering someone who wasn't mesmerized by the television camera's cyclopean eye.

Hunt hurried past, but it was too late. Damn her. He felt fury's familiar sting as he slammed his rigging bag down. It *was* too late, he should have realized that yesterday. Still, the anger pumping through him was an old friend, one that had served him well over the past months, fueling him with the unrelenting will to win. He let it wash over him, knowing he would start off the Finals with another good ride. Knowing, and not caring.

Chapter 19

On day eight of the Finals, Shallie reflected on how easy it had been to fool everyone around her. They all treated her just as if she were a normal human being. Only she was aware that her heart had stopped pumping when she willed herself to cease feeling and that ice water lay frozen in her veins. But then the only people in Las Vegas who knew her well enough to realize that an android had taken her place were too preoccupied to notice: Walter was like a lovestruck teenager. Petey was absorbed in hero worship as he trailed Hunt from one end of the arena to the other. Hunt might have noticed, but after their near encounter the first day, they had both become very careful to avoid one another. For her part, Shallie completely abdicated the bucking chutes to Hunt, retiring to Jake McIver's private box, where he kept a continuous party running, stocked with bourbon and buckle bunnies.

"Shalimar, you sweet thing." Jake greeted her as she

entered the private box on the night of the next-to-last performance. "You've been running yourself ragged. What you've got to learn about producing is delegating, the fine art of laying back and hiring someone else to run themselves to death."

A cute blonde at Jake's side giggled appreciatively, and Shallie wondered if she was a candidate for next year's Rodeo Sweetheart. Was Trish Stephans already in Hollywood?

"In case you've forgotten, Jake," Shallie said, remembering to throw in her "good old girl" laugh, "I'm the 'someone' you hired to run herself to death so you can sit up here and sip your bourbon and branch water."

Jake cackled, Walter and Miriam joining in at a more subdued level. Then the announcer was welcoming the twenty thousand spectators crowding the bleachers and telling them the first event would be bareback riding. The information was superfluous because the sellout crowd was composed of rodeo's aficionados, the die-hard fans who had flown and driven in from around the country to watch the roughest and the rankest collide.

"The bareback riding has generated more than its share of thrills over the past few days," the announcer went on, "and we're looking to see some more here tonight as our three leaders, Jesse Southerland, Emile Boulier, and Hunt McIver battle it out for that big golden buckle."

The three men rode like crazed artists, trying to push

their craft to its outer limits. In his riding style, each one revealed more than he would ever know about himself: Jesse Southerland hung on, hard and clutching. His mount was his enemy. Emile flapped loose and free, a happy ragdoll enjoying the jostling. But Shallie, in her most objective moment, realized that it was Hunt who was pushing back the boundaries, while the other two merely followed. He rode with an abstracted ferocity that lifted him above physical constraints.

Shallie appreciated the performance in the way a sports fan delights in seeing records broken and art lovers thrill to radical new innovations. But her elation had a hollow core. Panic clutched at Shallie as her thoughts drifted down toward that dangerous void. She jumped up from her seat.

"I'd better go down and make sure all the dogging steers have been sorted out." She escaped before Jake could order her to sit down and stop fidgeting. She had to get out.

Down in the labyrinth of pens, the steers she had culled out that afternoon waited patiently for their moment under the bright lights. A crew of livestock handlers, all as proficient at their jobs as any of the buckle-chasing contestants inside the arena, herded animals along a maze of metal alleyways.

"Need some help, ma'am?" a brawny cowboy she hadn't met asked her.

"No, I . . ." She shook her head. There was nothing for her to do there. She thrust her hands deep into her pockets, tucked her head into the collar of her jacket, and plowed into the wintry night. She was grateful for the blast of icy wind that bit into her, stunning her and clearing her head of all thoughts. Her hand leaped to her head to prevent the wind from blowing her hat away. She followed her feet, not thinking about where they were taking her, and not caring. The cheers of the crowd, the eight-second buzzer, the announcer's twang, all faded further and further away.

The sports complex was located at the University of Nevada, and as Shallie roamed the campus the stored tensions of the last several months gradually dissipated and she relaxed into an ambling gait. Just beyond the edge of the campus, Shallie spotted a diner, its neon sign blinking out a warm welcome as the winds bit into her.

Shallie picked a table by the window. The odors of frying hamburgers and yeasty doughnuts floated around her. A skinny waitress thrust a menu in front of her.

"Just coffee, please," Shallie said, declining the chicken-fried offerings. She pulled off her hat, carefully setting it down on its crown on an empty chair.

The waitress slid a steaming mug in front of Shallie. Shallie checked the time, astonished to find that she'd been walking for more than two hours. So, the rodeo was over. She swirled a trickle of cream into her coffee and cupped the icy twigs of her fingers around the mug. She imagined that the festivities in the hospitality suite and throughout the hotels, taken over by cowboys and their retinues of hangers-on, were probably in full swing by now. She hoisted her cup, a wry toast to the bacchanalia she'd fled. Undoubtedly Hunt would be enjoying it to the fullest without the onerous chore of avoiding her at every turn.

At the next table, the three occupants had chosen to keep their cowboy hats on. Their voices rose above the clatter of spatulas hitting the grill and coffee cups rattling against saucers.

"Can you believe that ride McIver put on that bareback?"

The other two chimed in with expressions of incredulity.

"What I can't believe is that he came from so far behind. I mean, he **was** *thousands* of dollars behind Southerland and Boulier when he went in and he's damn near closed the gap now. That big buckle is up for grabs. Either one of those three could take it away tomorrow night."

"Yeah," the first speaker agreed, "that McIver is really something."

Shallie closed her eyes as if she could shut out the name. She was so weary of it, of hearing about him, of seeing Hunt's face on billboards, newspapers, magazines, in her dreams. She opened her eyes and blinked twice, wondering if her suppressed longings hadn't burst forth in full hallucinatory flower. Hunt McIver was outside, his lanky strides gobbling up the city pavement. In the violet light cast by the crime lights, Shallie saw him veer toward the diner as if summoned by the force of her deepest yearnings. Shallie ducked her head as his gloved hand reached out to push open the door.

"Hey, isn't that McIver now?" A blast of cold air and the whispered question marked his entrance. Shallie didn't need to be told that Hunt McIver was in the same room with her. His presence bore down on her with a pressure that stole the air from her lungs. The arrow points of his boots approached, then stopped. They were aimed straight at her. She followed the impossibly long columns of blue-jeaned legs up past an extravagance of muscled shoulders to a pair of eyes filled with anger.

"Where the hell did you hide the grain mixture?" he demanded, dispensing with the frills of greeting.

"I didn't 'hide' it anywhere," Shallie blazed with a fury to match his. "It's where it's always been, in the back of the storage room. Walter knew that."

"Unfortunately, Walter followed your lead and was nowhere to be found either. And since you kept the grain formula your own little secret, no one knew what to give the broncs."

The clanging and clattering in the small diner stopped

as every ear tuned in to the fiery exchange. Shallie was ready to leap to her own defense, but Hunt cut her off.

"Because everyone else was busy, *I* was the lucky one who got to slog out in this miserable weather trying to track you down. Fortunately there aren't many places open at night in this part of town, and since you don't have transportation, it wasn't too difficult to track you down. But if you hadn't tried to turn this into a one-woman show, none of this would have happened. I'm surprised you haven't learned by now that rodeo is a team effort. A good contractor gets to be the best by being able to work *with* people, not against them."

Shallie thought of the nights spent worrying and the days cooped up in the rolling oven of a semi's cab, the dust she'd eaten, the pride she'd swallowed for the Circle M. She exploded. *"You're* talking to *me* about working with people? Precisely what do you think I've been doing for the past six months? Your damned contracts were filled because it was *me* out there charming cranky committeemen and disgruntled calf ropers. *I* was the one who coaxed the cowboys on the labor lists into making the extra effort in 110-degree heat that it took to ensure that *your* rodeos ran smoothly. Meanwhile, you've been the one in the spotlight. You've . . ."

Shallie heard the quaver in her voice and stood quickly, laying a handful of bills down on the formica tabletop. Tears were already collecting in her eyes, turning the city scene outside into a rippling underwater world as she left the diner.

"Hold on." She shook Hunt's hand from her shoulder and willed her tears back to their source. She had shown this callous, brutish man too much of herself as it was.

"Why?" she snapped. "So that I can be treated to more of your opinions as to my worth as a contractor? No thanks. I've heard quite enough already."

"Oh, slow down," Hunt commanded. "You were foolish enough to walk here by yourself, at least I can see to it that you make it back safely. In case you haven't noticed, this isn't Mountain View, New Mexico, where an unaccompanied woman can stroll down the street at midnight, or any other damned time the fancy strikes her."

"Thank you for that most illuminating geography lecture." Sarcasm flavored Shallie's words with a bitterness uncharacteristic of her.

"Where do you think you're going?" Hunt asked as Shallie set off to retrace the route she'd taken. "The arena is only a few blocks the other way."

Shallie fell in beside him without a word. Once again he had made a fool of her.

The silent streets echoed the lonely sound of two people walking together, yet utterly apart.

When they reached the arena, Hunt stopped and asked, "Shallie, why?" His question hung, untouched, in the cold, still night.

"Why what?" Shallie asked. Alternating currents of anger, longing, humiliation, desire, hostility, and regret swept through her. The crowds had thinned, but there were still clumps of fans, cowboys, and laborers nearby.

"Why are we acting like this? Look, I'm sorry for exploding. I've been under tremendous pressure. Plus, it's been so lonely these past few months."

"Oh? I would have thought that Trish Stephans would have provided ample companionship. Or did you mean that it's been lonely since she moved on to other interests?" Shallie's response was chilling. It slithered out of her like a serpent she couldn't control. But she wanted Hunt to know that she was fully aware of what the situation was.

"So, I'm still just a junior Jake McIver to you. Well, maybe you're right. And maybe it would be better if I were. Find your own way back to the hotel, but feed the broncs before you do."

He left her at the edge of the maze of pens. A steer lowed mournfully. Desolation washed over Shallie as the tall figure dissolved into darkness. She wanted to bite her shrewish tongue. He had been lonely. Lonely? She mocked her gullibility. Hadn't she seen the pictures of him and Trish? Seen the ever-present platoons of female fans?

The answers to her questions were swamped by a wave of hope that rose spontaneously at her first notice

281

of a shuffling sound coming toward her in the darkness. It was Hunt, he was coming back to her! This time she would bite back the hurt festering within her. She would listen. She would forgive. She would apologize. She would howl her love to the pale moon. She would do anything to have Hunt McIver back again.

"Shalimar, it's me." Shallie plummeted from the illusory peak of her stupid dreams at the sound of Jake McIver's voice. Her disappointment was quickly replaced by acute embarrassment, however, when she realized that Jake must have witnessed the entire exchange.

"I apologize," Jake said, confirming her worst fears. "I certainly didn't intend to be lurking out here spying on you and my grandson. I just thought I might know where that damn feed was everyone was looking for and I've gotten so tired of no one ever asking me to do anything, that I thought I'd just come down here and find it myself. I couldn't hear what you two were saying, but it obviously wasn't good."

Shallie desperately wanted to flee, to be done forever with this torment. But Jake went on, "You're wrong about Hunt. I know you don't approve of me. Don't think I really care too much for the women who do. Hunt doesn't either, you know. That's where you're wrong."

"Jake," she sighed, "like everyone else who reads newspapers, I've seen the pictures of him and Trish together."

Jake let a howl of laughter rip through the still night. "Trish Stephans? Hunt can't stand the woman. They both have the same agent. It was this agent fellow that started all that 'crown prince and princess of rodeo' nonsense. Wait a minute. Is that why you thought I was worried about Hunt hating me?"

Shallie didn't answer.

"It is, isn't it? Shallie, I only told you half the story when you were down at the Circle M. I see now you deserve to know the other half."

Jake's words were condensing into frozen puffs in the cold air, but neither of them noticed the temperature as Jake began speaking.

"I told you about adopting Hunt. What I didn't tell you was why. Having a wife didn't slow my son down one whit. Hunt was just a little boy then, but he hated his father for all the nights he'd leave him alone with his mother while she cried her eyes out. Hated him even more when his mama ran off.

"After that, Hunt's daddy really cut loose. A week or two after she left, I stopped by the house I'd had built for my son and his bride in a far corner of the ranch. Hunt was there all alone, just a little bitty boy, eating crackers out of a box. It was all he'd had for a couple of days. I finally found his father, drunk as a skunk, with the wife of one of his rodeo buddies.

"Courts declared him an unfit father and he never

contested the decision. Didn't even show up at the trial. Just lit out. We didn't hear much more about him, just that he drank himself to death a few years later."

Shallie tried to incorporate this information into the image she'd always carried of Hunt, the golden boy, untouched by pain.

"That's why I was wondering if Hunt hates me, for running around the way his father did. I know he loved Maggie as much as I did. She's what made the boy what he is, gave him his class and his heart. After she died," Jake went on with his merciless confession, "I just couldn't stand to be by myself. Oh, I'm not denying that I always appreciated a beauty when I saw one. But what I did out of need, Hunt's father had always done for sheer amusement."

"I'm sure Hunt understands." Shallie tried to comfort the old man, but it cost her an effort. Her mind was whirling with the secrets Jake had revealed. Hunt and Trish had never been involved! He detested the stereotypical womanizing rodeo cowboy as much as she did!

Shallie grappled with these new facts, trying to decide what she should do about them. From the murky turmoil only one clear thought emerged—it might very well be too late to do anything at all.

Chapter 20

As the National Anthem boomed out, announcing the final performance of the National Finals, Shallie felt practically unhinged with nervousness. Her life was hanging in the balance and she was paralyzed with indecision. She knew it was her turn to act. If there were any chance at all left, she would have to be the one to seize it. But she didn't know how. Perhaps things were irretrievably lost between her and Hunt. Maybe nothing she did would make any difference. The question she had to answer was—could she live the rest of her life knowing that she had let even the slimmest of chances slip past her?

"You know what would have made a hell of a match?" Jake asked the gathering in his box. "Hunt and Pegasus."

Shallie had been so scrupulous in avoiding any areas where she might have encountered Hunt that she hadn't even checked with the rodeo secretary to learn which horses had been drawn that night. It was a letdown to find out that she would never see Hunt on Pegasus again.

"Ladies and gentlemen," the announcer squawked, "we are coming right down to the wire here tonight on the bareback riding. With the size of the purse riding on this final performance, it could go to any one of our top three contenders. Let's lead off with a very tough cowboy from up Canada way . . ."

Shallie's attention drifted and she barely recorded Emile's stunning performance. She vacillated wildly between utter despair and the frail beginnings of hope. Jesse Southerland's ride was just as spectacular as Boulier's had been, and just as lost on Shallie. She focused on the chutes only when Hunt's name was called. This would be the ride to decide his future, whether he would lay claim once more to the title "champion of the world."

The sound of the gate cracking open and the crowd gasping in unison were simultaneous as Hunt's horse reared back, rather than darting out into the arena. A chute fighter. The dreaded label flashed across Shallie's mind. Fortunately, Petey was right beside his boss on the catwalks and jerked him free, hauling him up and off the horse before the renegade bronc could crush Hunt.

"The judges have awarded Hunt McIver a re-ride," the announcer told the startled crowd. "He will draw for another mount to ride after all the other bronc riders have gone."

Shallie felt her old insecurities rise up within her as she thought of confronting Hunt. *He doesn't want you*, they sneered. What *would* she be letting herself in for if she went to him? *More humiliation and hurt*, the phantoms answered. There was so much she didn't know, so much she was unsure of. She couldn't go to him. Better a life of not knowing than having to endure that one soul-killing moment when he turned away, leaving her with the deadening certainty of his rejection.

It's better this way. She attempted to comfort herself with the old familiar chant. In the final analysis, her desperate love for Hunt was just what made it impossible. What kind of relationship could they ever have with Hunt able to wield such frightening power over her? No, it would be much better for her to remain alone until the day when she made a comfortably affectionate marriage. It was a relief to have finally reached a decision. Shallie let a deep breath escape. In a distant corner of her awareness she thought she heard something, something important.

"What did the announcer just say?" she asked her uncle.

"Hunt's re-ride," her uncle sputtered in excitement. "It's going to be Pegasus."

A thrill of exhilaration managed to fight its way through the layers of resignation Shallie had already blanketed her emotions in. Hunt and Pegasus! Destiny had demanded a rematch between the two, Shallie reflected, just as she had dictated that there was to be no reunion for her and Hunt. Only this meeting of the finest horse and finest rider to grace a rodeo arena could have stirred Shallie. A hush fell over the crowd as they anticipated the collision of two legends.

Petey led Pegasus in. Shallie's discovery shone like the star he had become, tossing his shimmering white mane as if defying the man bold enough to challenge his supremacy in the ring.

At the sight of the majestic beast, Shallie felt her responses tear in two directions. On one side was pride in the animal she'd discovered. On the other was a rapidly mounting apprehension. Would Pegasus prove more than even Hunt could handle? Had his brush with the chute fighter moments before unnerved him? Would he freeze again, ripping open the wounds of humiliation inflicted in this very ring two years ago? For a second, Shallie felt she was back in the Circle M's moonlit arena wanting to plead with Hunt not to endanger himself.

One glimpse of Hunt's face, however, and all of Shallie's fears melted away. He looked like a little boy about to dive into a truckload of Christmas booty. Gone was the ferocious intensity of the past months. He was a man who had labored long and hard and was now about to enjoy his reward. Shallie knew there wasn't another bronc rider alive who would greet the prospect of eight seconds on board Pegasus with that kind of relish.

The roan was quickly rigged, tension building in the crowd with the delay. By the time Hunt had settled onto the blue-flaked back, everyone in the cavernous coliseum was hunching forward expectantly.

Shallie bit her lower lip, oblivious to the pain. She had no thought of sides, winning and losing, whether she should root for Hunt to best Pegasus or for her horse to vanquish Hunt. This match transcended such considerations. All she hoped for was that each would realize his potential.

Every pair of eyes in the coliseum was trained on Hunt as he nodded for the gate. From the first buck, Shallie knew that she was witnessing rodeo history. Hunt rode as well as Shallie knew he could, which is to say he rode better than any bronc rider ever had. Hunt pushed back the limit of the sport and Pegasus tested every new frontier. The ride was an elegy written in muscle and motion, composed on the common ground where man and beast met as fellow creatures.

The buzzer sounded and the coliseum exploded like Times Square at midnight on New Year's Eve. Shallie too was on her feet, exhilarated by the dramatic lesson Hunt had just graphically demonstrated for her. She couldn't even put it into words, all she knew was that it contradicted the gloomy conclusions she had just reached about Hunt's wielding power over her because of her intense love for him. What she had just seen in the arena was a display of profound respect, not power. She slid through the cheering fans, driven by a compelling urgency, a certainty that she had one chance left and must seize it now or it would fade forever.

She slipped around to the back, to the labyrinth of stock pens. Light from the arena seeped out through the entryway where two- and four-legged contestants came and went. Her heart drummed a pounding beat. Pegasus was driven out through the metal alleyway. He carried his foam-white head high and proud, as if he knew he had just set a standard by which all other horses would be judged. Not far behind was Hunt McIver.

"Whoa," he yelled, chasing the retreating horse that still wore his rigging.

All Shallie's newly formed assurance leaked out of her at the sight of Hunt. She couldn't go through with it. She would slip back into the shadows.

"Shallie, that you?" Hunt cocked his head toward her.

"Uh . . . yes." God, why was she hovering behind the chutes like some buckle bunny? "I . . . uh . . . Congratulations on your ride," she finally blurted out. Hunt came closer.

For a second they faced each other like shy and uncertain strangers, neither one knowing what to expect.

"Thank you. That means a lot coming from my old riding teacher." Hunt's laugh was awkward. Neither one spoke. The vague thoughts that had formed during his ride stuck in Shallie's mind. "Well, I better go get my rigging," Hunt said, but he didn't move.

"Yeah, some fan will probably try to take it as a souvenir," Shallie agreed lamely.

"Yeah, well, so long." Slowly, Hunt turned away from her in just the way Shallie had dreaded he would. He started to leave.

"Hunt." Her shout was louder than she'd intended, a desperate preamble to thoughts she was too confused or scared to express.

He stopped. "Yes?"

"Don't leave," Shallie asked.

A smile crept across Hunt's face. "Not if you don't want me to."

"Hunt." With that one word, Shallie laid herself bare. There was no point in hiding any longer.

She was in his arms, lost in his encircling strength. She drank in his presence with all her senses, drowning in his scent, his voice, his body heat, his touch.

"I was just waiting for you to speak," he said, his mouth close to her ear. "It wouldn't have worked if you hadn't made that first move. If you hadn't stopped me. But there are some things we have to get straight. In Albuquerque you accused me of being like my grandfather—"

"No, Hunt," Shallie broke in. "I was wrong, I didn't know. I was hurt, angry. It wasn't fair—"

"It was *very* fair," he concluded solemnly. "Very fair

291

and, as it turned out, very accurate. After Albuquerque, I started doing just what Jake has done ever since my grandmother died—trying to make a dozen women fill the empty spot left by the one he really loved."

Love. The word stunned Shallie. For months she had been tiptoeing around it. Now she couldn't believe she was hearing it on Hunt's lips.

"The woman Jake loved died. I suppose that's an excuse of some kind. But the one I love is very much alive."

Shallie felt locked in a kind of paralysis, afraid to move, even to breathe for fear that she would betray herself, that even the tiniest hint of her longing would deflect forever the words she ached to hear, hurling them into oblivion.

Hunt tilted her face up to his. The distant arena lights illuminated it with an incandescent warmth. Hunt took her hands. They were icy in his. When he saw the trembling vulnerability shimmering in the tears that trickled softly down her cheeks, he felt his own defenselessness. He took Shallie in his arms again, seeking to shelter them both.

"I love you, Shalimar Larkin."

At last Shallie inhaled, no longer afraid of breaking the spell. They were both under it. She felt as if champagne were coursing through her bloodstream, bubbling up from her toes, effervescing through her entire body, and leaving her mind in a state of tingling intoxication. Hunt McIver loved her!

"Hunt." She laughed a giddy, tipsy laugh that was as much incredulous relief as it was elation. The quizzical expression that crossed Hunt's face surprised her. "Of course I love you," she explained. "It's been so painfully obvious to me for so long that I assumed you must know."

"Shallie, I'm no mind reader. And you certainly didn't make your feelings obvious. You were so cold our first morning together," he went on, "then so incredibly warm that afternoon at the hot springs." Shallie saw in Hunt's face that he cherished the memory of that afternoon as much as she did.

"Then you froze me out again in Albuquerque. You wouldn't even listen to me. Wouldn't believe me."

"Hunt, forgive me. It was my insecurity."

"At first I thought you were trying to charm me so I'd help you get Pegasus. Being raised by Jake McIver, I've become very wary of women who want things. I've seen what they'll do to get them and how easy it is to prey on the male ego." Hunt's words made a comforting rumble deep in his chest, next to Shallie's ear.

"I probably loved you from the moment back at that podunk rodeo when you helped me pull my rigging," Hunt confessed. "But I wouldn't admit it to myself, wouldn't let myself feel it until you showed me that you would never just love me for what I could do for you or give you. After watching you in action, I knew you were perfectly capable of getting anything you really wanted without any help from me. That's when I decided you were the one I wanted. But not before you came to me."

"It was hard, Hunt," Shallie admitted. "I could never have believed you loved me." Saying it aloud put a seal on Hunt's words. Shallie began to accept their reality. She found further confirmation in the brush of his lips.

"Lord, I've missed you, woman."

Shallie let her kiss tell him of the long months of loneliness, of wanting him. Of desire and desperation. Their tongues exchanged the messages each had harbored unspoken for so long, and the bitter taste of heartaches unshared melted in the sweetness of union.

Through the distance, the announcer's voice echoed. "That's it, folks, it's official. Hunt McIver is our world champion in the bareback riding, with Emile Boulier taking second and Jesse Southerland in third place."

"Marry me, Shallie," Hunt breathed.

The crowd erupted in pounding, hooting cheers, calling for the new champion.

"They want you back in the arena."

"Answer me," Hunt insisted. "We'll merge the Double L and the Circle M under a joint brand. You won't have to give up anything. What do you say?"

Shallie thought that the sound of forty thousand hands clapping out wild approval provided just the right accompaniment as she accepted Hunt's proposal.

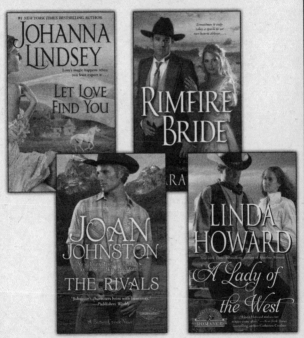